THE SNOW LEOPARDS CROWN

KIM KERR

SCIENCE FICTION AND FANTASY PUBLICATIONS

For my sister, Kathy

1

ADDICTION

Being punched in the face really hurts. Golden's fist was clenched by his side, and I glimpsed it briefly on its trajectory toward my cheek. At the time, I was smiling with my arms open. It was pleasing to see him, though the memory is hazy. I had just had my second pipe of opium for the day when my tall friend appeared through the curtain of smoke. Captain Waldheigheim stood behind him in his dark blue cape. Around me, other patrons of Oscar's Parlour lay semi-comatose on a variety of couches or cushions. Golden's different-coloured eyes were slits, his mouth set in a thin line, yet in my drug-induced state, I had failed to read the warning signs. The blow lifted me off my feet and slammed me into the wall.

I don't remember Golden carrying me to the Bookstore or strapping me to my bed. Nor do I recall the captain chasing away the security guards at Oscar's Opium Den. That was told to me later. I do remember waking up with a swollen jaw and a cramp in my stomach. My body craved opium, but I couldn't move as my arms and legs were tied firmly to the mattress.

"What have you done to yourself?" Golden asked.

He sat on a chair near the end of my bed. The sloped roof peaked above his head, and the large frosted glass windows of my attic let in the thin light of dawn.

"Let me go. I need to go out for a while."

"You're not going anywhere," Golden said.

I whined. "You don't understand."

"I understand perfectly," Golden growled.

It had been a long hot summer, followed by one of the mildest autumns in many years. After Miranda left, I found myself alone at the store, copying manuscripts of authors long dead and staring at the walls. Customers stopped coming to the store after Rackhime's death, and though Captain Waldheigheim gave me some work, I often had little to do. I wandered down to Docklands on occasion and saw Stella and the other girls, but they were very busy. As spring turned to summer, the patronage of the inns, gambling dens, and brothels went up dramatically. The river and ocean were now flowing with trade, and the farmers of the south and cattlemen of the plains all brought their produce to the great city of Hope. Yet, for all the bustle, I felt empty.

Given my race, it was always hard for me to find acceptance amongst the humans of Hope. Many of the other races wandered the narrow streets of Hope. However dark elves were viewed with suspicion, now more than ever. In the south, my people had burst from their mountain plateau, and in alliance with the Original Men from the Great Jungle, recaptured their ancestral hills. Then they'd pushed north against the southern duchies. Hope was far enough away to avoid entanglement in the war, but there were many in the city who advocated supporting the Dukes. The conflict made my presence in the city more problematic. Various individuals spat at me and called me a spy. I had cut my long white hair short, but nothing could disguise the dark skin and slightly pointed ears.

The dreams returned. I saw Cassie's swollen face nearly every night. Reaching out to her, I tried to pull the rope from around her neck, but she died again and again. The Scarred Man and Lord Vorhelm laughed at my efforts and pushed me away. I cursed them, and they became creatures of rotting flesh who yelled about my failure. Sometimes Trix would visit me in my sleep and ask why I hadn't saved her. Long sheets of skin would hang from her arms and back like pieces of crumpled parchment, and I would scream until I woke up. Often I would see Elhnora, but these nights were soothing. She would gently chide me for my guilt and point out the sacrifices I made in solving the mystery of her murder. The solace she gave me was only temporary.

Maybe I should have gone to find Golden, Kat, and Tearwyn and joined them adventuring in the east, but Hope was my home, and I had put down roots. I didn't want to abandon the shop as it was mine now, and the thought of boarding it up and leaving somehow felt like a betrayal. So I stayed and let the loneliness eat me. I had never been by myself before, except for an extended period after I was exiled from the mountains. If Golden hadn't dragged me into the wilderness then, I would have probably ended up as a permanent fixture in one of the cheaper inns near the waterfront.

Stella invited me to a party in the Merchant Quarter on the slopes of the Devil's Peaks, probably out of pity. She was to dance for the rich traders who crossed the oceans from the Old World and snuck me in. It wasn't the first occasion I saw humans smoking opium, but it was the first time someone offered it to me. The Old World humans didn't view dark elves with the same mistrust as those who lived in Hope and treated me as a curiosity. A bald man wrapped in expensive grey silk passed me the hookah pipe, and I inhaled the smoke almost without thinking. I felt a wave of bliss roll over me, and the tension that festered inside escaped.

"This is good stuff," the bald man said. "But I only have it every so often. Otherwise, it can be habit-forming."

I nodded vaguely and sucked down more smoke. The rest of the evening passed in a haze.

Stella walked me home, warning me about the side effects of smoking opium. "I had it a few times when I started working for Grandfather but saw what it did to some of the other girls and stopped. The women who didn't would walk around in a trance getting thinner and thinner until one day they seemed to disappear. Nobody could say where they went, but there were plenty of rumours. Teal said they just fell asleep and never woke up, but Aneeta believed Grandfather got rid of them as they were a bad look for his business."

Her conversation and warnings drifted over me like a gentle breeze. I smiled at her. The following day, while delivering parchments to the captain at the watchhouse, I caught a hint of the sweet smell of opium smoke. I followed my nose down a short alley and found Oscar's. Smoking opium is not illegal in Hope, just frowned upon, so I paid a copper to the large fat man on the door and went inside. People lay on benches and couches with long-stemmed pipes dangling from their lips. Most of them looked as though they were in a trance, and I felt a moment of fear, but then the owner of the establishment appeared and smiled at me. Oscar was a thin man, and his two front teeth were gold. His hair was a mop of sandy coloured curls, and his long fingers covered in a variety of rings, some no doubt magical. He found me a position near the rear door of the establishment and asked for a small amount of silver. I remember handing over the coins and then sucking on the metal stem of the pipe. At that moment, all my pain and loneliness disappeared.

"Why did you do it?" Golden asked, dragging me back from my memories.

"There was nothing else to do," I snarled.

"Are you telling me you became an addict because you were bored?"

I lapsed into a sullen silence. Part of me wanted him to go so I could attempt to free myself and make my way back to Oscar's. But I also wanted him to stay and make everything right again.

"Rackhime is gone, Miranda hasn't returned, and you were out plundering tombs in the East. What else was I supposed to do?"

"You could have come with us!"

"I live here. This is my home now, not the road. Besides, I don't want to see any more friends die under the club of a giant or in the breath of a dragon."

"No, you would rather kill yourself slowly with the pipe. That makes a lot more sense."

I just wished he would leave me alone so I could satisfy the cravings. Desperation took hold, and I longed to feel the delicious smoke working its way into my lungs, numbing my body, making me float free.

"Look, Golden, I won't have anymore. I'll stop smoking and follow you back East."

"Do you know why I'm so angry with you? It's something I never talk about with anyone. My father was an addict, and it's what killed him. He used to steal from his own wife and children to satisfy his cravings. He would lie, cheat, do anything as long as he could get more opium."

"I thought he died fighting hobgoblins when you were young."

"That's what I tell everybody because I'm too ashamed of what he really was. And now I find you travelling down the same path."

The tale was irrelevant. I needed to feel the long metal stem between my teeth. The desire consumed me.

"I won't be like your father, I swear by Trix's memory. I'll stop as long as you let me go."

"That's how desperate you are. You would even go as low as to use the memory of our dead friend to escape and make your way to Oscar's. You have just convinced me the money I'm about to spend will be worth it."

I felt a stab of ice in my belly as the cravings wracked me physically.

"Let me go, or I'll kill you," I screamed.

"You'll have to go through the withdrawal stage, and then the alchemist will be called. He can mix brews, which will put you off opium and other substances for a certain period of time. Of course, there are side effects, but seeing how the drug has taken you, I have no choice. At least I'll be able to get you eating again. You're skin and bones at the moment."

"You can't do this! I need the smoke to keep the dreams away. I still see them and feel their pain."

Golden's eyes softened. "That's probably the first honest thing you have said. I didn't see Cassie die, but she was important to me. I can't imagine what it was like to see her strangled."

Then my friend's brow folded in on itself. "It doesn't mean I'm going to let you slowly kill yourself. Lord Alder sent word to me of what you were becoming, and Captain Waldheigheim tracked you down. Now Kat and Tearwyn are bringing an alchemist from the edge of the Great Woods to fix this problem – well, at least in the short term."

"You do this, and you are no longer my friend," I hissed.

"That is the opium talking, though this will probably come between us in the future. Still, it's a price I'm willing to pay if it saves your life."

I hated them all. My body shook. I craved the pipe and the sweet bliss it would bring. The thought of taking my own life or perhaps killing one of those who cared for me floated in my skull like a corpse in the river, but the pain was too great.

At one stage, I remember Stella bending over me. I begged her to release me, but she shook her head. Screaming, I called her every foul name I could think of, and her face became pale. There were other visitors, and I learnt later Lord Alder visited with Teal. I didn't remember them as I was deep in delirium, and all I saw were the dead. Sweat dripped from my body, soaking the bed and pooling in the valleys and crevices of my body. All I wanted to do was crawl from my room and down the street to Oscar's. Nothing else mattered.

Insanity crept up on me, but soft cool fingers brought me back from the brink. I knew I was in a dream, but relaxed. My head was in the lap of a beautiful girl with bright blue eyes. For a moment, I thought it was Miranda, but her eyes were green.

"I can't keep you here with me for very long," Elhnora said.

"Where am I? I thought you couldn't come back."

"I can cross back over only once or twice. This place was created to comfort you. It took something of my soul to make it, but it's the least I could do for the one who brought the monster who was my father to justice."

Elhnora's hair floated around her head, and the light made it shine. She smiled and stroked my cheek.

"You feel too much, Ash, and though it defines you, it could also destroy your sanity. Someone is coming who may save you."

"I don't want to drink the alchemist's potion."

"I'm not talking of the magician. Miranda is returning."

My bonds held me to the bed. The rope burns on my arms and legs itched, and my mouth was dry; otherwise, I felt clear for the first time in days. At the end of my bed stood Tearwyn and Kat. She frowned at me and moved a little closer while my large friend stayed in the shadows.

"Golden is getting some rest. He's all done-in from trying to keep you under control for the last ten days," Kat said.

There seemed to be a tone of reproach in her voice, but I ignored it.

"Can I have some water, please?" I asked.

Tearwyn walked down the stairs and returned with a clay jug. He carefully lifted my head and poured some into my mouth. I swallowed greedily before coughing half of the liquid onto my chest.

"Take it slowly," my big friend suggested.

His hair and beard had grown back since I had last seen him. I briefly remembered when Aneeta had shaved his whole body one drunken evening and how he complained about being itchy for days afterward as the stubble pushed its way up through his bare skin.

"We need to get some food into him before the alchemist gets here," Kat said.

"You are too skinny, Ash, and that's saying something for a dark elf," Tearwyn said.

"I still don't feel hungry," I said.

"Your appetite will return," Kat said. "Golden mentioned the last thing that comes back is the desire for food. But we don't have time to wait. We need to get some bread into your stomach before you take the potion, so you're going to have to force it down."

I ate the bread slowly, and though it was warm and covered with honey, I struggled to swallow. As it hit my stomach, I felt waves of nausea roll over me. I drank a little more and slumped back onto my bed.

"It's not enough," Kat said. "Your stomach needs to be full before you can take the potion."

"I feel sick."

"I don't care," the elf snapped. "This is the price you pay for being weak."

"That's a little harsh," Tearwyn said.

"Is it? Ash seems to think he's the only one who has experienced trauma. Golden's youth was filled with watching his father steal to support his habit before he was eventually hanged. My own family was…"

Kat stopped talking, and her eyes filled with tears.

"Anyway, we don't all choose to crawl into the bottle or take to the pipe when things get hard."

"No, but some of us walk the tightrope of sanity. Not everyone responds to tragedy in the same way," Tearwyn whispered.

I remembered when I had first met my big friend and how the death of a woman had unhinged his mind.

"I'm sorry, Tearwyn, I just see how this has affected Golden, and I get a little angry," Kat said.

The big man nodded and cut up some more bread. My stomach settled a little, and I chewed it slowly. The nausea wasn't as bad this time.

My friends left me lying strapped to the mattress, and I wondered what I had done. Part of me still longed to make my way to Oscar's, but the craving had subsided enough for me to consider a number of choices. Kat and Golden were clearly distressed at my state, and it came to me that I had damaged a number of friendships. My descent into addiction was so fast I never considered the repercussions of my actions. Then I thought about how much money I'd spent. My buried strongbox was almost empty. I probably had a few hundred pieces of chopped silver and a handful of coins. Under normal circumstances, this would last me a season. I had not only been spending silver on myself, but a few of the other addicts managed to latch onto me, and I paid for their supply of opium as well.

Susal, a young merchant's daughter, became an addict before I did. Her family snatched her from the streets not long before my friends came for me. She used to be a pretty, if slightly plump, woman before the lack of appetite drained away her weight. She stole from her family and friends, to begin with, then after they rejected her, she turned to me, and I paid for her habit. We slept together more than once, but without passion. She was lucky her family decided to give her one more chance.

There had been others as well, a port worker named Dragel and an old soldier called Lentrish. I could remember their faces and visualise them sucking on a metal pipe, but I couldn't remember what they were like. Their personalities were lost in a fog. Susal presented as nervous and passive, but that might not have been the real her. I wondered what they thought of me and then realised their memories were probably as vague as mine.

It didn't matter anymore as I would probably never see any of them again. If this potion worked, then my desire for opium would be gone for some time, which was just as well, because I could feel the urge for it returning as I lay still. I had to make myself think of something else, and the first thing that jumped into my mind was Miranda. Elhnora said she was returning, though I didn't know if it was wise to take the word of a spirit which only spoke to me in my dreams. Trying to sort through my feelings toward her, I decided they ranged between anger and longing. I missed her when I woke up in the morning, and thoughts of her were akin to physical pain. Then I became angry because Miranda wasn't there. She said her honeymoon would only be short, and now she had been gone more than a season. A couple of letters arrived, explaining the small holdings her husband Sir Petar owned were in a mess, and she was putting them in order to guarantee their future income.

I was angry she had married the nobleman. It was true my rejection of her and the circumstances at the time pushed them together, but that didn't soothe my wounded pride. Now she was coming back to Hope, probably to live in the small mansion owned by Sir Petar up on the Devil's Peak. It would be possible to visit her regularly but whether she would want to have me around remained an open question. I was certainly glad she couldn't see me in my present state.

The magician was a round man whose eyes seemed to disappear into the folds of skin on his face. He wore a green and brown stained cape and wiped his nose a lot.

"You didn't tell me he was a dark elf," he said to Golden.

"I didn't think you would come if I did."

The fat man shrugged. "Your silver is as good as anyone's. It just might affect the response of the potion."

"You mean it has a different outcome for non-humans?" Kat asked.

"Of course, but if you want me to continue, I can. I have a rough idea of what variations are needed. If you change your mind, there will still be the matter of expenses, of course. I have incurred costs getting here, and then there is the matter of my time."

The fat man wiped his nose on his sleeve and smiled at everyone. I could see gold teeth, and they reminded me of Oscar.

"I don't know if this is such a good idea," I mumbled.

"The side effects won't kill him, will they?" Golden asked.

"No, at least I don't think so. Usually, for humans, there are ongoing mild headaches and some dizziness. For the different elf races, these problems are exacerbated."

"We don't have much choice," Golden said. "If this isn't done, he will probably be dead in a few years anyway."

"Don't I get a say?" I asked.

"Not this time, Ash. We still don't know what's motivating you. The opium could influence any decision you make," Kat said.

I held my tall friend's mismatched eyes with my own. He was taking a risk with my life and was battling his own demons, which were probably affecting his judgment. Yet his statement about my likely future, if I did nothing, shocked me, and self-preservation stepped in. It sounded like this was the only way.

"The potion will only work for four to five seasons, maybe a little longer for a dark elf, and after that, the cravings will return. They won't be nearly as strong as they are now, but they will still be there. I could give the potion a second time if the patient was human, but I wouldn't want to risk it on your friend. The headaches would be strong enough to kill him with a second dose." The magician smiled before sneezing loudly.

The concoction forced down my throat was the worst taste I have ever experienced. The nausea was close to the feeling when the Scarred Man fed me my own little finger. Golden held my mouth closed while Kat pinched my nostrils shut, forcing me to swallow. Tearwyn and the magician held me down while I thrashed. My body contorted into all sorts of strange shapes, and my big friend struggled to keep me pinned to the mattress.

"This is all quite normal," the fat magician said. "A little more violent than usual but still within the realm of an acceptable reaction."

The potion hit my stomach and then ran through my body like fire. I felt as though I would burst and shower my friends with scalding blood. Heat flooded my skull, and I believed my eyeballs were going to pop. Screaming, I tried to shake everybody off, but they were too strong. The urge to vomit disappeared, but the burning sensation continued to grow. I yelled that I was catching fire, but the magician told everybody not to worry.

"The potion is destroying the toxins in his body, and it just feels like its burning."

"I will kill you, fat man!" I shrieked.

The magician paled, and his eyes grew wide. "Your protection was guaranteed. You said no harm could come to me."

"We won't let him up until you are on your way home," Golden said.

I screamed again as the burning reached a new high, and my body bent upward like a bow.

Then I fell to the mattress and felt the heat fade away. My muscles slackened, and waves of exhaustion rolled over me. Soon I was asleep.

I lay in bed for a number of days, recovering my strength as the unseasonably warm weather continued. Thunderstorms lashed the city the day I went downstairs and made some food. I was ravenously hungry, and the meals my friends brought me didn't keep pace with my appetite. Golden smiled at me, and I patted his shoulder. Part of me wanted to be angry at him, but his motivation to save my life was pure. Kat, however, remained frosty. I saw Spike for the first time and ruffled the dire wolf's fur. He had stayed downstairs throughout my recovery, and I only heard him growl at the occasional visitor. The big animal licked my hand before curling up on the rug. As I shovelled food into my mouth, Tearwyn entered the shop.

"I have to leave, Ash. There's business in the east I need to tend to, and if I don't go soon, winter will lock me in the west," he said.

"What sort of business?" I asked.

"The type that puts coin in my hand."

He pulled me into a tight hug, and I could smell wood smoke and bread. I didn't want the big man to leave, but he didn't have the resource to stay in Hope without more money.

"I'll miss you," I managed to say.

My strength returned gradually until one day, Golden decided we should all go to Barnabus's Inn and have some of his famous goat curry. As we walked, my friend told me about the season of adventuring, which he, Kat, and Tearwyn abruptly left.

"We came home early because of you, but I must admit, it was quiet out East. Our group found a few minor tombs belonging to some long-dead hobgoblin chieftains, and we plundered them, then we fought the ogres at the edge of the moors, but the pickings were slim. I don't think we made more than a few hundred silver pieces each, and then there was the cost of the potion maker."

"I'll pay you back," I said.

"Yes, you will," Kat growled.

"Plenty of time for that later, for now, let's just enjoy the food," Golden said.

My tastebuds were reinvigorated by the curry. The heat rolled down my throat into my stomach while the meat melted in my mouth. Outside, the thunderstorms returned, and the street through the window came into view with each flash. It hadn't rained yet but moisture hung in the air. The door slammed shut as the wind caught it, and Golden hissed beside me. I looked up and saw a dark elf wearing a bearskin in the entrance, his long hair gathered in a ponytail. A chainmail vest glittered in the candlelight of the inn. Only the small lines at the corner of his eyes hinted at the dark elf's age. He stood erect and stared at me. I swallowed and wobbled to my feet.

"Hello, father," I said.

2

FAMILY

My father waited, framed in the doorway. Behind him, lightning flashed, illuminating the street and houses outside, followed by a boom. He stood a fingernail shorter than I but was broader in the shoulders. His chin looked like the point of a sword, and his eyes were flat and hard. My sisters often described them as orbs, which never smiled. He wore striped pants in the red and blue colours of our family, and his bearskin cloak swept the floor. As he walked toward me, I noted the longsword tied into its scabbard with a peace knot.

"*You do not seem pleased to see me, Ashen Gwenverliy,*" my father said in our tongue.

"Here I'm known as Ash," I replied in Westerian, the language of Hope.

He frowned, and his eyes flew over my friends. "You have been many things in your life, son, but never rude."

He had changed languages, so now everyone could understand him.

"Of course, you are right, father. I apologise."

Feeling as though I had transgressed, I quickly introduced my friends, beginning with Golden. Spike looked up from the floor and growled softly, which earned him a swift rebuke from Kat.

"I heard you associate with Hunters and Adventurers and made your fortune killing a dragon."

"We didn't kill the dragon, but escaped with some of its treasure."

"So, the job was half done, and the beast will have marked you for life."

"No one has heard or seen the dragon in years. Anyway, most of the money is gone."

"Already?"

"Your son owns a business which copies scrolls and books," Kat said.

The implication was I had bought Rackhime's shop and that that's where my money had been invested. I let the lie sit and silently thanked Kat for her quick thinking. My father glanced at the elf, and a certain tightening occurred around the eyes. He ignored Kat but not the statement she made.

"It is good to hear you have made something of yourself. I would stay with you at this establishment if that is alright. I'm not welcome in this city."

"The war is making it more difficult than usual for those of our race," I said.

"Indeed, it was a hard journey, and I had to make many detours to circumvent the battle zone."

"And what would be the purpose of your journey, Jarl Gravenson?" Kat asked.

This time Father turned and stared at the elf, and his eyes blazed.

"That is between me and my son, and not something I would share with you."

Kat's smile fell from her face, her hands tightened on the table, and Golden tensed next to me.

"Father, the animosity between us and our sister race is an anachronism."

"Not for me," he growled.

"I know a little about your son, Jarl, having fought and bled at his side for many years, and I'm guessing you're here because you need his help. Ash has loyal friends in Hope who have stuck with him in the absence of family, even supporting him with his recent illness. We respect that you are his father but will not tolerate rudeness to any of our group. I know the dark elves have their code of honour, and you need to understand, so do we." Golden's little speech touched the one area of vulnerability in my father's personal armour.

"I have heard of the Code of the Hunters, though I understand not all adhere to it. It is something I admire and apologise if I have transgressed. The implied criticism of my family I do not accept. *Ashen Gwenverliy* chose to leave his people."

"I had little choice," I mumbled.

"You could have regained your honour," my father said.

"He never lost it in the first place," Golden said.

"Leave it," I snapped at my tall friend.

Golden and Miranda were the only people alive who knew the true story of my disgrace.

My father gave me a questioning look but, seeing no response, shrugged. For a moment, there was silence, and I could see he was becoming uncomfortable. He switched back to our tongue.

"Your youngest sister has disappeared, and I believe she is in Hope."

I excused myself and walked with my father to a booth at the rear of the room. Thoughts of my sister *Tanvaily*, or Shade, as she was known to the human world, came flooding back. If I had shamed my father, her behaviour had driven him to the point of insanity. My younger brother and other sister had chosen sensible life partners and found acceptable positions within dark elf society, but my youngest sister should have been thrown in prison on many occasions. Shade liked to steal items of value. It would be complimentary to call her a thief as she was never skilful in her endeavours. Although she tried to escape capture by spreading a web of lies, Shade usually tripped herself up and would then beg for forgiveness from beneath a shower of her own tears.

Anywin's wedding was the last occasion I witnessed her larceny. My younger brother pledged himself to his life partner beneath the Hanging Rock of the Highlands on a cloudy day just before High Sun. Felt-covered family yurts surrounded the gaily coloured celebration tent.

I remembered the weather had been mild for a change, and the long tables set out with plates of roast deer, boar, and goat. Plates of steaming potatoes, carrots, and beans covered in cream filled the air with an aroma that made everyone's mouths water. The wine and ale flowed freely as the guests placed their gifts on the Rug of Gold. My sister stood next to me when the Harlsforest family placed a delicate tiara with the other presents. I heard my sister's intake of breath and understood her appreciation. The design of this particular piece of jewellery caught the eye. A large opal sat in the centre of the design, surrounded by many small emeralds. The whole structure was held together with thin bands of gold. I knew the item would have been very expensive to create, as emeralds were not found on the high plateau of my people and would have been purchased from the tribes of the Original Men who lived in the jungles to the south of our homeland.

The celebrations grew as the evening progressed, and the temperature stayed above freezing, rare for the mountains. My people danced on the rock platform smoothed by thousands of similar celebrations, and I remember seeing Father and Mother gliding across the polished stone, smiling into each other's eyes. Nobody noticed my sister slip away.

In the morning, the tiara was gone. Other guests left during the night, so suspicion didn't automatically fall on my sister. Well, not from the other families anyway. I knew it was her from the moment the theft was discovered and took the belief to father. This was before my disgrace when he still respected my opinion. My mother didn't want to believe Shade had stolen again as my sister often promised to change her ways. Father knew I was right and immediately dispatched riders to find her.

She was found at a trading emporium on the edge of the Golden Hills. In those days of peace, human caravans would often visit our lands with a vast array of goods, bringing in wine, silk, and cotton items and leaving with furs, gold, and opals. Shade wore a dress of green silk and had purchased a few kegs of the finest red wines. She already sold the tiara, and it was heading north. Shade denied everything at first, claiming she saved the money, which allowed her to purchase the expensive items. Nobody believed her, as my sister had needed to borrow silver from my mother only a few days before the celebration. My father paid the Harlsforest family the cost of the tiara, though it took most of the gold he had stockpiled. They sent my sister, in disgrace, to the training centre at High Peak, though she was lucky not to have been thrown into Greystone Prison.

I always felt sympathy for my sister as she was the only one of my family who showed any sympathy when I had besmirched my family's honour. They assumed I disobeyed the long-standing taboo and led my command into The Demon Caves, where my warriors were slaughtered, yet I survived. Shade had never believed my story about what occurred in that cavern of fire and death. Being a consummate liar herself enabled her to see the untruths of others. In the end, I think she was glad the focus of the family's derision was no longer on her.

"What has she done this time?" I asked as we sat down on opposite sides of the rough wooden table.

"Stolen from the Snow Leopard himself."

"The War Leader who commands the army?"

"Shade took the Crown of Kings and disappeared. This time she was long gone before I could start looking for her. The Snow Leopard has charged our family with the Crown's return. Our position within the new order is at stake. We could all be made exiles unless the item is recovered. ."

This was a critical situation for our family. To be cast out of the mountains during this time of conflict would destroy our clan, and the shame would devastate Father. The Crown of Kings was a relic of our people to be held in trust in the Temple of The Moon and only brought out in times of great conflict. The Snow Leopard had united our people and created the alliance with the Original Men. He called for the Crown after reconquering The Golden Hills, but Shade had stolen it en route to his army. She travelled as part of the escort and seduced the commander of the convoy before drugging him and slipping away with the Crown.

"How do you know she is here in Hope?"

"The War Leader has agents in this city. They are not dark elves, so they blend in, but their loyalty is unquestionable. They are known as the Fists of the Snow Leopard and are ruthless warriors and assassins. A black mountain pony was found for sale at the horse markets outside the Southern Gates of the city. Our mounts are rarely sold far from the mountain range, and your sister's pony was black. It's the best lead I've had so far."

Part of me wanted to ask why I should care. My family had turned its back on me after one supposed error. Being the eldest and most successful of my father's children, my fall from grace was spectacular. The fact I covered up for the mistakes of my dead lover was something none of my people knew, though my sister suspected. I couldn't let my clan be cast from our Homeland – I remembered how I wandered lost and homeless until Golden found me.

"I have some contacts in Hope, and our people stand out here. Shade shouldn't be too hard to find."

"There is a catch," my father said. "The agents of the Snow Leopard are looking for Shade too. If they find her first, they will not be gentle, and our chance to rehabilitate our clan will be lost."

"Do you know who these agents are?"

"No, but they are completely loyal to our leader. They're Original Men. The Snow Leopard lifted these people up and treats them with respect. He convinced them the enemy are the fair-skinned humans which flood across the Western Ocean."

I was interested in the identifying feature of the Snow Leopard's agents, not their politics.

"Has she sold the Crown?" I asked.

"I don't know," my father said.

"Is she alone?"

"We think so. She committed the crime alone, but there is no way of knowing if Shade has picked up any accomplices since she left the Golden Hills."

I nodded and tried to think of where to start. It would be necessary to visit the captain at the watchhouse, and maybe Lord Alder could ask some of his trading partners to see if they had heard anything. Maybe Grandfather and his underworld connections knew something, but I didn't want to visit him unless it was really necessary. I wasn't very popular at his fortified mansion anymore.

"I will find her and the Crown, Father. I will not allow the clan to be cast out."

"This could regain your position in society."

"That's not why I'm doing it," I snapped. "I don't want to see Mother and the rest of the family exiled. The humans will slaughter you unless you went south into the jungles of the Original Men, and I don't think the climate there would agree with you."

"It's where we came from originally," my father said.

"Those stories are so old nobody is even sure if the legends are true."

"All of that doesn't matter. I'm just relieved you're going to help me. In the end, your motivation is your own affair."

I wasn't sure if he believed my reasons or not. In his mind, the chance to regain lost honour would be the most important consideration in choosing to help or not, but I didn't think that way, not anymore.

We ate slowly, and I enjoyed the taste of the curry while my father picked at a slice of lamb pie. The conversation was stilted, with father volunteering nothing. I asked about my mother, brother, and other sister, and then about the Battle Leader who had taken the title Snow Leopard as he led our people northward.

"How did he get the Original Men to join us?" I asked.

"The Snow Leopard lived with his clan on the southern slopes of the mountains which surround the high plateau. He had many dealings with the Original Men who live in the jungles and swamps. At the same time, the fair-skinned humans from across the sea were starting to cut down the trees along the jungle's eastern edge, despite pleas from the

Original Men to stop. He gathered a number of the jungle chiefs together and promised to equip them with swords and armour. They don't need missile weapons as their black bows are deadly."

"When will the Snow Leopard stop? I mean, he's taken back the Golden Hills, hasn't he?"

"It is his stated intention to drive the fair-skinned humans as far north as he can."

"Well, he wants to be careful. Hope and a group of the northern cities have stayed out of the conflict so far, but if the War Leader inflicts too many defeats on the Dukes and Southern States, that might change. In the end, numbers will prevail, I don't care how good a general he is."

"He has won three major battles and been successful with a number of sieges. Castle after castle has fallen to us." Father's eyes shone as he spoke.

"But now he has stalled before the gates of Kathel. The towns of the peninsula are well fortified and impossible to put under a full siege without a navy, and we have never had one of those."

"The Snow Leopard will find a way."

I grunted. My father's blind faith in the leader of our people was out of character. The dark elf who led the army must be very charismatic to sway the leaders of the two hundred clans.

The dizziness hit me suddenly, and I almost collapsed into the gravy on my trencher.

My father called out, but I didn't register what he said. Waves of pain rolled from my skull and down into my neck. Then Golden was next to me, speaking softly in my ear. I don't remember how I ended up back at the bookshop; I can only recall the pain which swamped my senses. Finally, I regained some control of my body as I lay on a couch near the front shutters of the store. Golden lit the fire and while Kat ground up some herbs with a mortar and pestle.

"The magician indicated these would help control the side effects of the potion," the elf said.

My father stood to one side, looking from Kat to Golden.

"What is this illness which so debilitates you?" he asked.

"It's an old fever from the swamps to the east," Golden said quickly.

Kat frowned and continued grinding, and I glanced at the floor.

"I see," my father said. "Well, I pray it is something which passes quickly."

I hoped it would, but suspected the pain would become an ongoing issue, one which I had brought on myself.

3

A WELL-DRESSED THIEF

The herbs Kat brewed for me became a bitter-tasting tea, which gave me a good night's sleep. When I woke in the morning, I didn't immediately remember my father's presence. Going downstairs, I found him cooking eggs and bread in a large skillet. A pot sat on the coals nearby, dribbling steam.

"I awoke early and became hungry. The food was in the larder under the stairs, so I helped myself. I hope you don't mind," my father said.

"Not at all," I said.

"Your timing is excellent, as there is enough for both of us."

I smiled at a memory. "Rackhime said I had an amazing skill of turning up just as he had finished cooking."

"Who is Rackhime?"

"He was the old man who used to own this establishment. He's dead now."

"And the store is yours. I don't know a lot about businesses such as these. All I've seen are travelling fairs. Your shop looks orderly and well run.

"Thanks to my friends. In my illness, I let the place slip, but they cleaned it up."

"Their loyalty is to be commended."

Nodding, I moved toward the food.

"The Captain will help. He's a friend in the City Watch," I said. "He may be able to give us an indication of where Shade is. After all, dark elves don't exactly fade into the background in Hope."

"I shall come with you," my father said.

Not being sure how it would look with two dark elves wandering around the city together, I hesitated, then nodded and retrieved my cloak. Quickly I slipped the Cold Blade from its hiding place behind a loose beam and put a dagger in my boot. My father's eyes became wide when he saw the shortsword.

"Is that what I think it is?" he asked.

"If by that you mean, 'is it a Cold Blade,' then the answer is yes."

"Where did you get it from?"

"It's a long story," I said.

I remembered the skeletal fingers of the dwarf, breaking as I slid the blade from its hands. The cave had been almost dark except for the dim circle of light which came from Golden's torch. Ahead the cavern turned a sharp corner. Somewhere the tunnel entered the dragon's lair, and then we would stare at death. Golden had whispered to me, "We now both hold Cold Blades." I held a finger to my lips and gestured for him to take point.

"There are only twelve, aren't there?" father asked.

"Yes, all made by elves."

Father shook his head and pulled his cloak tightly around his neck.

"The weather turned overnight, and the rain now comes from the Northest. It will mean snow at home."

I nodded and imagined the stunted pines and rowan trees coated in the first layer of white for the year. The memory brought a burst of melancholy to me, so I pushed it away.

We drew stares from people on the streets, but luckily the number of folk outdoors was down due to the weather. Captain Waldheigheim wasn't at the watchhouse, and the office staff directed me to a small alley off Fish Street. My tall thin friend stood towering over the other blue cloaked members of the Watch. They gathered in doorways talking in muted tones and tried to stay dry. Next to a large broken crate, lay the body of a young man. He lay on his back, and I could see a straight red gash in the side of his neck. The rain washed all the blood away, and the wound stood out clearly. The death stroke appeared to be precise and probably came from a dagger or shortsword. The man seemed to have been young, barely more than eighteen years old. His hair stuck to pale skin, and large eyes stared up at the weeping sky. Contorted features marked the boy's face giving the impression he had died in great pain, yet the wound looked clean. He would have been considered handsome before his death. His clothes were well-tailored; the cloak trimmed with rabbit fur and the pants made of deerskin. A woollen shirt, dyed dark red, covered a thin torso. By his side lay an old longsword with a battered wooden hilt.

"Ah, Ashley, it's good to see you up and about. And who is this distinguished figure who walks next to you?" the captain asked.

I cringed at the use of the name, as I hated it and only tolerated it from this man.

"This is my father, Jarl Gravenson," I answered.

"It is a pleasure to meet you, sir."

I introduced the Captain, and my father's eyes widened again when I said the rank.

Smiling inside, I felt my back straighten. My father seemed to be impressed that I was not washed up and on the scrap heap of Hope society. Then I remembered how close I had come to destroying myself, and my smugness evaporated.

"And how may I help you?" the Captain asked.

Explaining my sister was missing and probably in Hope, he agreed to make some inquiries. I left out why she had come to the city but did say that she might not want to be found. Captain Waldheigheim raised one end of his long single eyebrow but said nothing.

He then turned and gestured at the body. "What do you think?"

"I would ask why a thief is wearing such expensive clothing," I said.

"How do you know he's a thief?"

"The sword is old and worn. If he was a dock worker or someone of a similar profession, he would have rough hands and wouldn't carry anything larger than a dagger. I also notice his shoes are soft-soled and are a lot older than the rest of his attire."

"I do wish you were working for me, Ashley. We noticed the same things, of course, but what about the wound?"

"Somebody who knew their job," I said.

"Ah, yes, but you probably wouldn't have noticed the broken fingers, as they are hidden by the cloak."

"He was tortured?"

"It would seem so. Every one of his fingers has been smashed by a hammer."

"Why would someone torment him?" my father asked.

"That, Jarl, is one of the questions I would like answered."

I watched as the sketch artist set up an easel in the shelter of a doorway, and a watchman flipped the cape away from the fingers. Now I could see how they had been squashed along the line of the knuckles.

"It wasn't anything to do with money, as they left his coin pouch," the Captain said. "Not that he had much, just a few cut pieces of silver and this small gold coin."

He heard the intake of my father's breath, and I dragged my eyes away from the corpse. Between Captain Waldheigheim's thumb and index finger was a shiny gold coin emblazoned with the head of an eagle.

"A Dremon," I hissed.

"Sorry?" the Captain said.

"It's a coin my people mint in our homeland to pay for the goods we buy from humans. We only use them rarely as your people are happier with chopped gold," my father said.

"It could be a coincidence," Captain Waldheigheim said. "But we don't believe in coincidences, do we, Ashley?"

I nodded and wiped the rain from my eyes.

We walked away from the Captain toward the book shop. There were a number of questions buzzing around in my head. I had a lead on my sister, but I wasn't sure where to start my search. Perhaps I should question the tailors of Jailer's Road or find Wink and ask him if he knew if any of his young street friends had recently struck it lucky.

"Why would she give money to a thief?" my father asked.

I had been so wrapped in my own thoughts I hadn't considered what he must be thinking. "*Tanvaily* needs help if she is to stay hidden. She must have found this young thief and offered him some sort of deal."

"And he spent the money on new clothes."

"I was thinking about that," I said. "If a young man suddenly comes into money, new attire is not usually the first thing he spends it on. Also, when a commoner does buy expensive clothes, they tend to be very tasteless and often, the result is a riot of colour. Our corpse seemed to have uncommonly good fashion sense."

Father nodded. "You have done this type of thing before, haven't you? Otherwise, why would the captain of the City Watch know you, and why would he be asking your opinion and suggesting you work for him?"

"Captain Waldheigheim and I have helped each other in the past."

Father didn't say another word until we were inside the shop. He sat down and ran his fingers through long white hair.

"I think with your help, we will find your sister before the Snow Leopard's agents. But you must understand if we do, I need to take her back to the southern mountains to stand trial."

"Father, our chances of finding Shade first are slim. Who do you think was torturing that young man, and why? They were almost certainly these agents your leader sent north, and if our young corpse broke before he died, then they have information we are yet to find."

"He is your leader too."

"What?"

"The Snow Leopard is your leader too."

I shook my head. Is that all father had heard? Clenching my teeth, I went upstairs. I needed to get some silver from its hidden place amongst the thatch to pay some bribes. My father's opinion was not important, or that's what I tried to tell myself.

Jailer's Road is not appropriately named anymore. Long ago, condemned prisoners were taken from the Citadel down a wide track to a square near the massive southern gate where they were executed by axe. Now prisoners are killed by rope in front of the watchhouse. Hovels line the road at its bottom end, but as it rises up the side of the peaks, the houses become more affluent. It was here the tailors set up their businesses. The response of the proprietors to a pair of dark elves gracing their establishments was cold, to say the least. It took a few pieces of silver to change their attitudes to something more cooperative. By the time we reached the fourth shop, my funds were running low.

"If this next owner doesn't know anything, we are going to have to return to the shop. I don't have the coin to keep paying these tailors to talk," I said.

"The clan can pay. I don't expect you to shoulder the burden of our inquiries by yourself."

I almost refused the offer but realised I didn't have the silver I once possessed. Nodding wearily, I stepped inside a shop called 'The Well-Dressed Gentleman'. The interior glowed. Bright lamps which burned sandalwood oil hung from a dozen locations within the store. The smell filled my nostrils, and for a moment, I was back in the Far East.

"We probably don't have the type of clothes you are looking for," a cold voice said.

A small man with a long piece of ribbon around his neck approached us. His bald head shone, but his chin was covered with a sharp-pointed beard. Silk and soft leather covered him, and his boots were made from snakeskin.

"We are not here for clothes," my father said.

He held a small polished piece of opal in front of the man's nose and let him have a good look at it. The shopkeeper's expression softened. His eyes glinted, and he took a step backward.

"How can I help you?" the bald man asked.

I caught a glimpse of the opal and understood the change in attitude. With the gem, Father could have purchased five outfits.

"We are interested in a young man who might have bought an

outfit at your store recently. A cloak lined with rabbit fur, deerskin pants, and a red shirt," I said.

"And a dark elf woman," my father said.

The shopkeeper looked strangely at my father and then stroked his beard.

"I don't know about the woman, although..." The man straightened his jacket. "There were four young men in here about eight or nine days ago. All of them were dressed in rough clothing, and I was going to ask them to leave when a cloaked figure dropped a pouch full of silver on my table. The young men then told me they wanted the best outfits I had to offer. They wanted clothes I had already made, saying they were in a hurry. The cloaked figure chose the outfits but never said a thing. I could tell by the shape and the way she moved it was a woman."

"There were four young men?" my father asked.

"That is what I said," the shopkeeper answered.

"How did they pay?" I asked.

"It was all in the silver coin of Hope. Freshly minted, though I could tell some of it was from the gambling halls."

"How do you know that?" I asked.

"The men and women who run the various tables bite the corners of the coins to check they are not fakes. It's faster than weighing them."

"Grandfather," I growled.

The shopkeeper heard me and stepped away, but this time he held his hands up in front of his chest.

"I don't want anything to do with that man. I haven't done anything wrong."

"You are safe," I said. "You have just opened another line of inquiry, one that will have no impact on you. Thank you for your assistance."

I nodded at father, and he dropped the gem into the man's hand. The opal disappeared, and we were back on the street, standing in the doorway as a shower of rain hid the Peaks behind a grey curtain.

"This just got a lot more complicated," I said.

"Why?"

"Because she has sold the Crown, and I think the buyer is one of Hope's most ruthless criminals."

The only way I could think such a large number of coins from the gambling dens ended up in the hands of a mysterious cloaked woman was if my sister had sold the item to Grandfather. That would also explain how Shade managed to find a group of young thieves who were willing to do her bidding. Not content with her hired help protecting her, they had to look the part as well. It had been Shade's first mistake, and knowing my sister, it wouldn't be her last. I received a description of all the young men from the shopkeeper before we left and knew the blond-haired one now lay on a stone slab in the basement of the watchhouse. How much he had told the agents of the Snow Leopard before his death was anyone's guess. My best chance of finding these young men might be by talking to Wink, and he wouldn't open up unless I gave him a lot of coin. I hoped my father had a number of opals in his purse, as it looked as though we might need them.

We were just entering the bookstore when a voice hailed us from across the street. A well-built man wearing a cloak approached us with his hands raised. Glancing around, I noticed a woman leaning against the wall of a house a little further up the street and another smaller man peering at us from the mouth of an alley. I reached for my sword, but my father grabbed my arm and pushed it away from the hilt of the Cold Blade.

"They are Original Men, agents of the Snow Leopard."

The man continued to walk forward slowly. I could now see his brown skin and curly dark hair. He continued to keep his hand well clear of his cape, but his companions would have concealed weapons close by and could rush to the agent's side if he was threatened.

"I have new orders for the Jarl, from the Snow Leopard," the man said.

He slowly reached inside his cloak and withdrew a folded

parchment sealed with white wax. My father took the letter and opened it. He read slowly and then sighed.

"I've been ordered back to the army. The agents are to find your sister and retrieve the Crown."

My father looked grey and washed out. His shoulders slumped, and he leaned against the wall.

"My chance to rescue our family's honour is at an end."

I owed Father very little, but felt sorry for him and had never seen him so vulnerable and defeated. So I made a promise which would almost destroy me.

"Father, I will find Shade and the Crown."

He turned, looked at me, and smiled. I hadn't seen him do that for as long as I could remember.

"You are not to become involved," the agent snapped.

We both turned and stared at the man. I could now see his brown eyes, which were flat and empty.

"The Snow Leopard doesn't command me," I said.

The man held my eyes. I saw a flash behind those orbs and knew he had just become an enemy, but I didn't care. The smile Father had just given me was more important than any threat the agent represented. He turned and walked to the woman who gave him a nod before following. The smaller man disappeared but would be somewhere close by.

"They will kill you if you get in their path," father said.

"I know this city, they don't, and I have some powerful friends. Maybe they need to be careful."

"You have been sick, don't place yourself at risk."

"Do you want me to find Shade and get the Crown back?" I asked.

"Of course I do, my son, and I want our good name restored, but not at the cost of your life."

I had to turn away so my father wouldn't see the moisture in my eyes. We had our differences, and there was still anger and disappointment directed at me over my exile, but this was something new. Our family believed the loss of the squad I commanded was my fault, and I hadn't said anything to challenge that position, but the few days Father spent with me seemed to have softened his feelings. I didn't for a heartbeat believe everything was repaired between the two of us, but at least he cared.

He left the following day just after dawn. The weather cleared, and warmth returned, causing a mist to rise from the cobbles of the street. Golden was there as well as Spike, but the dire wolf stayed inside so as not to scare the horses. I hugged Father briefly as Golden checked the clinch and reigns. I was surprised he showed concern at the Jarl's wellbeing but surmised perhaps he noticed the improvement in Father's attitude. My heart beat a little faster at our parting, and I wished we had more time together. These feelings surprised me, and I wondered at my ability to forgive. The previous evening I broached the topic of my father disobeying orders and staying with me, but the idea had been firmly rejected.

"If you fail, then our family's best chance to win back the Snow Leopard's good grace is by our clan's achievements on the battlefield, and to do that, I must lead our warriors."

This statement concerned me, as it suggested, Father might take unnecessary risks with his own life or those of his soldiers to win back the favour of his leader.

We hugged, and the Jarl of Gravenson Clan cantered down the street toward the West Gate. Golden gave my shoulder a squeeze before going inside to make tea. We sat together in silence, nursing our mugs for a while staring at the flames.

"So, do you think these agents will come for you?" my friend asked eventually.

"I don't think so. If I get in their way, they might attack me."

"And they'll have no hesitation about killing your sister?"

"None. They want the Crown, and they won't care what happens to her. Once she tells them where it is, they'll probably slit her throat. That's when the fun will start for Grandfather. Once they know he has the Crown, they'll go after him."

"If it wasn't for your sister, I'd encourage them," Golden said.

"I agree. If they managed to kill the old man, I'd celebrate for ten days, but that's all a dream. I've made a promise to my father, and I intend to fulfil it."

Later, I set out to find Wink. I would have gone earlier, but one of my dizzy spells hit soon after Golden left, and I was forced to make myself some herbal paste to keep the headache, which followed at bay. It took some time before the foul-tasting concoction took affect, so I spent time copying wanted pictures for the Captain. Losing my little finger had forced me to adjust my quill style, and I could write as well as before. The drawing helped soothe the pain in my skull. I watched as the quill flowed over the parchment, and as each new line appeared, the throbbing decreased. By the time I felt well enough to move, the picture of Adrie Cathlos, a wanted murderer and outlaw, had been completed.

I found Wink in front of the Mermaid talking to Aneeta. She was flirting with the poor boy, and I could see that he was red in the face and seemed to be hopping from one foot to the other.

"Are you tormenting him again?" I asked.

Aneeta put her hand in front of her chest and opened her eyes wide. "If I did, I would help to put the poor lad out of his misery. I couldn't just leave him in such a state, could I?"

I smiled and considered paying for the boy to watch the tall, long-haired woman dance. Aneeta performed at the Mermaid most afternoons and evenings and had been a friend of mine for almost three years. This game she played with Wink was getting more provocative. He turned sixteen a few days ago, and I heard Aneeta promising an extraordinary present.

"You will need to make good on your commitments to the lad one day," I said.

"Oh, I plan to, eventually."

A security guard stuck his head out of the gold-painted door.

"You're up next," the thickset man said.

Aneeta turned, winked at the boy, and then swayed up the steps before disappearing inside the Mermaid.

"I'd pay for you to watch her dance, but I think it would only make your situation worse," I said.

"Do you think she will ever keep her promise?" the red-headed boy asked.

"Who knows? If it was Stella, I would say definitely, but with Aneeta, it's hard to be sure. Anyway, that's not why I'm here."

Gesturing to Wink, I took him into a side alley. The smell of rotting garbage and horse shit was strong, but I ignored it and moved close to him.

"I need to know if any of your friends got lucky lately. You know, came into money. They would probably be good looking lads."

Wink leaned away from me and looked back out into the street. Carts and pedestrians flowed in both directions at the alley's mouth, but nobody even glanced at us.

"I don't know anything."

By the way he moved I knew he was lying.

"Yes, you do. I'll make it worth your while. I need to track these boys down as their lives are in danger."

"This is tied up with Grandfather, so I can't talk."

Well, that confirmed one of my suspicions; the old man was definitely involved.

"I know the boys have got themselves a rich and attractive patron, and I guess that Grandfather helped set up the deal, but the person they work for is not what she seems. The boys are in over their heads."

Wink chewed on his lip before glancing out of the alley again. He then bit on a fingernail and shook his head.

"I'll give you enough coin so you can spend some quality time with Aneeta," I said.

Wink rolled his eyes and looked at the door to the Mermaid. He gave a brief nod and then put his hand out. I dropped the small opal my father had left me, into his palm.

"Stitch, Jolen, Tucker, and Struts all got this job with some woman who pays well. She did a deal with Grandfather, and then he whistled up the boys. After that, they all disappeared for a while. I saw Jolen at the markets buying food not long ago and he was dressed like a noble. He told me his client was real easy on the eyes and paid well for his silence. Wouldn't say any more, but then later, I heard he turned up dead in an alley. I started to get worried, so I asked around. That's when Grandfather sent Mugs and that new woman Sabella to warn me about asking too many questions."

"Do you know where the boys are?"

"I'm not certain, but they always used to sleep around the warehouses near the Port District."

That was enough. I would find them with this information unless the agents of the Snow Leopard already had. I hoped Golden and Kat would come with me, but I knew I couldn't count on their assistance.

"Should I go and see if Aneeta is available now?"

I smiled. A young man's mind is usually dominated by one thing.

"She'll be dancing at the moment, but that opal should be enough to get you through the door to watch her, and enough to get you upstairs with her as well."

Wink didn't even say goodbye. He ran across the road into the Mermaid and disappeared inside.

4

A GREEN DRESS

The Port district had always been the darkest area of the city once the sun set, and I was in my element. My eyes adjusted like those of a cat and the corners and hidden places all became clear. I wore my Cold Blade and carried the double-shot crossbow I had had specially made while adventuring in the East. The weapon was small and its range short, but the bolts could inflict grievous wounds at close range. Golden and Spike were with me, but Kat had refused to help.

"She's still not happy with you. Says you need more time to recover before taking on jobs like this," Golden said.

I grunted thinking about it. Kat's anger was understandable. She was very protective of Golden and viewed my slide into addiction as a betrayal of our friendship. I suppose in some regards she was right. As for taking on this task, I couldn't control the arrival of my father and the urgency of finding my sister any more than I could stop the Great River.

"Any idea where they're hiding?" Golden asked.

I nodded and signalled that I would take the lead position. Running down a number of narrow alleys, we climbed over piles of crates. Taking the three of us through a maze of piled goods, we eventually reached the piers which stuck out into the river. Ahead I could see cogs and three-masted lanterns tied to barges and longboats. All of them were dark and quiet. The wooden treadle crane sat idle with its large round wheel creaking slightly. I focused on the sound and searched. My eyes spotted movement, but then the shape disappeared amongst piles of cut timber, which sat on the pier.

"There's somebody down there," I said into Golden's ear.

He nodded and drew a blackened dagger. Neither of us wanted to draw our Cold Blades yet as they might catch the moonlight and give our position away.

Using my sister's love of comfort, I had tracked her here. I knew she wouldn't want to stay in a warehouse. They were generally smelly buildings, full of rats and hard to keep secure. A boat, on the other hand, could be comfortable and provide you with a means of escape. The only problem was due to the benign weather, many had made late-season voyages and were now tied together in such numbers that only those at the very outside would be able to move. None of the boats on the inside could maneuverer away from the jetties.

I signalled to Golden, and we crept in short bursts between piles of crates and the cut wood. Spike knew we were trying to be stealthy, and his instincts became that of a hunter. I searched the area near the crane and eventually saw movement on the deck of a lantern ship which was tied up nearby. The boat's sails were furled and the deck covered in bundles of furs. I watched as a figure dashed across the wooden planking and jumped to the deck of a riverboat tied to the ship's other side. This smaller craft was piled high with bags of potatoes and pumpkins, which were all bound for the markets of Hope. I heard a soft clicking, and Golden pointed at the start of the pier. Two men carrying burning torches walked along the waterfront. Their long cloaks hung to their boots, and crossbows rested on their shoulders. They were obviously from the Watch and making their rounds. A small amount of goods were stolen from ships while they rested at port, but the vigilance of the guards meant the pilfering would always remain small-scale, and anything of real value was not left on board.

Dropping into a crouch, I ran toward the first boat. Golden, Spike, and I had to find some cover before the two men wandered down the pier. Our quarry moved onto another boat, this one a flat-bottomed barge. It was tied to another ship, and these boats formed a bridge between one pier and the next. I worried the figure we followed might be able to slip away, presuming he knew he was being followed. At this stage, I didn't know if the fleeing individual was one of the missing boys or an agent of the Snow Leopard. We took cover behind the furled sail on the lantern and waited for the members of the City Watch to move on. They seemed to take forever to walk to the end of the jetty and return to dry land. I heard snatches of conversation between the two men which drifted on the breeze as they disappeared amongst the warehouses.

By the time we were on the deck of the flat-bottomed barge, the moon had disappeared behind clouds. A small rope ladder hung from the side of another lantern. This ship was large, with three masts and a bow spit and would have been able to cross the western sea to The Old World. I climbed to the deck and crouched low. A built-in area at the stern was big enough to contain the captain's quarters and a dining area, and maybe another cabin or two. From the light shining through a small glass window, I saw a body sprawled in the doorway. White crushed powder lay scattered across the deck. I reached out and picked up some of the substance, noting that it was eggshell. Golden left Spike on the lower boat, climbed over the rail, and dropped down next to me. Pointing at the eggshell, I slid forward, sweeping it from my path. The pieces would have given away the footfall of any intruders on the deck. It was only my acute eyesight that allowed me to spot it.

A dark pool of blood surrounded the body in the doorway. I was almost at the opening when a short man with a shaved head stepped out. He gave a gasp of surprise, and I dove sideways. I heard the click of a crossbow, and a bolt whizzed past my feet and cracked into the mainmast. I fired a bolt from my handheld crossbow, but I couldn't tell if I had hit anyone. Then Golden yelled, and Spike growled. The wolf tried to leap to the deck of the higher ship but couldn't make it. I glimpsed combat behind me before darting into the captain's cabin, my Cold Blade in one hand and crossbow in the other. I saw a dagger spinning toward me and swayed aside. My crossbow tracked a shape across the room, and I pulled the trigger. There was a grunt, and a body collapsed onto the floor. A corpse lay near a small open trap door.

I sensed movement behind me. My hand just made it in front of my throat as a wire tightened. The thin steel bit into my flesh, and liquid ran down my arm. My assailant pulled back, but I shifted my weight and threw myself forward, rolling. The move tossed my attacker over my head and onto a chest. Long dark hair and curved hips. A woman. She recovered quickly and sprang backward toward the window, drawing her blade.

"We are not enemies," I said, taking a step forward.

"You have killed Shiny and interfere in the Snow Leopard's business. We warned you to stay out of this," she growled.

"She is my sister."

The woman slashed at my head, and I caught her blade on mine. I focused my thoughts on a raging blizzard and pushed the image into my sword. Frost appeared on my blade and ran down onto the woman's weapon. She screamed and dropped the sword, hugging her blackened fingers to her chest.

"It's over," I said. "Surrender, and we'll work this out."

The woman seemed to relax, and I stepped away in order to move around the chest between us. She turned quickly and dove through the rear window of the cabin and into the water. By the time I reached the smashed glass, she had disappeared, but I heard splashing and Golden's voice by the side of the ship. I ran through the cabin and back onto the deck, where I noticed a large Cold Blade buried in the railing. Golden yelled for help. I stepped to the side of the ship and peered down. Spike was doing the same from the barge. Between the two vessels, my friend floundered around in the murky water.

"Help me out," he yelled.

"Where is the man you were fighting?" I asked.

"We both went over the side, but he dived under, and I lost him. He came out of the front hatch."

I lowered one of the ropes on the ship down to him. Golden climbed up and stood next to me on the deck. Water ran from his hair and clothes and formed a puddle around his feet.

"One of his companions had the same idea, but I finished the other," I said.

"I slashed at him, but my sword got stuck when it hit the rail."

I grunted. It was rare that Golden missed with the Cold Blade, so his opponent must have been skilled.

I found a small oil lantern and lit it from the light source in the smaller cabin. This room held a bed covered in women's clothing. On top of them lay a sheer green dress made from silk.

"This was my sister's room."

"How do you know?" Golden asked.

"Green is her favourite colour, and she loves silk."

"Don't all women?"

"True, but this pendant on the shoulder is a mountain wolf. It is one of the symbols of my clan."

Taking the pendant, I walked back into the main cabin. The body of the bald man lay near the head of a double bed, my bolt embedded under his chin. A good-looking boy laid on his side near the trap door, in his hand an old cutlass. His brown curls covered one eye, but the other stared without seeing. Golden turned the body onto its back and pushed one of the arms aside. Then he closed the young man's eyes and stepped away from the corpse.

"He has only one wound, straight through the heart. The lad hasn't gone stiff yet, so this didn't happen very long before we arrived."

I nodded and climbed through the trap door into the hold. Walking toward the bow, I moved around large kegs of wine. Another of the boys lay near the forward hatch. He had a cut on his arm and another on his hip. The killing blow was through the throat. Blood drenched the large boy's fine new clothes. He obviously held this position while someone went up and out of the front portal. I guessed the boys had died so my sister could make her escape.

I returned to Golden.

"They heard the eggshells, and one of them went to check. It was a smart move scattering the pieces on the deck, but the boy was shot as he opened the door. Then Shade positioned each of the lads at a hatch to slow those who were pursuing them. It looks like she got away. I'm guessing the agents were searching for the Crown when we interrupted them," I said.

"So she threw those boys to the wolves. Nice. You sure you're from the same family?" Golden asked.

"Shade always puts herself first."

"Well, what do we do now? Your friends have swum away except for the bald one, who isn't going anywhere, and your sister looks like she escaped."

"One of the agents isn't here and might be trying to pick up Shade's trail, though I don't like his chances."

"Why's that?"

"Shade is fast and well-trained. She will be armed and a match for any agent in a one-on-one confrontation, if her courage holds. Besides, she will have gone straight to Grandfather."

"That won't make him happy," Golden said.

"No, I'm not sure what he will do. He might kill her, or he could decide the agents of the Snow Leopard are intruding on his patch."

I knew he'd killed perceived rivals before when one of the dark elf clans paid for my assassination as revenge for the death of their sons after my command had been destroyed in the caves. He ordered the destruction of the team sent to kill me and then informed me I owed him a favour. I considered that debt paid with interest by my actions the previous winter.

"Why don't you go and get Spike while I have a look around," I said.

Golden nodded and left while I started to pick through the jumble of clothes on the captain's bed. I thought the ship probably belonged to Grandfather or an associate of his. They must have made this location available to my sister.

My hand still bled from the wire, so I wrapped a cotton scarf around it. The steel had bit into the flesh just above where my little finger used to be. It stung and would probably need a stitch or two. I began to carefully search through my sister's possessions. It was a strange feeling as some of the items brought back powerful memories. The wolf pendant, for example, given to both of us on the same day we graduated from the associated combat style. There were three disciplines the children of clan leaders could train in; wolf, hunting cat, and eagle. I was proficient in all three, though trained with my sister in the skills of the wolf. She started training in the methods of an Eagle Warrior but had quit halfway through because of an argument with an instructor. The next item, Shade's jade necklace of leaping trout, had been given to her by Father when a trade delegation of humans from the north visited our encampment. She was only a child at the time, and I could remember her squealing with delight after she took it from the leather pouch.

A small brown parchment peeked out among expensive fur gloves and leather shoes. It was in the language of our people and appeared torn and ripped at the corners.

It is agreed. The guards will be drugged and sleep heavily on the night when the moon is full. The item will then be yours to take. Move swiftly for the drug will only give you a night's start. Sell the item in the human city of Hope to the previously mentioned contact. We will be watching.

No signature, but it was immediately obvious to me Shade had not acted alone. There must be those of my people who did not support the Snow Leopard. Why they believed the theft of the Crown would undermine his leadership was something which eluded me. Part of me felt glad not all the dark elves blindly followed the war leader. I wondered what Shade was caught up in. Then I realised whatever it was, she'd now dragged me into it too.

Water dripping from Golden's sodden frame announced his arrival. Then Spike's wet nose push against my hand. I read the note to him while he used some of the bedding to dry his hair.

"So, your sister was actually working for someone else, one of the other clan leaders maybe," Golden said.

"It's possible. Why steal the Crown, though? Why is it so important?"

"Perhaps they wanted to embarrass the Snow Leopard?"

"That's probably true, but it won't undermine his leadership. I wish I knew more about the law associated with the Crown. My father would have been able to tell me, but it's too late to ask him now."

"What about Petar's old books? They might tell you something,"

Golden said. "He's due back in Hope any day now, and so is Miranda."

I slowly chewed on my lip. It would give me a legitimate reason to visit her, but I wasn't sure if I was ready.

"I'll think about it," I muttered.

We left the ship and bodies where they were and returned to the shop. I slept heavily that night for the first time in an age and woke refreshed to the sound of the wind. It was blowing a gale outside, and I could see the white caps of high waves on the river through my window. The sound whistled through the streets and rustled the thatch in the roof. The air had a bite to it, and dark clouds piled up to the north. The weather was about to change.

After having a bowl of pumpkin soup at Barnabus's Place, I paid Captain Waldheigheim a visit. I informed him of the bodies on the ship, and though I tried to keep the story vague, the man's intellect was sharp, and he went straight to the heart of the matter.

"Your sister is a thief and has brought trouble to our city," he said.

"That's true, but there's more to this than just a snatch and sell. The politics of my people are involved, as is a major crime figure. I'm going to need time to sort this out," I said.

"So why are you telling me all this, Ashley?"

"Because I trust you, and I don't want you wasting your time trying to solve a crime you have no background on. I don't want you walking into a situation where you don't understand what is at stake."

"I now have the background, and I can't ignore murder."

"I know that. I just thought we could help each other."

The Captain stroked his eyebrow and then leaned back in his chair. "I believe we can, but any cooperation would be off the books. If I find your sister, I will arrest her, though I'm not sure what the charge will be."

"Of course! Actually, a prison cell might be the safest place for her," I said.

I needed to see Grandfather but wondered if the risks were worth it. As I walked along Fish Street, shielding my eyes from flying dust, I thought of our last meeting. On that occasion, I handed him three thousand silver so that Miranda could marry Old Petar. If it was his last memory of me, maybe he wouldn't kill me on sight. The storm broke just as I reached the shop, and I dashed inside. Standing looking at a number of scrolls was a dark elf woman with short-cropped white hair. She wore a light blue cloak that hugged her figure, and I noted a buckskin coat tossed over the leather couch. I was struck speechless as this woman's features were almost identical to those of my long-dead lover, Zenta. Her cool eyes swept over me before coming to rest on my face.

"I bring greetings from the Sunspear Clan and the Battle Leader, and beg the hospitality of your house," she said.

It was a formal greeting and one I was supposed to reply to with a set phrase, but I had been away from my people for so long I couldn't remember the words.

Her eyes narrowed, and she took a step toward the door.

"Of course, if there is no welcome for my clan…"

"I can't remember the words," I blurted out.

Her eyes softened, and she turned and smiled at me. "Maybe you have been away too long, *Ashen*, the Softly Spoken."

I felt a lump form in my throat. "Nobody has called me that in a very long time."

"I believe it was your name at the academies. The words you are searching for are *my hearth is yours. My house is yours until the next setting sun.* Do you remember now?"

"You are welcome to stay, but please don't call me that name. It drags back too many old memories."

"The past is full of all manner of feelings, but none of them should be shut away," she said.

I didn't want to talk about this anymore.

"I don't know your name, though your clan is one I have had some association with as we trained together at the Lodge of the Hunting

Cat. As a group, we roamed the forests together on the outer slopes. I saw the sea for the first time from amongst the pines with warriors from your people."

"It is good to know the memories you associate with my clan are pleasant ones. My name is Kedria, and I'm here to help you find the Crown."

I was stunned and hopeful. Maybe the Snow Leopard had changed his mind about killing my sister. She handed me a sheet of parchment. There was no wax seal, but I could see the mark of a dark elf leader.

"I don't know this sign," I said.

"It is from the Snow Leopard, and it authorises me to assist you in finding the Crown. Unfortunately, it doesn't withdraw the mandate given to previous groups. I believe our leader wishes to explore all options in retrieving the stolen item."

"He is not my leader," I said.

I expected a reaction to that but Kedria only raised an eyebrow.

"Indeed, there are a small number amongst our people who feel the same way."

"I was wondering why the Crown is so important. It's an ancient relic, but surely a Great War leader would need his army more than an old piece of silver."

"He cannot be crowned king while it's in the hand of our enemies. That is the law."

I whistled and threw back my head. "The Snow Leopard wants to be crowned king! We haven't had a hereditary ruling family for many, many generations. No wonder some dark elves are not very happy."

"Those in opposition are few."

This didn't seem right. I was getting drawn back into a world I had fled – been pushed from. My head started to spin, and pain burst behind my eyes. I collapsed with a thud and woke up naked in bed. The room spun, and my mouth felt as though I had been licking Spike's coat. Three or four candles lit my loft bedroom, and I could see Golden sitting on a stool at the end of my bed, eating flatbread rolled around some meat.

"These are delicious, Ash. That houseguest of yours certainly is a great cook."

"I need my herbs," I croaked.

Golden disappeared, and I heard his heavy footfall on the steps. There was a distant conversation, and then my friend returned, carrying a steaming mug. He handed it to me and sat back down.

"Her common tongue is a bit formal, but we're managing to understand each other. She must be strong, dragging you up here and putting you to bed, but your people have always had great strength. It must be the mountain air. I suppose she got a bit of an eyeful, though your race has never been big on modesty."

"That's the elves," I muttered.

"Anyway, a few seasons ago, I would have been competing with you for her attentions – and winning, of course. Now I'm with Kat, though, so that sort of behaviour is out of the question."

"I'm not interested in her."

"Yeah, I know, you're still hooked on Miranda. But she's not here, and after all, she is married, so it's not like you would be breaking any of the rules."

"Shut up, Golden."

"I mean, she has more curves than your average dark elf, and I know you like that, and now she has seen your package, maybe she'll be interested in purchasing."

"My head is pounding, and I think I want to kill you."

"Well, the pain is self-inflicted, but at least the response shows you're returning to normal."

"Kedria will be going in the morning."

"But she said she is here to help you find the Crown."

"She works for the Snow Leopard and will get in my way. Anyway, how do I know I can trust her?"

"I would have thought that's why you would want to keep her close. That way it won't matter if you trust her or not."

"I plan to keep a very close eye on her, don't worry about that."

5

THE PRICE OF TREASON

I had to agree, keeping Kedria close was probably wise. She knew the ways of my people better than I did and understood the current politics. Her clan was not one of the larger ones, and in many ways, they were isolated from most of the powerful groups which roamed the high plateau. The main range surrounds our high plains, but there is a spur of lower mountains that run west from the taller peaks. It can be reached from the high country by only two lofty passes. The dark elves who live on the spur make their homes in the forested valleys that cut through the low mountains. Kedria called that area home.

The smell of frying mushrooms and the buzz of conversation brought me downstairs. Kat was there with Golden and Lord Alder. Teal sat on the nobleman's knee while Kedria fed them all fried vegetables and flatbread. It looked far too cosy.

"I hope you are feeling better, Ashen; your friends told me about your illness."

She spoke in the tongue of my people, so everybody stopped talking and looked at me. I translated quietly and sat at one of the worktables.

"I'm sorry, I must improve my command of the Western language," Kedria said.

"I think you speak it as well as I do," Kat said.

I wondered if the elf would have been so friendly if she had known about the conversation between Golden and I the previous evening.

"Lord Alder, though I'm always pleased to see you, I can't help wondering; what are you doing here at this time of day?" I asked.

"I have brought you some work to do, and this is a good place to meet with Teal. We get to have breakfast together so rarely."

"What have you brought me?"

"Six volumes of the history of Lorekril, the Lost City of the Dwarves. I would like two copies of each."

I looked over one of the books, marvelling at the illustrations and maps. These were rare volumes and would be a joy to transcribe.

"I will take good care of them. Will you be selling the copies, or are they for your personal collection?" I asked.

"Some will be going to Petar and the rest to a temple library which is opening on the Peaks. I will pay you thirty silver per book, but it must be your best work."

It was above what I usually charged, but he asked for high-quality copies. I nodded and continued to flip through them.

"We understand Kedria is here to help you find your sister," Teal said.

I didn't want to have this conversation, not in front of everybody, but I suppose there never had been a very strong concept of privacy amongst my friends.

"She is here to find the Crown, not my sister."

I said it a little more harshly than I intended to, and everybody stopped and stared. Kedria's eyes went hard, but then she turned to my friends, and I saw her expression change. She now looked puzzled and slightly hurt.

"But of course, her assistance will be greatly appreciated, for, in the end, our goals overlap."

Kedria's eyes gleamed. She smiled, and I was transported back to my lover's bed ten years earlier. My friends seemed to bathe in her radiance too, and they all relaxed and started to talk amongst themselves. I turned back to the books, though I could feel someone watching me. Turning slightly, I saw Kedria's eyes; they met mine and held them. I felt small, as though I wanted to hide. These feelings were new to me, so I quickly looked away.

Eventually, everyone left, though it was late in the morning before they did. I borrowed a magical ring and a shattered stone and hid both of them in the heel of my boot. The ring was small and flat, so it was possible to tuck it alongside the stone. I thought of hiding it in my mouth, but I had used that trick once before with Grandfather. Walking down the hill, I turned at Crab Way before taking the final turn that would take me to Grandfather's mansion. There were six men at the gate, all armed with crossbows and swords. On the roof of the mansion, I saw strolling archers. Guard dogs and their handlers patrolled the cobbled courtyard before turning into the garden, which ran by the flanks of the structure. Piles of cut timber lay outside the compound where a row of trees had once stood.

I called through to the guards on the other side and asked to see Grandfather. They ignored me for a while but eventually, one of them scurried off. A short while later, a tall woman with blonde hair tied into a long plait appeared. She had slightly pointed ears and high cheekbones, suggesting elven blood somewhere in her past.

"What do you want, Owl? Grandfather is busy."

"Getting over an attack, is he? Is that why the oaks are coming down? I must say I have never seen so many guards here, not even when the war with The Dance Master was in full swing."

The tall woman took her crossbow off her shoulder and brought it to rest in front of her.

"You know it is funny, you turning up here today. A really strange coincidence," she said.

"Maybe it isn't. Maybe I planned the whole thing," I replied.

"I doubt if your drug-addled brain would be able to work out something as complex as an attack on Grandfather's compound."

Word had obviously spread about my time in the opium dens.

"Perhaps I know something that could help find those who attacked the old man. I mean, you didn't get them all, did you, Sabella?"

"My fame is spreading, I see; you have heard my name," the tall woman said, tossing her head. I thought I saw the corner of her mouth turn up but couldn't decide if it was a smile or a sneer.

"I don't know how welcome you'll be, but you better come in, Owl. Maybe you could be of some assistance."

She nodded at a swarthy man standing at her side, and he turned and strolled toward the front door of the mansion.

"Hurry it up, Crowler, I haven't got all day," she barked.

The man scowled back over his shoulder, then broke into a trot.

"Just can't get good help these days," Sabella said.

They took me upstairs via the back entrance, which was something new for me at Grandfather's. He must have something in the front rooms, he didn't want me to see, but by changing the routine, the old man had given me a clue. There were ways of finding out his secrets. They frisked me five times, and even my mouth was searched. As I approached the main study where Grandfather met all his visitors and conducted most of his business, Sabella instructed me to remove my boots. I kept my face neutral because if anything went wrong now, I had no magical protection.

The fire was only a pile of glowing embers, but the room was warm. A stooped man in long robes trimmed with gold eyed me from beside the window. He held a staff carved from ivory in his left hand. This magician was powerful. I could tell from the glowing gem on top of the staff.

"He has no magic on him, Gerald," the man said.

"Thank you, magus. And your help in the other matter is greatly appreciated," Grandfather said.

"Gold will, of course, show me how pleased you are with my assistance," the magician said.

Grandfather nodded and waited until the man shuffled slowly out of the room.

The crime lord looked older than when I had last seen him.

"Why shouldn't I kill you, Ash?"

"For old time's sake, maybe."

The old man sighed and walked toward a set of massive windows that overlooked the city.

"Just ask your question and leave," he said. "I doubt if you really have any information about last night's attack."

"What, no offer of a drink, questions after my health or about my friends?"

He half-turned and frowned. "I'm past your games. Last year your investigations almost destroyed my business. It's taken me the better part of the season to put things right."

"You asked me to look into the deaths of those girls. It wasn't my fault where it led."

He stared at me for a while, then stroked his short salt and pepper beard.

"I don't know where your sister is," he said.

I blinked a few times and shut my mouth.

"It's the only reason you would be here. Like your friend, the Captain, I don't believe in coincidences."

"But you met her?"

"Yes, and a charming young woman, she turned out to be. Very cooperative, if you get my meaning."

I wished I hadn't. The thought of Grandfather with my sister repulsed me.

"She was very friendly, but our relationship is now over," the old man said.

"Where is the Crown?" I asked.

"That particular item has moved on. You see, I was just a middleman who helped facilitate the sale."

"Who has it now?"

"I'm afraid the deal is subject to a confidentiality clause."

"So you took the Crown from my sister and set her up on the boat, but that didn't go so well. Then Shade would have come back here."

"I heard about the nasty business down in the port area. Those poor young men run through like pork sausages at a barbeque. Unfortunately for you, your sister didn't come here after the attack. As I said before, I don't know where she is."

"Do you think others thought she was here, and that is why you were attacked last night?" I asked.

"I have no idea."

I tried to read his face but couldn't tell if he was lying or not. He'd let me interview him so he could tell me of his relationship with my sister. Grandfather probably thought I would be outraged, but very little Shade did surprised me, though I was more than a little disgusted.

There was nothing more to be said, so I stood and walked to the door. I didn't say goodbye or even acknowledge Grandfather.

"I was sad to hear that you had become a drug-addled vagrant. You will be returning to the opium dens soon?"

I ignored the jibe but decided to store it away in case I ever felt the urge to start using the water pipe again.

As I turned the corner to Fish Street, I saw Kedria walking toward me. Her pace was fast, and her head down. Behind her, a group of men yelled abuse. They looked like dockworkers, but there were some merchants and stable hands present as well. I ran to her, ignoring the surge of dizziness, which came with sudden exertion. The men saw me and started to yell louder. I took Kedria by both arms, and she looked up at me.

"We are not at war with Hope. Why do they hate us?" she asked.

"Ignorance and stupidity. There are many in Hope who would like the city to join the Southern Dukes in their war. We need to get back to the shop."

I pulled Kedria into a side alley and pushed her before me just as the first rock flew in our direction. It hit a set of shutters to my right, breaking the thin wood with a crack.

"Hurry," I yelled.

Kedria moved quickly. A barrage of rocks and other missiles were hurled, but the alley protected us from the worst of them. I heard a roar as the enraged men realised their quarry was getting away. My head swam, but I closed my eyes and ran. We emerged into Ship Street just as the crowd surged into the far end of the alley. It wasn't far to the shop from here, but we still had to run through the Red Market. Kedria moved faster than I did, and if I fell behind and the crowd caught me, I would be dead in a few heartbeats. The market area was full of people buying fresh produce, and many of them stopped to stare in the direction of the sudden roar of noise. I weaved through the stalls as the growing mob smashed into the market from the other side, knocking over stands of food and pushing shoppers from their path. Realising even if we reached the bookshop, we would not be safe, I tried to think of a plan. Stalls appeared in front of me, and I dodged them and their owners. The sound grew to a deafening rumble as more people joined the mob. It was only the chaos enveloping the market area that saved Kedria and I. We ran around the corner and found a line of mounted watchmen confronting us.

I held up my hand and tried to regain my breath. A sergeant rode forward and lifted a club above his head.

"Stop, we have done nothing wrong!" I screamed.

The weapon fell toward Kedria, but she twisted aside, grabbed the man's arm, and pulled him from his horse. I was impressed by the speed of her attack on the sergeant. One of the other Watchmen lifted a crossbow and aimed it at her.

"Stop!" a voice yelled.

The Captain pushed a large grey horse through the line of mounted men and raised a curved sword.

"Hold your positions and do not fire," he ordered.

The watchman lowered his crossbow, and the Sergeant scrambled to his feet, his face red and hair wild.

At that moment, the crowd surged around the corner, screaming. They came to a halt and looked at the line of mounted men, their voices fading away.

"You will disperse and return to your homes," Captain Waldheigheim shouted.

The crowd slowly edged forward until one man in a bloodstained apron, carrying a large carving knife, pointed at us.

"What about the Owls?" he yelled.

The rest of the mob hissed and mumbled their ascent.

"Have they broken any laws?" the Captain asked.

"Their people burn and pillage the Southern Hills," a woman carrying a rolling pin screamed. Her hands were stained white, and she had arms like a dockworker's.

"We are not at war with the dark elves," the Captain said.

"But we should be," the butcher yelled.

"They shouldn't be walking freely around our streets," an older man said.

"Kill the spies," another yelled.

The crowd started to move toward us.

"Draw swords," the Captain said.

With a hiss of steel, twenty longswords left their scabbards. I scanned the mounted men and realised they were outnumbered by the mob by at least five to one.

I stepped in front of Captain Waldheigheim and raised my arms high.

"We surrender to the Watch," I yelled.

The Captain looked puzzled for a moment and then nodded.

"Take the dark elves into custody for disturbing the peace."

Four men dropped from their mounts and roughly tied our hands.

"We will take these two and question them," Captain Waldheigheim said.

The man in the butcher's apron nodded. "Make sure you punish 'em good."

The Captain gave a short nod and spun his mount on the spot. His men pushed us at sword-point toward the watchhouse. Kedria glanced over at me, and I nodded to her.

"It's alright. This is the best way. I know the Captain, and he is a fair man."

A group from the mob followed us. They seemed to think it was important to make sure the Captain did as he promised. We were hustled down to the cells and put in one of the bigger ones with a small barred window above our heads.

"I'm sorry, Ashely, but it is prudent I lock you up for a while. The crowd wants your blood, and though you haven't done anything wrong, I don't want that little group gathering their friends and burning half the city."

"I understand, we'll keep a low profile until this hatred dies down," I said.

"That might take some time. The McRobb family has been feeding the city stories for days now about the massacres performed by the armies of your Snow Leopard, or the Mountain Wolf as they prefer to call him. All very dramatic, I'm sure."

"He's not my Snow Leopard, and the dark elves have been devouring babies and burning villages, according to the stories, ever since human nobles decided that they wanted our hills."

Kedria cocked an eyebrow and glanced at me. I thought she smiled, but when I turned, her expression was neutral.

"Perhaps, but armies at war do terrible things. It really doesn't matter. You and your young female friend have committed no crime, so as soon as that little group wanders off, I'll let you go," the Captain said.

In the end, Golden came and took us back to the shop. Three or four of the mob had stayed, so we left the building through a rear entrance. Luckily the compound was a sprawling affair built around a grey square building, incorporating many other dwellings as well as stables, and there were consequently many ways in and out of it. My head pounded by the time I reached the work area of the shop, and I slumped on the couch, rubbing my temples.

"You need some of those herbs?" Golden asked.

I nodded, and he set the kettle to boil on the dying coals of the fire.

"I don't know how you live here, *Ashen*, when the pale humans hate our race," Kedria said.

"It's not usually this bad," I said. "The war has stirred up the crowd's emotions. Besides, I was exiled."

"But if you help find the Crown, then that could change," she said.

"One problem at a time," I mumbled.

Golden handed me a mug of tea, and I sipped the liquid. A little later, my head stopped pounding.

"Why were you out in the street anyway?" I asked.

"I wanted to stock up on food. We have no eggs and flour, but before I reached the market, I was attacked."

"But you were nowhere near the market," I said.

Kedria looked at the floor and laced her fingers together. "I got lost."

I shook my head. "The weather is changing. When it becomes really cold, we will be able to move around hooded without suspicion."

"What did you find out from Grandfather?" Golden asked.

I repeated the conversation, leaving out the part about the old man sleeping with my sister.

"Do you believe him?" Golden asked.

"I'm not sure. I got the feeling he was holding something back, just telling me enough to throw me off the trail without actually lying."

"Maybe your sister has left the city and taken the Crown again," Kedria said.

I looked sideways at her, wondering how she had drawn that conclusion.

"No, she is still here. The Crown, however, has been sold to a noble family."

"How do you know that?" Golden said.

"They are the only ones with the silver to purchase it. At this stage, I'm leaning toward a family which is involved in the war effort, someone who would like to humiliate the Snow Leopard."

"A noble family?" said Kedria. She paled and turned away.

"Don't worry. We'll get it back," I said.

That night I worried about security. The events of the day had left me concerned about the mood of the city, and I thought it possible a few angry citizens might target the shop. The lock on the front door was old, and I had to grease it with lard before it worked again. Then after barring the door from the inside, I did the same for the rear exit. Everyone left except for Kedria.

I wasn't sure what to make of the dark elf woman. She was very attractive and could handle herself in a fight, but I didn't know if I could trust her. I stirred the coals, shaking my head. Truth be told, I didn't really trust any of my race. They had thrown me out for a crime I hadn't committed. To be fair, I confessed to the deed to shield others, but the penalty had been harsh – exile for life. Now, one of my people sat in the leather armchair and eyed me speculatively. She swirled the wine around in her mug before glancing in my direction.

"You never tried to come home, did you?"

"Why would I? My family believes I have dishonoured them, and my people held me responsible for the death of twenty warriors. I had to start again or die," I said.

"You could have petitioned the Heads of Families."

"Only with my father's support, and he wasn't very happy with me. Anyway, Golden found me, and life took a different path."

"You don't seem to like the idea of the dark elves following a King. I would have thought you wouldn't care who led us now that you live apart," she said.

"I don't really, but I suppose the thought of my people being ruled by one individual cuts against the grain. It's hard to say why I feel this way. Maybe it's because I never like placing all my faith in one individual."

Kedria nodded, then stared at me until I looked away. Again she was making me feel uncomfortable.

"I suppose you better sleep here for now. It's not safe for you anywhere else. I will get some blankets, and you can sleep on the couch," I said.

"Thank you," she said.

6

HOUSE OF THE BLACK BOAR

I awoke with lips pressed against mine, and a warm body nestled in my arms.

"Kedria?"

"Quiet, lover. Just go with it."

And I did. Her body demanded, and mine responded. It had been a long time since I had lain with my own race; I had forgotten the feel and smell of it. Kedria's scent was of spicy herbs, not the milky smell which seemed to float around most humans, and I was transported back to the bed I had shared with Zenta before her death in the caves. I must admit I didn't even think of Miranda until the following day. In the morning, I awoke to the sight of a naked woman carrying a tray laden with fruit and steaming drinks. Her dark body seemed a shadow against the light streaming in through the window. I smiled at Kedria and accepted a mug of hot chocolate.

"You should do that more often," she said.

"What?"

"Smile."

That's when thoughts of Miranda intruded, as she had said something similar to me.

Kedria must have seen my face drop.

"I meant no offence."

"No, it's not you. Just that somebody else once said that to me."

"Another woman?"

"Yes."

"Are you still with her?"

"No. Well, I don't think so. It's very complicated," I said.

"I see. And I just made it more so, I'm guessing."

I rubbed my chin and sipped my hot chocolate. Miranda was due home any day now, and I had been looking forward to her arrival. Now I wasn't so sure I wanted to see her.

"It's not the time to think about her. I'm just happy to be here with you," I said.

Kedria smiled, though it didn't touch her eyes. She crawled under the blankets with me, and we ate hard-boiled eggs and fresh bread. Then we made love again.

I worked through the morning, copying the books left by Lord Alder while Kedria slept late. Then I boiled some water for her to bathe in while she cooked lunch. These domestic tasks almost swept away any thoughts about my sister or Miranda. This illusion was broken when Wink appeared at the door.

"Can you lend me some silver?" he asked.

"Why?"

"I need to see Aneeta again, and I've spent all my money."

"The opal is gone?"

"Yes, but it was worth it. I didn't know it could be like that."

Wink had a serious case of lust for the tall dancer, and after a short conversation, I realised he was consumed with thoughts of her.

"You know she is a working girl, and your time with her is a business transaction?" I asked.

"I don't care, I just have to see her."

"I'm not just going to give you silver to support your addiction."

As I said it, I thought my choice of words was ironic and Wink, to his credit, made the connection.

"You'd know about that," he mumbled.

I let the jibe pass and wondered how I could help the teenager. Kedria listened to the exchange with a slight smile on her face.

"Lend him the money Ashen. The boy has it bad," she said in our tongue.

I didn't translate but softened.

"Alright, but I need information. You have to answer some questions, and if you don't know them, find out."

When he readily agreed, I saw how desperate his need was. Usually, Wink was more cautious.

"Who attacked Grandfather's?"

"A group of the Original Men. Though one of them was killed by the new head of security."

"Sabella?"

"Yeah, she is one tough bitch and knows how to handle a blade. I wouldn't get on the wrong side of her," Wink said.

"Does he know why he was attacked?"

Wink's caution returned. He shook his head and stepped away from me.

"Do you want the silver?" I asked.

Wink groaned. "He put out the story it was the Dance Master's men, but I know different. This mob that attacked was better than well-trained thieves, and their skin was brown like they were from the south. Also, they wanted something. I think they were after the Crown."

"What do you know about the Crown," Kedria snapped.

"Just what I heard the top guards saying. That there was this old Crown Grandfather got from some dark elf, and he was goin' to sell it on."

"Who too?" I asked.

"I don't know," Wink said.

I thought for a moment, then went upstairs and found a small bag of silver for the boy.

I handed it to him. "There will be more if you can find out who he sold it to."

Wink grabbed the bag and nodded before sprinting off down the street.

"Well, I see the minds of young men vary little between the races," Kedria said.

It was a few days before I heard from Wink again. I tried to make some inquiries myself about the location of the Crown but found nothing new. There were no new leads, and I fell into a domestic routine with Kedria. I worked on the books while she cooked and read. She had a better understanding of the symbols which represented the human tongue than I did and also understood the Dwarven language. Golden and Kat dropped in occasionally, but otherwise, we were left to our own devices. I developed an appreciation of how 'normal' couples lived, and though I hardly knew Kedria, I began to understand her mannerisms and moods very quickly. She had a disconcerting habit of drifting away during conversations, leaving you with the distinct impression you were talking to yourself, and then suddenly she would be with you again. Kedria would smile and repeat my last sentence, and I would be left wondering if she had been paying attention the whole time.

The note from Wink asked me to meet him at the rear of Dodger's Inn. This was near the port area and close to where Shade's boat had been moored. It usually sold food and drink to the dockworkers, but at the time of night, Wink wanted to meet me, it would only have a few patrons. There was a hint of snow in the air, not just the chill of previous days but a tingle on your skin, which warned the first storms were winging their way south.

Leaving the shop just before twelve bells, I made my way through the darkened streets, sticking to the shadows. I took a route less direct than usual in case someone followed me, as Kedria said she had noticed a few men watching the shop during the day. She had encouraged caution and told me not to go straight to the meeting place. I only saw a few watchmen and some late-night drunks making their way home from Docklands.

When I reached Dodger's, I called softly for Wink, but there was no answer. I moved along a very narrow alley to a small wooden shed at the rear of the building and whistled gently. The only sound was the wind in the rigging of the ships moored at the nearby piers. The hair on the back of my neck went up, and I reached inside my cloak for the Cold Blade. Something felt amiss, so I pulled the deadly steel from its scabbard, and it glowed softly in the darkness. Slipping around the edge of four stacked crates, I saw the body. My catlike eyes picked out a single wound just below the ribs. There was no sign of a struggle, and Wink's eyes were wide open in shock and pain.

Sighing, I stepped over to the body. The teenager lay on his back, sprawled amongst rubbish and coils of rope. His coat was open, and his shirt undone. Somebody had killed and then searched him. I closed his eyes and then did the same, knowing whatever he carried would be well hidden. I thought I had a good idea of where to look. First, I tried the heels of his shoes, and even though one contained a wire lockpick, there were no clues as to why he had been killed. Then I tried his belt buckle. After fiddling with the small plate at the front, I found a catch that revealed a hidden compartment under the metal. It was a thin area, only enough to hold a sheet of paper or maybe a very thin blade. What I found was a small piece of material. I unfolded it and looked cautiously. On it was the head of a black boar with gleaming yellow tusks. The eyes of the animal were red and seemed to glare at me. It was the symbol of the house McRobb, and I knew it was probably the reason why Wink had been killed.

I didn't know who had killed the boy, but I suspected Grandfather immediately. Carrying the body to the front of the crime lord's mansion, I left it propped up against the wall. One of the guards yelled at me, but I was gone before he got close enough to recognise who I was. As I walked home, I felt the anger that had built within me surge forward, and I reeled. The side effects of the potion which prevented my return to the opium dens hit me, and I dropped to my knees. Pulling myself up, I staggered the rest of the way to the shop. I made it through the door and walked over to the coals of the fire. Kedria heard the noise and came down the stairs wrapped in a robe.

"Are you alright?" she asked.

"I need my herbs. My head is pounding. I feel like passing out."

Kedria gently moved me to the couch and then blew on the coals. She fed small pieces of kindling into the growing flames until it was hot enough to warm water. I laid back and closed my eyes. Eventually, the tea was ready, and I inhaled the steam. Slowly as I drank, my head cleared, and I felt as though I could talk.

"Wink is dead. I think Grandfather killed him so he couldn't pass along any information. I thought the boy was safe, believing the old man might give him a pounding for talking, but I never dreamed he would murder him."

"So, you have hit another dead end?"

"No. I found this on Wink."

When I showed her the parchment, a look of anger washed across her face.

"Yes, this is the family stirring the people of Hope into hatred against our clan, so it fits that they have the Crown. The McRobb House aligned with the Vorhelms in the belief it was in the city's best interest to enter the war against our people. When what was left of the Vorhelm family withdrew from political life, the McRobbs took their place," I said.

Kedria's face was twisted, and her hands clenched.

"We have to control our emotions, Kedria, and plan our next step carefully."

Her face slowly relaxed, though her eyes still blazed. She nodded and moved to me.

"You are right. We must do what is right for our people."

She kissed me and led me upstairs.

The McRobb mansion was one of the oldest buildings in Hope. It looked like a small keep and even had the remains of a moat running around the edge of the high iron fence. It was no more than a shallow ditch now covered with moss and short grass. The building could be viewed clearly through the bars of the fence even though a hedge grew on the other side. I suppose it had been planted to provide some privacy for the courtyard and gardens of the compound, but it was a ragged affair with gaps every few paces. Gaining access to the grounds would not be very difficult, but getting inside the mansion was going to be tough. There was only one entry point, and narrow arrow slits lined the lower level of the structure. The upper windows were promising as they were recent modifications, probably created to make the mansion more comfortable. The problem would be opening them from the outside without alerting any guards.

I had no idea where the Crown would be kept but guessed it was well guarded. Deciding not to try and steal the artefact now, I needed more information and wanted to watch and learn. It wasn't long before I noticed someone else observing the McRobb mansion as well. A woman pushing a hand cart loaded with fruit stopped across from the gate and attempted to sell her wares to the guards at the front of the mansion. When they showed no interest in purchasing anything, she moved a little way down the street to the corner and tried to sell her goods. There was only a small amount of traffic on the streets of the Peaks, and it struck me as an unusual place to trade from. It didn't take me long to realise the young woman was not trying very hard to sell anything. I moved a little closer to her, approaching from behind through the cover provided by the parklands which surround the Sacred Lake.

Though she was well covered by her cape, I got a glimpse of curly hair and brown skin. She was one of the Original Men, and I surmised part of the squad which had attacked my sister and assaulted Grandfather's mansion. I decided to take a chance and stepped out of the park behind her with the Cold Blade in my hand. Folding my cloak over the steel, I tried to make it almost invisible.

"Pity you failed to kill Grandfather," I said.

The woman spun around, and her hand went for a dagger hidden in her sleeve.

"Don't," I barked and let her see the Cold Blade.

It was covered in a thin layer of frost that chilled my gloved hand.

"You would be dead before you could make the throw," I said.

"I'm pretty fast, *Ashen,*" the woman said.

I was surprised she spoke my tongue and used my name. Then I got my first close look at her as we now stood only two paces apart. She was pretty, with short curly hair and wide cheeks. Her eyes were brown and flecked with gold. She reminded me of Cassie though her nose and chin were more pointed.

"So am I," I said.

I watched as her hand moved away from her sleeve and came to rest on the cart.

"I am not your enemy," I said.

"You are the brother of the traitor Shade. She stole an item which prevents our leader from assuming his rightful position."

"Why do you support a dark elf? He is not of your race."

"He has lifted our people from the repression of the pale skins. The men from across the sea pushed us into the jungles and stole our land. Now we strike back."

"The Mountain Wolf must be special if he can elicit such loyalty from your people."

"That name was given to him by the Southern Dukes. He is the Snow Leopard and leads us to our rightful place."

She sounded like a fanatic. I guessed the war leader of my people must have handpicked a number of the Original Men for special favour and treatment. The tales were the jungle tribes fought with him for plunder and high-quality weapons, but the commitment of some of these people to him seemed to run very deep.

"Where is my sister?" I asked.

"We don't know. If we did, we would kill her. She is protected by Grandfather."

"No, she isn't. He's abandoned her."

"If not by him then by one high in his company. She would not be able to hide from us so successfully without help."

I nodded. That fitted with the evasion I felt when questioning the old man.

"If I help you get the Crown, will you leave and not trouble my sister?"

The woman's face shifted. My offer had thrown her.

"Why should the Fists of the Snow Leopard trust you?"

"Because you need my help. Your little group of five is at least down to three, and you can't do this alone. I know this city, and I just want to keep my sister from being thrown from the Black Cliffs."

In my mind, I could see Shade falling to the jagged rocks after the executioners threw her over the drop.

"She doesn't deserve any mercy."

"Maybe you're right, but she is family, and I don't want her to die."

The woman grimaced but then nodded once. "I will take your offer to my…"

She stopped talking and peered behind me.

"Are you alone?" she asked.

"Yes."

Then she dove sideways. A bolt flew through the air and embedded itself in her cart. A second one followed, and a grunt of pain rang out. I ran to the woman and saw the small crossbow bolt sticking out of her thigh. It hadn't hit a major artery, but it was deep.

"Keep pressure on it," I said as I pushed a cloth around the wound.

The woman groaned, and I scanned the bushes for movement. I caught a glimpse of a figure some fifty paces from the path. It was kneeling and reloading a crossbow.

"I'll be back," I said and jumped to my feet.

The street and park were empty, but I didn't know how long they would remain that way. I had to deal with the sniper before any passers-by called the Watch.

The cloaked figure heard my pounding feet and fled. We ran along a gravel path toward the bridge over the Sacred Lake. The sniper jumped a low hedge and ran through the scrub and bushes which lay in the middle of the park. I moved quickly, trying to ignore the building sensation of my pounding head. Cursing the potion's side effects, I tried to anticipate the course the mysterious assailant might take. The streets on the southern flank of the Peaks were twisted affairs with many alleys, and I decided it was the probable direction the attacker would take. Pushing through some bracken, I crashed into a man in a brown cape. I immediately realised this was not the sniper I was chasing as the cape was the wrong colour. There was a flash of recognition in his eyes, and I knew I'd crashed into one of the Fist that the Snow Leopard had sent to Hope. He probably was on the way to check on the curly-haired woman. My blade was out, and I waved it in his face.

"I don't want you," I yelled. "I'm after the sniper."

His brow came together in confusion, and a hand axe appeared from under his cloak. It flashed toward my head, but I caught it on the sword and flicked the blow away. My left fist came around to hit the man on the chin, but he rolled with the punch, and I only clipped him. He stepped into me and delivered a vicious headbutt that landed on my nose. I fell backward over a low bush and rolled to my feet. My opponent ran around the shrub and swung at my head. I caught it on the Cold Blade and willed the power of the blizzard into my weapon. The frost spread down his axe, and the man screamed as the cold found his fingers. If his weapon had not had a wooden handle, he probably would have never been able to use them again. The axe fell from his hand, but he recovered quickly, punching me in the stomach. I tensed, but the blow still hurt. Stepping backward, I tasted my own blood as it streamed down my face and into my mouth from the scalp wound. My head pounded. I waved my sword at the man, and he took a pace toward the path. Then he was running. I took a couple of steps to follow him, but the world swayed, and I fell to the ground.

It took me a while to slow my breathing, and then longer to clean the blood from my face. I staggered back to the lake and washed off what I could before returning down the mountain via side streets and back alleys until I could see the sign of the scroll which hung in front of my shop. Kedria wasn't there, so I washed my face and made a pot of tea for my pounding head. I lay on the old couch and fell asleep. I was woken by Spike licking my face. Golden stood next to the dire wolf, inspecting my forehead.

"That was some punch. You almost need a stitch," he said.

"It was a headbutt, but I've had worse."

I then told him what had happened during the day and asked where Kedria was. He had no idea. The wolf padded over and sat in front of the fire.

"I came to tell you that Grandfather wants to see you. He found Kat and me gambling at The Sleepy Lion and told me to get you."

"Since when did you start to do the old man's bidding?"

"Well, he asked nicely and cleared our bill. He also said he had information and work for you."

The Grandfather would have sent Wink in the past, but now he had killed him I supposed he needed to send other messengers.

"I'll go in the morning."

"I'd go now if I were you. He seemed upset and kept saying something about everybody always thinking the worst of him. I almost laughed at that, but considering he was paying off my debt for the night, I thought I'd better keep a straight face."

Kedria burst through the door in her dark cape. She looked around and shut the door behind her.

"What's going on?" I asked.

"A second Fist has arrived in Hope, and they are here to take you into custody."

"But Ash hasn't done anything," Golden said.

"They think he is working with his sister and can't be trusted."

"You need to talk to them, Kedria. They need to know I'm trying to help recover the Crown."

"That's part of the problem. They don't trust me either. They think you have corrupted me and I'm no longer working for the cause."

Falling back on the couch, I rubbed the growing bump on my head. I cursed my sister and wondered how I was going to fix this mess.

7

GRANDFATHER'S DEAL

One problem at a time; first I needed to talk with the old man. I left the shop and walked through the gathering dusk. The wind picked up, and the temperature dropped. An autumn storm formed north of the river, crackling and spitting its fury over the plains as it sped south. It felt as though it might even carry snow in its black towers. I pulled my cloak tightly around me and pushed on. By the time I reached Grandfather's mansion, it had started to snow. Big wet flakes swirled around me, plastering my eyelashes and finding their way into my boots. I cursed and banged on the front gate with the back of my dagger.

Eventually, a guard left the small stone gatehouse and let me in.

"We were told to expect you, Owl, but weren't sure if you'd come in this weather."

Grunting, I shook myself like a dog as they led me into the foyer. I underwent the usual security precautions with ill grace and glanced around for the new head of security.

"Where's Sabella?" I asked.

Two of the guards exchanged a glance but didn't answer. That got my interest. If Sabella had fallen from favour, then Grandfather would have lost his second Security Chief in under a year, the last one having betrayed him to the Dance Master. It didn't say much for the old man's ability to judge people's character.

I was taken to Grandfather, who stood in front of his giant windows watching the fury of the storm. He didn't turn around.

"You know, when I watch the displays, nature can put on it leads me to think we are nothing."

"Very philosophical, Grandfather."

He spun, and his mouth curled up at one corner.

"I've been told it is one of the side effects of ageing," he said.

The old man did look older. His neck had become flabby, and he was thickening around the stomach. His skin seemed to hang below his eyes as though he hadn't been sleeping well. I tried to feel sorry for him.

"What did you drag me here for?" I asked.

"Drag you? Come now, Ash, you have always had a choice where your relationship with me is concerned. You just like to pretend to others you don't."

I felt my heart clench at the brutal honesty of his statement. It was true, in all my dealings with Grandfather he never forced me to do anything against my will. Yes, he manipulated me or put pressure on, but I always had a choice.

He sighed before continuing. "Despite the word on the street, I had nothing to do with poor Wink's death and would like nothing better than to see his killer brought to account. I had a soft spot for the kid and hoped that one day he would rise up through the ranks of thieves. I knew he was leaking you the odd piece of information but turned a blind eye to most of it, knowing if I wanted to pull him into line I just had to ban him from the Docklands area. His infatuation with Aneeta would have been all the motivation needed."

My eyes must have widened.

"I knew of his interest in the dancer and can't say I blame him. She is attractive in many different ways, but I digress. The fact is, I didn't kill him, and I want to find out who did."

I was thrown. Grandfather had been my prime suspect for Wink's death, but his denial was heartfelt, and I couldn't see why he would put this much effort into lying to me. Still, I was wary.

"Do you want me to look into it?"

"No, I want you to find my Security Chief."

I nodded, now we were getting closer to the heart of the matter.

"Sabella disappeared a few days back, not long after your sister fled her attackers whilst staying on one of my ships."

"Is there a connection?"

"Yes, it seems your sister not only used her wiles on me, she also charmed my Security Chief."

Shade had been known to have female lovers when she lived on the high plateau and especially favoured the bold women who travelled with the entertainment fairs.

"Sabella is a very intelligent person who is deadly with both blade and bow. She didn't like men, and that seemed a positive attribute when I first employed her. I never anticipated her being seduced by a dark elf woman, and I don't appreciate my employees leaving without permission."

"I remember. It often surprised me that you let Kat go so easily."

"The elf was just under contract and never knew a lot about my organisation."

"If I find Sabella, what do you want me to do?"

"Just tell me where she is, and I'll handle the rest."

I knew what that meant. He would kill the woman quickly.

"My sister is likely to be with her."

"That is the sweetener on the deal. You can take your sister away. I promise she will not be harmed, and I will help you capture her as it is doubtful she will want to renew acquaintances with you willingly. I will also pay. One hundred silver now and another two hundred when you finish the job."

I whistled. That was a lot of money. He must want Sabella badly.

"You must have trusted her," I said, twisting the knife.

His eyes went black, and he turned to the storm.

"Why do you want me to do this? Why not your own people?"

Grandfather didn't turn to face me. "That's easy, Ash. You are the best in Hope at this type of work. I've heard even the captain of the

Watch thinks so. When you want to take down dangerous prey, hire the best hunter you can find."

I sat in the guardhouse, waiting for the worst of the storm to pass. The snow had become blinding sleet. Forks of lightning split the sky around the mansion, and for a heartbeat, I thought I could see Grandfather standing at his window. Two guards huddled in front of the small fireplace capturing most of its warmth. I didn't care; just glad they hadn't thrown me outside. The storm would have soaked me to the skin in no time if they had.

The revelation that Shade had taken up with Sabella didn't surprise me. The Chief of Security would be just another person who could protect her, someone she could use as a shield against her dangerous and indulgent choices. Shade had chosen a high-quality guardian this time. The rest of my interview with Grandfather led me to believe there was only one person in Hope who could beat Sabella with a blade, and that was Golden. The old man thought I would be very hard-pressed to survive a duel with his Security Chief, especially as she carried a Black Blade. The sword was ancient and supposed to have been made by the dwarves. It was immune to magic and indeed dispelled all arcane properties within a couple of paces. My Cold Blade would be useless against it.

I had taken the job because it placed some of the Grandfather's information sources at my disposal. If Kedria was right and another Fist had arrived, that meant there were at least seven fanatics in the city who would kill my sister on sight. I wondered what they would make of my offer to help them take back the Crown. They probably dismissed it after their agent had been shot while talking to me. If the Fist became desperate, they might revisit the proposal, but Kedria's information about the orders of the new group meant the spies of the Snow Leopard were probably best avoided.

Eventually, the sleet eased to steady rain, and I decided to brave the weather. My cloak was waterproof, but it didn't keep all of the moisture at bay, and by the time I got back to the shop, I was damp.

Kedria cooked a meal of curried chicken, and the aroma of the food filled the shop. My stomach growled as a reminder of my hunger. Golden was gone, but Spike remained.

"The wolf is here to watch over me, though I don't think he likes the task," Kedria said.

"Why do you believe that?"

"I tried to pat him, and he growled, so I thought if I fed him, he would accept me. But he didn't eat the food I offered him, and he still won't let me near him."

"He can be funny around strangers, but I guarantee if the Fist of the Snow Leopard tried to arrest you, he would stand by your side."

"That's good to know."

That night as she lay in my arms, I told Kedria about my deal with Grandfather. She seemed happy about the course of action I chose, even though it would mean I would have less time to retrieve the Crown.

"I'll get the artefact too, I just need a way into the McRobb Mansion," I said.

"But you mentioned it was built like a castle."

"If there is one thing my years of adventuring taught me is there is always a solution," I said.

"Isn't your work for the Grandfather top priority now?"

"Not necessarily. Besides, I thought you would want me to take the Crown. The quicker I retrieve it, the quicker the Snow Leopard can be crowned King. Isn't that right?"

Kedria stiffened in my arms. "Yes, yes, of course, you're right. I just don't want you spreading yourself too thin. You are still getting over your illness after all."

She rolled in my arms and kissed me. The embrace became more passionate, and soon all thoughts of Grandfather or my sister vanished.

The next morning I visited the Peaks to have another look at the McRobb's mansion. I wondered if I would see any members of the Fist in the vicinity, but the area seemed empty. The roof of the mansion was flat with a large battlement running around the edge. Golden could probably throw a padded grappling hook that far, but it would be useless if there were guards stationed in the area. During the day, I could clearly see two men walking around the old battlements, but it didn't mean they would be there when the sun set.

The Captain sat on his bay mare, watching as the sketch artist from the Watch drew the door of the three-storey building.

"Last night a large group of men broke into this building and dragged out a dark elf family from the Far Ranges. They weren't from your mountains but the other homeland of your people far to the southeast," he said.

"I know of it, though I have never been there. It's a very isolated location. What were they doing in Hope?" I asked.

"They were the representatives of a trading group selling copper and diamonds. I believe they hadn't been here long. I gather you didn't know them?"

"No."

The question didn't offend me. There were few dark elves in Hope and most tended to clump together. I was the exception to the rule, but the Captain wouldn't know that.

"Well, they were dragged onto the street and butchered last night. The male and female were beaten to death, and the children had their throats cut."

I closed my eyes and tried not to think of the terror the family would have felt before their deaths.

"I'm sorry. I should have spared you those details," he said.

Shaking my head, I tried to drive away the disturbing thoughts.

"I'm actually here to ask you about another dark elf."

"Your sister?"

"Yes, have you heard anything?"

"I know that a dark elf woman was seen on the Peaks a while back. She was involved with a disturbance near the McRobb mansion."

That got my interest. Maybe she had taken a shot at the female member of the Fist I spoke to. If it was her, then she had taken a huge risk, which was not out of character. I filled the Captain in on my deal with Grandfather and told him about my sister hiding out with his head of security.

"I'm willing to give some of the money to a charity associated with the Watch if your information helps me find them."

"That will not be necessary," the Captain said stiffly.

I shook my head and smiled. "I know you would give me the information willingly as long as it doesn't compromise any of your other cases. I'm just trying to be fair."

Captain Waldeigheim's shoulders relaxed, and he patted his horse's neck.

"As you say, I would help a friend regardless. Your donation can go to the temple's poor box if you like. I find that some of those without are less likely to steal when they have food in their bellies. As for what I would like as a reward for any information, tell me where the Head of Security is first before you inform Grandfather."

"You would like me to hand Sabella to you?"

"I will offer her a deal which helps her keep head on her shoulders. Then Grandfather might find his life becoming very difficult."

I liked the sound of that. "I think that can be arranged, though we will need to make it look accidental. Otherwise, he will come after me."

The Captain nodded. "I'll leave it in your capable hands, Ashley."

As he rode away, I realised he called me a friend.

I needed to look around by myself to see what I could uncover, as it was common knowledge Sabella had spent a lot of time around the port. The docks were quieter as many boats had returned to their home ports before winter set in. There appeared to be little movement amongst the piers and jetties that stuck out into the river since the storms of late fall, but there was still the odd ship that made its way to Hope from the small ports and towns of the West Coast. Traffic from the Old World had stopped completely. Only a madman would try and cross the wide ocean this late in the season.

Sailor's Rest was a comfortable inn set back from the river on a small rise. It boasted some of the finest ale of the city and cooked a delicious fish stew. I had often eaten there with Golden and knew the owner, a dwarf named Snuffles.

The heads of a few old sailors rose as I walked into the well-lit inn after the first bell of the afternoon. A couple of the men glared but soon turned away and sunk back into their ale.

"Don't mind them," Snuffles wheezed. "They has nothin' better to do then stare these days."

A couple of the sailors muttered at the comment.

Snuffles beamed at me. His long red-brown hair was tied back with a leather band, and his beard tucked into a belt. He cleaned his thick meaty fingers on an apron before wrapping me in a back-breaking hug. I looked at his creased face and twinkling grey eyes and decided I needed to get to the Sailor's Rest more often.

"Haven't seen you in a long time, Ash. Golden still comes, and his wolf steals my soup bones, but I never sees you."

"I've been sick," I said.

"Heard what happened, but we won't talk about that. Time has moved on, and you're back with us now," the dwarf said.

As Snuffles eased his rotund frame onto a barstool, I reflected on how I felt about my addiction being common knowledge. I had only myself to blame. If I hadn't become an addict, then I wouldn't have to go through these uncomfortable conversations.

We talked for a while about mutual friends and the unusually warm autumn. Snuffles predicted the dry spell was an indicator that we were in for a harsh winter.

"That storm is but a warning. Last winter was bad, but this one will be worse," he said.

I decided I would broach the topic of my sister and Sabella, and told the old dwarf the whole story and how my sister's life appeared to be in danger.

"Knew Sabella when she was a little dock rat. Tough little mite back then but after she grew and went adventuring she became a force to be reckoned with. Sabella used the silver found in the north to train with some of the best fighters around. Even travelled to the Old World to work with the Blade Masters. Then she went north again to make her fortune, but her band was cut to pieces by trolls on the Ever Fens. Anyway, she returned, broke and out of work. No other Hunters would trust her as there were rumours of her abandoning her comrades. Anyone who knew her would never say that. Sabella is brave to a fault. If anything, she bites off more than she can chew."

"Did you know she only liked women?"

"There were rumours but hells, it's not uncommon these days. Sabella spent a lot of her money at Docklands, and that's how she met Grandfather."

"Any idea where she might hide out?"

"I like Sabella. I don't want her to end up at the bottom of the river."

"I'm not going to give her to the old man," I said honestly.

"But he's payin' you."

"Some of the money was given to me upfront, the rest I don't care about."

"You're playing a dangerous game, Ash."

"But I mean to win. Besides, the more I hear about Sabella, the more I admire her and want to rescue her from my sister."

"Alright then. She used to play by the old woolsheds as a kid. I know she had a hidden room in the loft of one that was comfortable. Below the barns, the main sewer for the city runs in all directions. If I was her, I'd hide there. Grandfather doesn't know about it, and only a few of her friends do."

"Thanks, Snuffles. I won't leave it so long next time before I visit."

"See that you don't," the dwarf said with a smile.

A small metal chimney leaked smoke from the roof of the last of the six woolsheds. It could have been a merchant keeping warm while he did his accounts, but I doubted it. There was no way to reach the loft except through the barn itself, and at the moment there were men working nearby. The barns were full, and this wool would either be moved to the southern slopes of the Devil's Peaks where women would spin the thread, or it would stay put until the seasons changed and it was shipped across the ocean. The bales would provide cover for me inside the sheds. I would investigate the area when darkness fell and see if my sister was hiding there with her new lover.

The crowd gathered just outside Docklands and chanted slogans of hate against my people. I pulled the hood tighter around my face and stayed in the shadows. From there, I watched as a wide-shouldered man of middle years climbed onto a large crate. He had the blue eyes and pale skin of the men who crossed the sea. On his hip, he wore a longsword encrusted in gems, and his surcoat was emblazoned with the head of a boar. Yellow tusks and blazing red eyes made the creature appear fierce and dangerous. Jamie McRobb cleared his throat.

"Why do we wait!" he boomed.

The crowd growled like a beast.

"These Dark Owls are burning their way north, destroying castles and villages, stealing, raping, murdering, and yet Hope does nothing!"

The crowd fell silent but moved closer to the big knight.

"We have waited for those that lead our great city to pick up the axe, the bow, the lance, but we have waited in vain. The Wolf is bringing his army to us. He will not stop until we are driven from these lands, back into the sea that brought us here. His aim is our absolute destruction. Well, I, for one, cannot stand by any longer. I will protect what is mine. I'm proposing we form a crusade. I will gather an army outside the jurisdiction of this city and supply it with arms and food. This force will swell until it is the size of an ocean. With it, we will swamp the dark elf army and its allies and drive it back into the mountains where we'll destroy this threat once and for all. The Owls are an abomination, and I will not stop until every last one of them is killed."

The crowd screamed and howled, and Jamie McRobb smiled.

"The Mountain Wolf would be king of his people, yet he cannot be crowned without an artefact which his people hold dear. I have stolen this item and challenge him to take it. While I wait, I urge you to purge this city. Driveaway every dark elf you can find, and when it is done, meet me on the plain near the Small Woods. There, the crusade will gather before it heads south. Bring food and weapons, but if you have neither do not fear. I will provide."

McRobb paused, and the crowd yelled and bayed.

"Now cleanse the city!"

With that, the crowd streamed from the large square and into docklands.

8

NIGHT OF FIRE

Was Jamie McRobb insane? He had defied the Council of Notable Elders and unleashed a mob on the city that would tear Hope apart. Kedria and I were in great danger. My shop was well known, and it wouldn't be long before one of the great unwashed remembered where I lived. I pitied the small number of dark elves in the city. Most of them would die before the sun rose, but I realised my sister was probably the safest of all my kind. She and Sabella would have to wait. I needed to think of a safe place to hide for the night. Grandfather wouldn't risk protecting me in the face of the mob, and I didn't trust the Watch either. Not all their members were as open-minded as Captain Waldheigheim when it came to the other races. I made my way into an alley as a group of men and women started hurling abuse at a group of elves. It wasn't long before insults became rocks and timber. Then the mob attacked. I saw a young female elf make it to the mouth of the alley before she was hauled backwards by the hair. Two large men held her to the ground while another kicked her. Then one of them turned and looked at me.

"An Owl," he yelled.

I ran. The elf broke free, but then she was out of sight. Only one place might be safe tonight, but making it there would be difficult.

Lord Alder could hide me if we slipped into his mansion quietly. I sprinted up Fish Street and felt my head start to spin. Not now, I thought. The side effects of the potion couldn't have chosen a more unfortunate time to hit me. Staggering to the entrance of the shop, I found Golden waiting for me. He hauled me inside and slammed the door before barring it with a thick piece of timber. Spike licked my hand and curled around me.

"I need my tea," I gasped.

"I'll make it," Kedria said.

She placed the kettle in the coals of the fire and added wood.

"We can't stay here," I said. "They know a dark elf runs this shop and it won't be long before they come for us."

"Where should we go?" Golden asked.

"To Lord Alder's mansion. If we can get in unobserved, we should be alright. Finding a safe way, there will be the problem."

"Well, it's almost completely dark. That should help," Kedria said.

I looked around. "Where is Kat?"

"She'll be here soon, but she won't be troubled. The mob are after dark elves aren't they?" Golden asked.

"The crowd is killing anyone, not human. I saw elves attacked and it wouldn't surprise me if dwarves and the Original Men are next," I said. "Jamie McRobb stirred the crowd to a fever pitch, and now he has set them loose."

There was banging on the door and then a yell. Golden pulled the plank free and found Kat holding off four men with her shortsword. Golden jumped into the fray swinging the lump of wood which had held the door shut. He hit one man in the side of the head, and the timber splintered. The man toppled and lay still. Spike leapt through the doorway, and the other men turned and fled; the sight of a snarling dire wolf too much for them. Spike jumped on one and tripped him. The wolf grabbed the man by the back of the neck and shook him like a rag doll. I heard something snap and watched as the man went limp.

"We have to go. Those who escaped will bring more," I said.

Kedria shoved a wooden mug into my hands while Golden checked on Kat. The elf had suffered a little bruising but had no serious injuries. Spike danced around her excitedly, trying to push his nose into her face.

"I'm alright, you hairy monster," Kat said, scratching the dire wolf behind the ear.

I scalded my tongue on the hot tea but forced myself to drink. It didn't taste as strong as I was used to and I wondered if it had brewed for long enough; I wouldn't have time to make another pot.

Hiding a few of the most precious books and my money in a large strongbox beneath the bricks at the rear of the shop, I then grabbed my weapons. By the time I returned a large group of people carrying torches had appeared at the end of the street. Golden led us across the road into an alley, but we were seen. The moon was out, and there were no clouds, so the streets were brighter than usual. I heard the roar behind us and screamed for everyone to run. I still felt lightheaded and dizzy. Forcing myself to sprint, I noticed Golden and the others were pulling ahead. A crossbow bolt flew from the crowd. It sung past my head and buried itself in the wooden boards of a house. I fired my handheld crossbow at the surging mass of humanity and heard a scream. The crowd roared and seemed to move faster.

"Come on, Ash!" Golden bellowed. "Don't waste your time trying to slow them!"

He stood at the end of the alley holding a hand axe. The first group of people ran into the narrow gap between the houses, but one of them tripped. Others fell, and soon the alley was jammed with heaving bodies. It gave us the chance we needed to break away from the pursuing mass and Golden led us into another series of twisting streets and alleys called the Rat's Maze on the lower slopes of the Devil's Peaks. Behind us, I could smell smoke and see the glow of beginning fires. The mob had set the torch to their city, and only the wet thatch from the recent storms would slow the progress of the growing flames. Unfortunately, the wind seemed to increase the fire, fanning it and helping it feed. I could hear screaming and the sound of howling, like that of a wounded dog.

Eventually, we left the Rat's Maze and sprinted along a wide street that ran at an angle up the smaller of the two peaks which sat at the centre of Hope. We reached a barricade manned by members of the

Watch. It was a thin affair made up of only a few carts and some empty crates and barrels. The barricade wouldn't hold the mob for more than a heartbeat. A corporal in a blue cloak hailed us, and Golden strode forward.

"We need to move up the Peaks to a friend's house. The mob is killing all non-humans."

"That ain't my problem. We got orders to enforce a curfew. Turn around and go home and we won't shoot you."

"I'm a friend of Captain Waldheigheim, and he would vouch for me," Golden said.

I thought that was a bit of a stretch, but my head was getting worse, so I didn't contradict him.

"I doubt it, pretty boy. Now turn around before I put a bolt in you."

The corporal lifted the crossbow casually to his shoulder and took aim. Kedria brought her handheld crossbow up and pulled the trigger before anyone could stop her. As the corporal died, he fired his weapon, and the bolt flashed past Golden's ear. We all dove for cover as more bolts flashed from behind the carts.

"What did you do that for?" Kat yelled. "There are other ways onto the Peaks."

Spike charged forward the ten paces which separated us from the barricade and leapt it in one bound. He landed on a Watch member loading his crossbow and tore his throat out. Another man ran at the wolf from behind holding a spear. Golden threw his hand axe. It hit the member of the Watch in the side of the head, spinning him around. Kedria had also run forward. She killed another man with the second shot from her small crossbow. Kat's dagger found the throat of another. I stumbled forward and stared at the carnage.

"Did we get them all?" Kedria asked.

"Yes," Kat said. "None escaped."

I shook my head and closed the eyes of the man Spike killed.

"Best we don't mention this to the Captain," Golden said.

"You think?" I snarled. "Kedria, this was unnecessary. These men died for no reason."

"They stood between me and safety, which is cause enough."

"They were just young and scared and following their orders," I said.

"When they tried to send us down into the mob, they became my enemy."

"We are not at war with these people!" I shouted.

"Well maybe we should be," Kedria muttered.

The sound of howling and screaming grew louder and somewhere close by a burning house collapsed into ruins.

"The discussion will have to wait," Kat snapped. "Luckily the mob will be blamed for this. We need to move."

The angry crowd found other paths onto the Devil's Peaks. Pitched battles broke out between small groups of guards from the mansions of the nobles and the artisans and workers of the Lower City. We passed groups of entangled bodies where soldiers lay in the embrace of butchers and dockworkers. Kat led us to a small garden at the front of the residence of a small noble house perched on the edge of the Peaks. Here the slope was less pronounced.

A group of the Knights of the Citadel galloped down the cobbled road and straight into a crowd of men and women carrying an assortment of weapons. The momentum of the charging horses carried the knights forward, and I watched as mace and sword fell on the mob. Eventually, the sheer number of people slowed the armoured men and then the crowd pulled them from their mounts. One by one the knights disappeared under a sea of writhing limbs. Woodmen's axes and workers' clubs rose and fell until the mob finished, and then they turned and jogged past our hidden position up into the Noble district. They didn't move with the same energy as before as many of them were bloody and carrying wounds.

I led the way and took our little group into the park between the two peaks. We followed well-worn paths around the edge of the Sacred Lake and then out to a line of hedges near the McRobb mansion. There we stopped and watched as soldiers wearing the surcoat emblazoned with the boar's head gave swords, axes, and crossbows to the mob. The citizens were now well-armed and would be more dangerous than ever.

"We are close, but the next part will be risky. The streets here are wide, but if we follow the edge of the park, we will only be a couple of blocks from Lord Alder's mansion. The problem is that we will be very close to the Citadel, and I don't think the knights will hesitate to ride us down if we cross their path," I said.

My head pounded, and I could barely stand. The tea hadn't worked, and I couldn't understand why. I didn't want to collapse. Even though Golden would carry me, it would slow our party, with perhaps fatal consequences. Small groups of people occupied the park, but they were dispersing. Golden crashed into three men and a woman as we crossed a path that led to the bridge over the lake. He cut down a big man wearing a leather apron carrying a stone mason's hammer, but the others ran into the bushes, yelling for help. We skirted the park until it ended at the road that ran up to the Citadel. Knights streamed from the open gates of the massive fortification in groups of ten and cantered down toward the fires of the city. Their armour seemed black and their faces were hidden under pig snouted helmets.

Kat led us across the road and down the street toward Lord Alder's mansion. We turned the corner to the great house which looked out over the city to find the front gates in ruins and corpses lying in the gutters. Golden took us through the courtyard and onto cobblestones covered with blood. Men in chain shirts and people in coats and rough jackets lay everywhere. Ahead of a small knot of men at the top of wide steps fought a group of between fifty to sixty men and women before the main door of the mansion. From an upper window, a woman threw heavy objects at the crowd. We attacked from behind. Kedria and I fired our crossbows until they were empty, then we fought with our swords. I could do little more than fend off blows as my head spun and legs wobbled. It was Kat, Golden, and Spike, who did the damage. The hand and a half Cold Blade cut right and left as Golden took arms from torsos and heads from bodies. Kat's light blade flicked in and out of the mass of writhing bodies and came away covered in blood. She guarded Golden's flank as he cut his way forward. The dire wolf, as always, was a force of nature. Spike tossed people aside as if they were old bones, snarling as he did so. Soon the crowd melted away from the terrible swords and destructive jaws, and then they were running. Lord Alder killed a man carrying a sword but wearing the tight-fitting jacket of a dockworker, then he stepped forward.

"Well met, Golden. I cannot say if your arrival could have been any better timed."

"We came here looking for safety, but it seems as if nowhere is free from bloodshed tonight," my tall friend said.

"The mob was led here by McRobb's soldiers, though I can't prove it. It seems as though someone was arming them," Lord Alder said as he kicked away the sword a dockworker had held.

"We saw the people being given weapons in front of his residence, by soldiers wearing the colours of McRobb," Kat said.

Lord Alder nodded. His shoulders slumped slightly, and he wiped the blood from his longsword on the cloak of a dead man. One of his soldiers bent and lifted a wounded man up by the chin to cut his throat.

"No," Lord Alder said. "Take all of the wounded to the main hall and call for healers. These people are citizens of Hope and were poisoned by words of hate."

Teal ran from the front door and took the blood-spattered noble in her arms.

"I'm alright," he murmured into her ear.

I realised she had been the woman throwing objects from the window at the crowd. Sitting heavily on the steps, I put a hand to my head and vomited.

Later, Kat brewed another pot of special tea, and I felt an immediate improvement in my condition. Lord Alder and Golden helped some of the remaining soldiers stack the dead. They laid out the corpse of the soldiers with their arms crossed and their swords on their chests and closed their eyes. Kat watched the entrance with two young guards and a few of the servants. They pulled the gates closed and barred the passage as best they could with large pieces of timber and an overturned cart. Inside, the wounded groaned and some died on the floor of the Great Hall while the cook and Teal tried to tend them. No healers came, as the streets were too dangerous for them to travel.

Slowly the noise of the mob died away, and only the crackle of fire and the smell of smoke was left. Toward morning, the rain blew in off the ocean from the Northwest saving the city from conflagration. I slept a shallow dream-wracked slumber filled with images of fire and blood. The others didn't sleep until the rain started to fall, and Lord Alder didn't rest at all. He searched for and found healers who stitched the wounds of those who had fallen in his grounds. Opium juice was liberally applied and eventually, the sounds of the wounded diminished.

The city awoke the next day as though it had a hangover. The streets were empty except for the surviving members of the Watch and the Knights of the Citadel. The smell of wet ash covered the stench of death. Most fires were out, but many houses had been burnt to the ground. In some areas, whole streets were gone leaving only gaping holes, like the black pits in a mouth of rotten teeth. We heard three or four thousand souls had gathered near the Small Woods. Hardly a crusading army that would trouble the Snow Leopard but the McRobbs reinforced the group with some of their own soldiers and hedge knights, and peasants were said to be moving in small clusters from the north to join it. The Council of Notable Elders met in the Round Chamber at the heart of the Citadel, but after the casualties the knights took, it seemed as if it would be powerless to do anything about the illegal army gathering just outside its borders. Kat put forward the hypothesis this was why Jamie McRobb stirred the city to chaos in the first place.

Meanwhile, I was no closer to finding my sister or recovering the Crown. I guessed the McRobbs would have moved it out of the city last night using the chaos of the riots as a cover. Golden went out briefly in the morning and noted their mansion stood empty. It made sense the family which had started the trouble would flee the city. If they stayed, Jamie McRobb would have been arrested immediately.

Kedria brought me hot bread and soup for lunch. She smiled and kissed me before moving off toward the kitchen to get her own food. On her hip, she wore the double-shot crossbow. Watching the lazy sway of her hips, I wondered how she fitted into my life. I didn't know if I loved her, and as soon as I examined my feelings, Miranda's face jumped into my mind. She was expected back in Hope any day now, and I still hadn't decided what I was going to do when she returned. Sighing, I realised it was another complication.

I wandered around Lord Alder's mansion until I found a north-facing window. The scars of the city stood out from here, with black marks against the greys and browns of the houses and other buildings. Only Docklands seemed to have escaped the effects of the fire.

"It's not a pretty sight, is it," Lord Alder said.

I jumped slightly, as I hadn't heard his footfalls. "No."

"I have been looking for you, as I have unexpected news." He smiled at me. "Not everything went the McRobb's way last night. It seems something they recently purchased has slipped through their fingers."

"The Crown?"

"As they tried to take it from the city, it was snatched away. Details are sketchy, but somehow a portion of the mob turned on the men guarding the Crown. In the attack, it was taken."

"How do you know?"

"Matron Snowfeld's spies heard the story and confirmed it from a captured McRobb man. She spread the tale to undermine the McRobbs' appeal to the masses. If they no longer hold the Crown, then their symbol of resistance against the dark elves is gone. Snowfelds are against the war, and their house was attacked last night too."

I nodded slowly. "So Jamie McRobb started a fire he couldn't control. The question is, who has the Crown now?"

Going over it in my mind, I tried to work through the list of candidates. It could have been the Fist of the Snow Leopard, but they would have been attacked by the mob. The Original Men, marked by their brown skin, were targeted last night, and as the Fist only consisted of this racial grouping, it would have been extremely dangerous for them to move about the city. Grandfather could have worked out what was going on and jumped at the chance to steal the Crown back, but would he want to upset the McRobb clan? Then there were Shade and Sabella. My sister wouldn't have dared walk the streets last night but maybe one resourceful woman who knew the city well would. Why would they want the Crown? My sister's reasons behind her actions never made much sense, but everything I had heard about Sabella led me to believe that she wouldn't take a risk without good reason. I would need to get down to the woolsheds as soon as possible to see if I could find the pair of them before they slipped away, and I probably should visit Grandfather again. If the Fist had the Crown, then it had probably already travelled south. My sister's fate and that of my family would be sealed.

The curfew on the Lower City was lifted the following day, and I felt strong enough to make my way down to the bookshop. Kat and Golden came with me. Spike bounded along in front of us, enjoying the nearly empty streets. Kedria stayed at Lord Alder's mansion and excused herself, saying she had correspondence she needed to complete. I didn't know how she was going to get mail through to our people and she told me not to ask.

"Your new girlfriend is a bit quick off the mark," Golden said as we walked through the blackened streets.

Wreckage lay everywhere, though some streets seemed completely untouched.

"What do you mean?"

"She shot the watchman down without much thought," Kat said.

"I know," I muttered.

"We were all put at risk by her actions," Kat continued.

"I didn't like her choice either, but she isn't from here and feels like she is in constant danger. I guess that makes her a bit jumpy."

"She's a strange one, I must say, Ash. I know you are together at the moment, and I don't mean to insult you, but sometimes I wonder about her," Golden said.

"You mean the faraway look she gets?" I asked.

"Yes, I suppose that's what I mean. Sometimes she looks right through people like they're not there."

"I think Kedria feels out of place here," I said.

"It's more than that," Kat added. "And Spike doesn't like her."

The big wolf ran back to the group at the sound of his name, almost knocking Golden over.

"Spike doesn't like a lot of people," I said.

"He likes Miranda," Kat said.

"I can't choose my partner based in the whims of a dire wolf," I snapped. "Besides, she made her choice."

The elf shrugged and helped Golden regain his balance.

"I always trust Spike's judgment," Golden said. "After all, he caught Kat for me."

"Yes, after I beat you up," the elf said, smiling.

My tall friend laughed and slipped his arm through hers.

The shop was a blackened ruin. The top floor had disappeared, leaving a gaping hole, and the front door and workshop area were covered with fallen timbers and soot. Only the stairwell and the rear of the shop remained relatively untouched. The large north-facing window was smashed and all the books and scrolls ruined either by fire or the rain that followed. I felt a hollow feeling in the pit of my stomach and moisture crept into the corner of my eyes. My last contact with Rackhime had been destroyed. Most of the work tools were burnt, and the precious bottles of ink broken. My favourite couch was blackened and waterlogged. I yelled in frustration and kicked at a ruined book which flew to pieces.

"I'm so sorry, Ash," Kat said.

"We need to scavenge what we can, and don't kick any more books," Golden said. "You know Rackhime would want you to save whatever you could."

"What's the point?" I mumbled.

"You start again, and don't give up."

"Golden's right. This place holds meaning, and we are not going to throw it away. We will rebuild it," Kat said.

My friends fossicked through the ruins while I recovered the large strongbox from the rear of the shop. The few scrolls and twelve books it contained were undamaged, and the silver and gems were safe. I hated Jamie McRobb, a man I had never met; he had destroyed something important to me. My reasons for denying him the Crown had just grown.

9

HIDEAWAY

Going to see Grandfather after finding the shop destroyed was probably not one of my wisest decisions, but it was on my to-do list. Kat and Golden went to check the condition of their own lodgings, while I made my way to the fortress where Grandfather ran his empire of vice, gambling, and smuggling. A row of houses to the north of the solid mansion had burnt to the ground. Some of the high stone walls which protected the building were scorched, but no damage had occurred inside the compound. I noticed on the walk from the Peaks that most of the damage had occurred in the artisans' or dockworkers' districts. The mob had burned down their own houses.

The guards told me Grandfather wasn't in but could be found at the Mermaid, one of his gambling and dance halls. I made my way to Docklands, skirting streets blocked by fallen rubble. The Watch was supervising prisoners clearing away the worst of it. They stood by as sullen men, and women dragged blackened beams into piles that were later loaded onto large wagons and moved to the riverbank. Captain Waldheigheim sat on his bay mare giving orders to a couple of sergeants and felt a surge of relief. I had been concerned about his fate during the riots.

"A bad business," I said, walking up to him.

He nodded, arm in a sling and bruising around one of his eyes. There was also blood and grazing on his single long eyebrow.

"McRobb has a lot to answer for," Captain Waldheigheim said.

"The mob burnt down the bookshop."

The Captain sighed, and his shoulders dropped. "Another reason for that clan to be brought to justice."

"I gather the mob ran over you," I said.

"A lump of thrown wood hit me above the eye, and I fell from my horse. It's nothing really."

That was doubtful. I could tell by the way the Captain moved he was in a lot of pain. It took some time to fill him in on all my news, leaving out our involvement in the death of five of the Watch.

"I wondered why McRobb sent some of his men back into town. We captured two a little earlier, and they both now reside in the deepest cells under the watchhouse. It fits with your story about the loss of the Crown. He must want the artefact badly if he is willing to risk some of his most trusted men to retrieve it."

I shook my head. Not only was I up against the Fist of the Snow Leopard, but now McRobb's best men would be thrown into the mix as well.

"You'll go after Sabella soon?" he asked.

"I have a lead I'm going to check out. If she did steal the Crown, then I suspect she and my sister are still hiding somewhere in the city. But first I want to visit Grandfather and try to find out if he was involved."

"Well, keep me informed. I must say, Ashley, your life is never dull. It makes me glad I'm just a humble policeman."

The noise coming from the Mermaid was muted by its usual standards. There were only a few girls dancing, and I didn't know any of them. Grandfather sat at a small gambling table holding playing cards. He had three cards on the table and four more in his hand, so I guessed he was playing the Hidden King, a game of bluff and counterbluff. I bought a drink and watched. In the corners of the room, four warriors stood and surveyed the crowd while three more men patrolled the premises. They saw me and nodded but kept their distance. Grandfather played an excellent game of cards. His face and body remained relaxed, and his expression of indifference never changed. Sometimes the eyes can give you away in a high stakes card game, but his only moved slowly around the room before settling back on his cards. They didn't dart around or stare intently at his hand. The other players were either nobles or rich merchants and were out of their depth. Grandfather slowly bid up the pot as though he was hesitant or unsure before sweeping away his opposition with a stunning hand that held three kings and a queen. As he gathered his winnings, he looked at me.

"Thanks for not interrupting, Ash. It is rare to get a hand like that."

"I must say, you hid its strength masterfully."

He smiled slightly. "I've had practise, but enough about cards. I'm betting that you are here about the disappearance of the Crown."

"Does the whole city know?"

"Only those with excellent intelligence sources and yours are obviously as good as mine, which of course is one of the reasons that I employ you," Grandfather said.

"Did you steal it?" I asked.

Grandfather looked at me round-eyed before laughing. "I have to say, Ash, your bluntness is refreshing. Everybody else tiptoes around me, but not you. Of course, a little more respect wouldn't go astray, but then we can't have everything."

I waited, staring at his face. His beard was greyer than I remembered it and his neck marked with dark spots.

"No, I'm not that stupid. The McRobbs are powerful enough to hurt me if I cross them and this city is not big enough that it wouldn't leak out if I tried to sell it to someone else."

"Do they believe you?"

"That is an excellent question. I think they are undecided, but I have offered to assist them in any way I can and have told them it is my belief that Sabella stole it."

"That must have been an embarrassing admission," I said.

Grandfather's face hardened. He gestured at one of his men, and the guard crossed the room and stood by his side.

"You are not going to spoil my good mood, Ash. This little chat is over. Graznor will escort you to the door."

"Don't the McRobbs want you to clean up your own mess?"

Graznor stepped forward, one of his bear-like hands reaching for the sword at his waist.

"That's why I'm paying you, Owl, remember? Now get out and don't return until you have found Sabella."

I turned and walked toward the exit, happy I had annoyed him. Grandfather doesn't like to be reminded of his mistakes, and his old security chief was turning out to be one of his biggest.

As we reached the door, Graznor gave me a push. That was a mistake. I hit the door frame hard but then spun to face the huge man. He grinned at me and held a large knife in front of him. Noting his missing teeth, I smelt his sour odour. I stepped into him, taking the dagger hand in one of mine and then I turned into his body. We both faced the same direction now and were so close for a heartbeat I could feel his breath on my ear. As usual for me, when I fought, time seemed to slow down. Hammering my elbow twice into his stomach, I slammed the heel of my boot down onto his toe. Graznor doubled over in pain, and I stepped around to face him. I kicked him once under the jaw, and he fell. His companions ran into the room but by the time they reached the door, I was in the street and running. Today the side effects of the potion didn't flood my brain, and I moved easily. Grandfather employed big men, but they weren't fast. They had no chance of catching me. Laughing, I slowed to a jog.

Grandfather probably told the truth. My needling wasn't only because I liked to annoy the old man; I also wanted to see how easy it would be to provoke a reaction. If Grandfather had stolen the Crown, then the mess wasn't because of Sabella, and he might not have become angry. It wasn't proof, and I had seen what a good card player Grandfather could be. I might still be wrong, but when a hunch combines with a little evidence, no matter how circumstantial it is, I go with it until something shows me I'm wrong.

The night was dark and still with a hint of frost. I would have preferred some wind or rain to cover the sounds of our approach but didn't think I had time. If Sabella and Shade were in the room above the woolshed, then they might not stay much longer. I only wanted to confirm the location of the two women before passing the information to Captain Waldheigheim. He would have the manpower to seal off all the possible exits from the building, and then he could take whatever information he could from Sabella about Grandfather's operations. The Captain said he would give the Crown and my sister to me. After all, he had no proof she had broken any of the laws of Hope.

Kedria heard of my little night expedition and announced she wanted to come with me. I hadn't been sure it was wise, but she could be stealthy when she wanted to. Kat would have been a better partner as she was probably even quieter than I, but I remained hesitant as I didn't want to involve her in the problems of my people. We dressed in black and strapped our weapons firmly to our bodies, hiding our white hair under hats of wool. Both of us greased and oiled our small but powerful handheld crossbows. I hoped they wouldn't be necessary, but I felt certain Sabella would fight anyone who invaded her sanctuary.

The area near the woolshed was quiet, with only the odd scurrying rat breaking the silence. Kedria and I walked quickly over the cobblestones to an area of beaten earth near the rear door. This was an obvious point of entry and one that was sure to be trapped if the small apartment near the roof was indeed the hideout of my sister and her lover. There were shuttered windows set well above the ground, which was how I planned to get inside. The walls of the building were made from long planks of wood that had split in many places. Though I could have easily pulled some away from the noise it would make during the process would alert anyone inside the building. Instead, I used the gaps in the timber as footholds to climb to the windows. Once I scaled the walls, I undid the shutter with a long thin piece of timber. Slipping inside, I found myself on top of a high stack of wool bales. My eyes took in all available light, and soon I could make out a central walkway which ran above the main room to what looked like an empty series of offices. All of them were open and overlooked the main wool storage area, but I couldn't see where the hidden room would be.

There was a soft creak on the rope, and Kedria slid alongside me. I knew she would be able to see whatever I could and decided perhaps she would be of more assistance than Kat. After all, everybody knows elves can't see in the dark.

I cupped my hands around Kedria's ear. "We need to move over the top of the bales to the walkway. The stairs will be trapped."

She nodded, and we moved carefully, climbing from the different stacks of wool until we were just under the walkway. Stretching carefully over my head, I found purchase on the bottom rail. I pulled myself upward and was glad to be wearing gloves as the railing consisted of long thick pieces of wire that had been pulled tight to prevent someone falling. Reaching down, I hauled Kedria up alongside me and flinched as her crossbow banged on the rail. It had come loose at some point, and I signalled for her to secure it before we moved on.

The first office was backed by a board on which chalk marks had been scratched. There were no parchment or writing tools in sight, as such items were far too valuable to be left lying around. Wooden chairs and two fold-up tables had been stacked against the wall. The floorboards were rough and worn and creaked softly under my feet. The next office looked the same as the first, except two barrels had been placed here. There were also buckets, mops and brooms leaning against the wall. Long coils of rope were looped carefully on the floor, and large block and tackles hung from hooks. A wall ran at right angles to the room, meaning that the office next door would be half the size of the one we were now in. There was no need for the room to be smaller than the others, and I started looking for a secret latch, or some other mechanism I suspected would open a door to the hidden chamber. Not planning on entering, I intended to leave and pass all the information to the Captain. I had just noticed that one of the hooks was free of rope and pulleys when there was a loud clatter and a bang behind me. Turning, I saw Kedria tangled in rope with a bucket and an errant mop lying nearby.

Gritting my teeth in frustration, I pulled on the empty hook. There was no choice now but to confront my sister and Sabella. A small door swung open. Two women were at a hatch at the far side of the room, one fair-skinned, and one black. Sabella grinned at me and then I heard the swish. I just had time to turn my head when a tied sack on a rope swung into the space I was occupying. It caught me with a glancing blow and knocked me off my feet, spinning me into the wall. The sack must have been filled with dirt or sand, but whatever it held made it heavy enough to hurt. Kedria's fall made so much noise I opened the door without looking for any traps. It took me only a few heartbeats to regain my feet. I sprang across the room to the trapdoor, down which the two women had disappeared. Pulling hard, I found the hatch wouldn't open. I felt a surge of frustration followed by a familiar pressure behind the eyes. My headache returned, and soon I would need some of my tea or I would become incapacitated. Spotting a shortsword leaning against a chair, I tried to use it to lever the trapdoor open, but it was wedged tightly shut. I hammered at the wood with the weapon and felt the pain in my skull grow. Eventually, the timber gave, and I tore the small door from its hinges. The smell of rotting garbage and sewage hit me in the face. A narrow tunnel descended into the dark, and a knotted rope hung from a spike that had been hammered into position at the top.

"They'll be long gone," Kedria said.

"Thanks to you," I yelled.

"It was an accident. I saw the mop but missed the bucket."

"How could you be so clumsy?"

"I was in a hurry to catch you."

"You will not be coming with me again," I snarled. "I'll take Kat. Even Golden would have been quieter."

Kedria hung her head, and I felt the pain explode behind my eyes. It dropped me to my knees in agony, and I groped in the pocket for my tea. Kedria spotted my distress and eased me onto a rumpled bed. Soon she had heated some water on a small iron stove and put a wooden mug in my hands. I blew on the liquid while it cooled and then sipped it until my head started to clear.

I was calmer now, and it seemed to help with the pain though I remained angry at Kedria for betraying our approach, but there wasn't any point holding onto the frustration. My sister and her lover had abandoned many possessions in their hurried departure. I was sure

Sabella would have an emergency supply of money, clothes, and weapons somewhere close by, but she would still miss some of the items left in her hidden room.

"Search everything," I said.

Standing slowly, I moved to a small table and pulled out a dagger. I felt that chasing my sister from her hidden dens was becoming a habit, but then I remembered who she had shared this place with.

"Watch out for any hidden surprises. Sabella will have left a few in order to incapacitate those who seek to track her," I said.

The first such device was attached to a stool in the corner of the room. Moving the offending piece of furniture removed a weight that triggered a mechanism in the floor. What would happen next we never found out as Kedria put a block of wood on the area, replacing the weight of the stool before the trap could go off.

"There's a coin pouch filled with silver and a sharpening stone. I've also found clothes, food, and some wineskins, but nothing of interest," Kedria said.

I took the money, old habits dying hard, and then searched through parchment on the bench. On one sheet described the Crown of the Snow Leopard. The second sheet was written in the western language but contained spelling mistakes and incorrect grammar.

"Agreed upon, yes. Bring the item to the place of your greatest failure."

I picked up both parchments and folded them before placing them under my leather vest. There was also a bone scroll container sealed with wax. Two small holes had been pushed through the seal with wire. I took out a dagger and started working at the wax when I hesitated. Why had the scroll remained unopened when the women had obviously been in the room for some time undisturbed? The container itself was worth more than a few silver pieces and the runes inscribed on it were old Dwarfish. I suspected it to be part of some plundered treasure Sabella had stumbled upon during her days as a hunter.

"Kedria, come here and stand ready with your sword."

She did so, and I placed the scroll container on the table. I picked off the wax quickly, and a large spider fell out onto the sheets of blank parchment. Kedria was ready and squashed the arachnid with the flat of her blade.

"A northern diamondback. Deadly with no known cure. They are very aggressive when cornered or surprised," I said.

I looked at the spider with its smooth patterned body shattered by the blade. Sabella had certainly gone to a lot of effort to hurt those who chased her. She must have expected to be discovered at some stage, the question was where she would relocate to.

The parchment indicated a deal had been struck, but it was unclear with whom. A location for exchange had been agreed upon, but I couldn't understand what the phrase "your greatest failure" meant. It led me to believe my time was running out and Sabella and my sister would soon be on the move.

"We need to return to Lord Alder's," I said. "There's nothing more we can do here."

Kedria put her finger to her lip and glanced around the room. "Why not stay here?"

I thought about it. The room appeared comfortable with a small stove and a ready-made security system. It was also well hidden and unknown. If the city went berserk again, it would be the sort of place where a couple of dark elves could hide. The traps could be reset, and I could add some of my own, in case Sabella decided to return. I doubted that she would. Sitting on the bed, I patted the pile of sheepskins. Kedria looked at me and raised one of her white eyebrows. I smiled and considered different ways she could make it up to me for giving away our approach.

The rubble around the ruined bookshop had been cleared away by the following afternoon. Kedria was somewhere in the city purchasing food supplies for our new base. I told Lord Alder and Golden, where I was staying and warned them about the locations of all the traps. Then I sent a note to Captain Waldheigheim, giving him similar information and telling him of my near-miss with Sabella. I collected the hidden strongbox and the books and scrolls and thought about what to do with them. The Dwarfish history books were Lord Alder's and the scrolls of Knowledge written by the Original Men were mine. The rolls of parchment had been copied by Rackhime and were some of his finest work. I caught a lift with a wagon carrying crates of chickens up to the market that ran in The Open just below the Noble District. Lord Alder was pleased to see me again and smiled as I handed him the book.

"I thought this would have been destroyed in the fire," he said.

"It was one of the few items I had the chance to put in the strongbox before we fled. It was out on the bench where I had been copying it, so it caught my eye."

He turned it over in his smooth hands. "It's funny you saved it, as I had originally purchased it from Golden."

"Where did he get it from?"

"He said it came from one of his old trips to the East and thought the gems embedded in the front cover might make it valuable, but its age is what makes it so important."

"I agree, and will finish copying it for you when I set myself set up again."

Lord Alder nodded. "There's no hurry. In the meantime, I might send it over to Sir Petar to study. Would you take it there for me?"

My heart started to hammer in my chest. "Are they back?"

"He and Miranda returned this morning and are in the process of settling in."

I agreed to deliver the book, and Lord Alder left me to meet with two iron merchants from the city of Deeport.

The knowledge Miranda had returned shouldn't have surprised me as I had known for a while they would be back any day now, but now she was back I felt unhinged. There were now issues I needed to deal with, the first one being my future with Kedria. I had entertained thoughts of returning to my people for the first time in years. The possibility of going to the mountains with Kedria and settling down with her amongst her clan was enticing. The isolation of her family amongst the mountains of the Eastern Spur interested me. I would be amongst the dark elves and yet be far removed from the politics of the clans of the high plateau. It would also be feasible to keep some distance from my own family. The reunion with my father had gone well, but I wasn't sure if I was ready to trust him. The destruction of the bookshop had removed my last physical bond with Hope and cleared the way for a return to my people.

I didn't know how Kedria felt about any of this as we hadn't discussed it and I wasn't sure if moving south was really what I wanted to do. Not seeing Golden would be hard but he had Kat now, and I didn't see him for half of the year anyway, as he was usually in the East searching old ruins for silver or gems. Hope felt like home, and I couldn't ignore that fact. I didn't think of the southern mountains or the windswept high plateau as anything but a chapter from my past. And there was Miranda. Even the thought of never seeing her again hurt. Our future was unknown, and she had married the old noble Sir Petar, a situation my own behaviour had precipitated.

Miranda's house stood as I remembered it, except the trees and shrubs were taller, and the barn had a new roof. As I walked up the steps to the wide veranda where we had spent an afternoon kissing, I almost fled. I felt the beginnings of a headache. I forced myself to be calm. My breathing slowed, and I cleared my mind of emotion. The pain receded, and I focused on what I was here to do. Lord Alder had wrapped the book in greased paper, and I would hand it to Sir Petar with Lord Alder's compliments, then I would go. I knocked loudly on the door and waited. It swung open and there stood Miranda.

10

WITHOUT A TRACE

Her hair was up in a bun with strands drifting around her face. She wore a blue dress that swept the ground and yet clung to her. Large eyes widened as she put her hand to her mouth. Behind Miranda, men moved in the hallway carrying furniture and large trunks. I stared at her and resisted the urge to take her in my arms. She patted her hair and smoothed down her dress.

"I'm sorry Ash, I wasn't expecting visitors."

"If I've come at a bad time, I can always return later," I said.

"No, it's not that. We're still getting organised, and Petar is hopeless. He has returned to his library and is engrossed in his books and scrolls already."

The sound of the old man's name sent a surge of jealousy coursing through me.

"Well if you give him this, then I'll be on my way," I muttered. "It's from Lord Alder."

Miranda frowned and then stepped up to me. A heady scent radiated from her, and I staggered slightly.

"You can give it to him yourself. I'm not going to let you escape that easily. I want to know everything that is happening. The house can wait."

She led me inside and knocked on the study door. Sir Petar answered, and she opened. The old man was a little more stooped and wrinkled than the last time I had seen him. Books and scrolls were scattered around the room, and a map lay spread across a large table. He looked at me with hooded eyes and slowly placed the scroll he had been holding on a chair.

"This room is already a mess, Petar. I had sorted it before we left, so you better put everything back where you got it from," Miranda scolded.

The old man's eyes stayed with me.

"The dark elf visits us first. I thought it would be so, yes, yes, I did. But so quickly, he has come."

I remembered the way Sir Petar spoke and frowned. The old man's strange mannerisms had not always annoyed me, but they did now.

"I have brought you a present from Lord Alder. He says you might be able to read the script and translate it, but I will need it back at some stage as I have been paid to copy it."

He took the book from me and unwrapped the paper. Slowly he caressed the gems embedded in the front cover.

"It is a copy of something from long ago, yes, yes. Old Dwarfish it is, but so much more."

The old man's eyes shone, and his hands shook.

"Copied it must be, but first I will translate, though time I'll need. It is from before people came from the West across the seas. So ancient is the writing. An old Dwarfish translation of something even more ancient."

Miranda smiled and nodded at me. "Tell Lord Alder we appreciate his gift."

She led me from the room as Petar carefully turned the pages of his new acquisition.

"He has already forgotten about you," she said as we walked into the kitchen. "Books and scrolls are his first love."

"Not you?" I asked.

Miranda's mouth became a thin line. "Don't start. We are together because he was lonely after the death of his daughter, and after you rejected me, I decided to find some security. We have travelled this road, and there is no need to walk along it again."

She was more direct than I remembered and cut straight to the central point. I had nothing to argue with, at least nothing logical. Tea was prepared, and we moved to the drawing-room.

"I want to know everything," Miranda said.

I started by telling her about Teal, and Lord Alder and the union looked as though it was going to produce a child. Then I told her about the visit from my father and the trouble my sister had caused. I didn't tell her about my addiction.

"Who is Kedria?"

I couldn't meet her eyes. "A dark elf agent sent here to find the Crown."

"She is more than that, isn't she?"

"You weren't here, and she offers me solace. I dropped into a very dark hole after you left, and she found me."

"Do you love her?"

I found the direct approach slightly unnerving and squirmed in my chair.

"While away, I had to deal with the managers of a number of small estates, with merchants, and even the odd banker. Petar's assets were a mess. I discovered plain talking usually got the best results when working with these people, so you better get used to it," Miranda said.

"I don't think I do," I said slowly, answering her original question. "She is important to me, but it's not love."

She nodded and linked her fingers in her lap. "I want to keep seeing you, Ash."

My feelings surged, and the headache exploded behind my eyes. I must have paled because Miranda spotted the change.

"Are you okay? You look ill."

I fumbled in my pocket for the tea leaves that would ease the pain.

"Please brew these. There is more I need to tell you."

The story of my addiction came out slowly, and Miranda listened as I tried to explain the pain and loneliness that had led me down that dark path. As I spoke, my shame grew, and I felt unworthy to be in her presence.

"I shouldn't be here," I said.

Her eyes never left mine. "This is exactly where you should be," she whispered.

Those few words comforted me more than anything that had been said since I had stopped smoking opium. Miranda's fingers clenched and unclenched in her lap as she sat before me.

"This may sound a little ruthless considering all that has happened, but Ash, I don't want to be without you."

At first, I didn't know what to say, and I sat there staring. Even my headache was forgotten as I tried to process what she was saying.

"But we are both with someone else," I said.

"Then, we will need to be discrete. Your dark elf friend will leave eventually, and Petar is happy with a companion. I've had a lot of time to think about this, and though there have been times when you have been a complete fool, you always thought you had my best interests at heart. The role of the Mistress of this house is something I have grown into, and it has made me decide to take what I want in life, and I need you."

Miranda stood and cocked her head sideways as though she was thinking, and then she stood and slid toward me. The kiss, when it came, was gentle and soft. I sighed into her mouth as though breathing out the tension I always carried. The kisses became more urgent and deeper, and we rolled into each other on the couch. When we stopped, Miranda laughed breathlessly.

"This is not discrete. There are workmen everywhere, and Petar is only a few paces away in his study. I'm staying tomorrow night at Lord Alder's mansion with Teal. You're invited to dine there as well."

I gasped. "So, Lord Alder and Teal know of your decision!"

"They have both encouraged me in it. Lord Alder says that after finding Teal, he realised it's important to grab happiness while you can."

We kissed one last time and then spent the rest of the meeting grinning at each other like happy children. I had my tea, though I didn't really need it in the end. We said goodbye, and I looked for a wagon which would take me down the hill. I couldn't stop thinking about my dinner invitation for the following evening. The sense of anticipation remained intense, and then I remembered Kedria and my feelings were tempered by guilt. I decided to end the relationship with her as soon as possible, but the timing was complicated by many factors, not the least of those being she had just set herself up in the woolshed with me. Then there was our joint search for the Crown and my sister that we were far from completing. In the end, I decided it didn't matter. If we had to continue our goals apart, then that's what I would do. Miranda's sense of putting herself first had inspired me to do to the same.

The hidden room at the woolshed smelt of rosemary and mint when I returned. A pan containing various herbs and the better part of a chicken awaited me. Kedria half smiled as I entered and then turned back to the meal.

"I thought I'd make something special," she said.

"It smells nice," I said.

We ate in silence and later Kedria took me to bed. I wanted to say no. But she was the gentlest and most engaged she had ever been with me, and I didn't want to spoil the moment. Later she lay in my arms and stroked the different scars on my chest and arms.

"You know I would never want to hurt you, *Ashen*," she whispered in my ear.

I nodded, feeling confused and guilty.

"I'm dedicated to my family and what is right for our people, and I want you to understand that."

I wasn't sure where she was going with this, but I didn't want her to worry.

"I realise your family and clan are very important to you," I said.

She rolled to face me. "It's more than that. I've done things I'm not proud of, but always with our people's best interests in the front of my mind."

She looked at me fiercely, and then we kissed again. Before I knew it her hand had stirred my passion, and we were soon joined. In the morning, when I woke, she was standing naked by the fire, warming her hands. I crossed to kiss her shoulder, but she stared into space and ignored me.

"I'm going out to find Snuffles to ask him some questions, and then

I have some other people I need to see. I probably won't be back today," I said.

"Do you really think the old dwarf will be able to help you?" she muttered.

"Help us, you mean. I don't know, but I hope so."

Kedria's mood was unsettling, but I decided to ignore it and concentrate on finding Snuffles before going up the hill to Lord Alder's mansion. Tomorrow I would look at finding another place to live.

The old dwarf lay on a wide cot in the infirmary of the Temple of The Lady of the Swan. Women in long black dresses swept around lines of white cots. The smell of lavender sat uneasily over a number of other scents. The metallic tang of blood lay just at the end of my senses as did the stench of death. Light filtered in through high windows. Long pillars of stone threw shadows over the sick and injured, hiding the ghostly pallor of their skin from all but the most observant. The women would bend and offer a sip of water or a quiet word to those that lay on the cots. They looked like dark angels shepherding their flock through a cloudy sky.

It had taken some time to find Snuffles and had only been by visiting all the temple's sickhouses that I had located him. His inn stood next to the river, a blackened husk. A dockworker had told me that the Watch had dug Snuffles from the wreckage, barely alive. My hatred of the McRobbs grew further. Snuffles' teeth appeared briefly in the forest of his beard before disappearing. The attempt at a smile became a groan of pain, and his eyes closed while he rode the waves of agony.

One of the Swans of the Temple appeared at my shoulder and whispered into my ear.

"He has burns to his feet and hands, but it's the crushing wounds that are killing him. He bleeds on the inside, and it is just a matter of time before the Collector takes him."

"Is there nothing you can do?"

"We ease his pain, but opium is expensive."

I gave the woman a pouch of silver, pushing the money into her pale hands.

"Make sure he gets as much as he needs."

The woman nodded and then glided away, her dress sweeping the marble floor as she left.

"They rolled down the road into the inn and attacked like rabid dogs, Ash. I fought them, but they hit me with clubs and rocks."

Looking into Snuffles' eyes, I sat and listened.

"I knew some of them, had fed 'em, drunk with 'em, but when they burst through me door, they looked as though they'd just jumped from hell. Their faces were red and twisted."

"Jamie McRobb filled their ears with poison; they were drunk with hatred," I whispered.

It was as though I hadn't spoken. Snuffles groaned once and tensed with pain before relaxing again.

"I called some of the sailors by name and asked for help, but they kicked me and hit me."

"It's over now," I said.

The dwarf sighed and looked at a fixed point above my head. It didn't feel right to ask him about Sabella, but I had to.

"Snuffles, I need to ask about Sabella."

He closed his eyes and then breathed deeply. "Yeah?"

"She has the Crown and is in a lot of trouble."

"Silly girl," he whispered.

"I need to find her and the only clue says something about her 'greatest failure', but I have no idea what that means."

The dwarf grinned and gestured for me to lean forward. His lips moved, but I needed to strain to catch his voice.

"Sabella only failed once. At the Ever Fens where she led a group of hunters, adventurers, whatever you'd like to call 'em, to their deaths."

I sat back. Whoever wrote the note knew of Sabella's past and had used it to set a meeting place for the exchange of the Crown. Now all I had to do was get to this location and find her and my sister. The place referred to wouldn't be the Fens themselves as the trolls were very fussy about who they let into their territory. It would be at the nearest large town or village. The chosen location was far enough away that none from Hope would interfere, or that's what the two groups believed.

Making sure Snuffles received a large dose of opium, I left the temple and made my way to Lord Alder's. He would have maps of the east that would suggest the most likely location of the rendezvous with the next potential owner of the Crown. I could have asked Sir Petar but decided I didn't want to see him on this particular day; after all, I was meeting Miranda tonight.

"You are a little early, my friend," Lord Alder said as he greeted me in his hall.

He was dressed in tight woollen pants and wore a loose white shirt. In his right hand, he held a sabre. "I was just getting some practice in with my trainer, but if you would care to take his place?"

I was tempted. The last time we had duelled, I had almost killed him, but that felt like it had happened in a previous life.

"Only if we change weapons. I'm not familiar with your fragile blades."

He threw back his head and laughed, a booming sound which pulled up the corners of my mouth.

"Longswords or short?"

"Short, please."

As we prepared, I questioned him about his knowledge of the northeast.

"The maps will tell us, but from memory, there is a fortified town and a castle out on the Red Pike River. It's about three days' ride from the edge of the Fens but its good wheat country in the summer. This is an awful time of year to go that way as the winter hits there before it does here."

"I know," I grumbled, "But I've got little choice."

We duelled in front of his swordmaster. The man surprised me with his youth, but when I heard he had fought on the eastern frontier, I realised he would have combat experience and understand more than the technicalities of using a blade. I changed into a white shirt.

"Bernard will keep score," Lord Alder said as he placed the helmet on his head.

It was of light construction and padded with sheepskin. I wore one as well, and the visibility was excellent between the wire slats, but I doubted it would save the head from a really serious blow.

We started at four paces apart, and the instructor watched intently. I attacked first, and Lord Alder defended. He easily swept aside my first thrust and danced forward, slashing at my neck and face. I swayed backward and took stock. His footwork was flawless, and I had no snow or buried branches to help me beat him this time. I slashed at his neck, and as our swords locked, I punched toward his head with my left fist. He blocked with his free arm and slashed at my flank. Catching the blow, I pushed it away, but as I did Lord Alder's left fist thundered into my ribs. The blow didn't count as a point, but I doubled over, and he flicked a quick attack from the wrist at my head. The helmet took the force, preventing my skull from being opened to the bone.

"One point, Lord Alder," Bernard called.

The bout lasted for twenty minutes, and by the end of it, I was exhausted. Lord Alder defeated me five points to one and looked as though he had barely worked up a sweat.

"You are as skilful as I remember, Ash, but you lack stamina."

"I'm unfit, though the last time we fought conditions were on my side."

"Still, you taught me that day there is always someone out there who is better than you. I thought I couldn't be defeated and yet you did."

"I got lucky."

"You out-thought me, and it almost cost me my life."

"I regret that now."

"There was no long-term harm done, and in the end, much good has become of it. If we hadn't fought, I wouldn't have met Teal."

"And I wouldn't be meeting Miranda here tonight."

"Indeed, it's funny how the wheel turns. Now we'd better bathe and find some suitable clothes for you to wear."

"I must admit I feel both nervous and a little guilty about this evening," I said.

"That is understandable, but push the guilt aside. Sir Petar really can't expect his young bride not to form romantic attachments. Their marriage is one of companionship. She is a beautiful young woman and was never going to be satisfied with just him. I'm just glad you both found each other. Besides, noblemen take lovers all the time, and they are the ones who married women their own age.

"What about you and Teal? Are your peers more open to your relationship?"

Lord Alder rubbed a wet cloth across his face before replacing his weapon in the rack.

"Some are, though I can never take her to official functions. We can never marry, though I plan to adopt any children we have so they can inherit after I die."

We crossed to the stairs and then moved down to a smaller room near the rear door. Lord Alder led me to two large tubs made from bronze. One was filled with steaming liquid, the other one-half empty but the depth grew as servants tipped buckets of warm water in. My noble friend stripped and plunged into one of the tubs and came up spurting water like the porpoises that live in the Great River. I saw the scars I had given him almost a year ago. They looked like pink lines on his flesh that started and ended abruptly on his shoulder and flank. I tried not to think about what I had done to him. The water was almost too hot, but after some initial pain, my skin soon adjusted, and I enjoyed the sensation.

"I do this often these days and even more frequently in summer. After strenuous exercise, it feels great to wash away the sweat. Of course, with Teal around that occurs more often than it did in the past."

"Too much information, my friend," I said.

Lord Alder laughed, and I felt my grin returning.

We looked briefly at his map collection before going to choose some clothes for me to wear for the evening. A brief study of the scroll confirmed his recollection of the region with only the village of Snote being closer to the fens than the town of Wallington. Large forests stood to the west of the area, and I noted the road I needed to take would lead me through the southern portion of one of these. The area was often raided by both hobgoblins and giants from the Stony Hills with the trolls joining them in summer.

"I hope Golden will come with me. That is not good country to travel alone in."

"What about your dark elf companion? Would she not accompany you?"

I glanced sideways at him, looking for some sign he was teasing me, but his face remained impassive.

"That relationship is about to end."

"Ah," he said. "A complication."

"My life has always had plenty of those," I muttered.

He slapped me on the back and led me to chests full of clothes.

"These are some of the items I wore while I was sick. They are too small for me now but should fit you with your narrow shoulders. I don't suppose it matters what you wear as they won't stay on very long."

He laughed again, and I joined him. I was starting to enjoy the day.

The atmosphere was very relaxed by the time the light faded. Staff started to drift around Lord Alder's mansion, lighting candles and oil lanterns. I spent some time reading scrolls in the huge study and sipping wine. When Miranda and Teal arrived together, I had moved to a rear balcony with my noble friend. Teal entered first, her eyes shining at Lord Alder. She wore a pale dress that was high around the neck and clung to her like a second skin. Her freckles danced around her face as her grin became a dazzling smile. Miranda moved forward slowly, her hands clasped in front of her. Her dress was dark red and plunged low at the front. She wore earrings made from small bells that tinkled as she walked. Her eyes held mine as she stopped in the doorway and then flicked away and looked down at her feet. Lord Alder stepped up to her and took both of her hands in his.

"Welcome to our house, Lady Miranda. Come and share the view of Hope with us."

He guided her to my side, putting Miranda's hand in mine. I smiled, and she squeezed my fingers gently. We turned and looked out over the city. Clouds flew quickly from the west, winging their way only a few hundred paces above the highest peak. The city spread across the slopes down toward the Great Sigh River. The shadow of the mountain fell across the eastern suburbs, hiding the Rat's Maze and the huge gatehouse which guards the road to the Small Woods. Smoke drifted upward from thousands of chimneys to be caught by the westerly breeze. I could follow the winding track of the various roads that cut back and forth across the flank of the mountain, all heading toward the noble estates that sat cradled between the two separate peaks. The brown waters of the river mixed with the blue of the ocean at the edge of my vision, and wagons could be seen winding their way back to the villages and farms that dotted the far side of the waterway; their drivers returning from the ferry where they had been delivering food to a hungry city. Barges sailed upriver to the various towns along its length, and small boats came with the current to drop off the last of the root crop harvest. The lumber yard which sat further upriver had just taken delivery of a consignment of logs that had been floated from the forests of the east, and men walked over the trunks of giant trees like ants pushing the timber towards the shore.

I took it all in as I inhaled Miranda's scent. The soft smell of lavender floated around me, and I turned to look at her. In profile, her nose tilted up slightly. Stray wisps of hair caught the breeze and twirled around her brow. She sensed my scrutiny and turned to face me. I kissed her gently on the lips and then stood back. The resulting smile made her teeth glow, and I thought of kissing her again.

"Let's sit and have a drink before dinner," Lord Alder said quietly.

Chairs were brought, and the staff served ale and wine as well as plates of thinly sliced nut bread. Teal led the conversation with tales of high society. Many nobles still shunned her, but others had invited her into their homes, either to garner the favour of Lord Alder, or to gain notoriety for having had an ex-dancer in their house. Then Lord Alder spoke briefly of his alliance with Matron Snowfeld and their determination to keep Hope out of the Southern War.

"We have sent scouts and a force of knights to watch the so-called crusading army, but as it has left our territory, the Council of Notable Elders want to shepherd it on its way."

"I've heard that McRobb's forces have grown," I said.

"That's true, though it still probably doesn't number more than six thousand fighting men. It looks larger because of all the families that are travelling with it. A group of hedge knights joined it from the north as did some crossbowmen from the eastern forests. McRobb even employs some elves as scouts. I'm surprised they work for him after what the mob did to the other races in Hope.

"Some of the tribes are hard-pressed for coin, and the food it will buy," I said.

"Well, the only other information we have gathered is that the Crusade is short on provisions."

Later, Miranda filled us in on her travels around Sir Petar's estates and her attempts to bring them to order.

"They are all doing well as the harvest has been acceptable, but most of the profit was being skimmed off by the stewards before any of it made it into Sir Petar's coffers. I had to remove a few of them and gave a warning to some of the others. I've employed a man from the city to ride around the estates twice a year and inspect the books. Then I'll check his work."

I felt uncomfortable listening to tales from Miranda's other life and was grateful when Lord Alder announced dinner was about to be served.

It was river trout and roast lamb on large trenchers of hard bread surrounded by a variety of vegetables. Different sauces steamed from clay jugs and expensive glasses held wines that ran smoothly down the throat. The table was not so large that we sat paces from each other, but big enough to comfortably hold all the food. The smells immediately set my mouth watering, and I remembered how hungry I was. We chatted through the meal, eating and laughing until the table was cleared. Then soft breads and cheeses were served. Afterward we retired to the study and drank port and played Hidden King using pine nut seeds as the stakes. Teal won nearly every hand and teased us as she did.

When the last card had been played, and the glasses cleared away Lord Alder and Teal exchanged a look.

"We are retiring now. Your room is at the top of the stairs to the left," Lord Alder said.

He led Teal from the room by the hand as she blew kisses at Miranda and I until she disappeared through the doorway.

There was an awkward moment after the door closed. Miranda walked quickly across the room and started kissing me. Her hands tore my shirt open, and for a brief instant, I wondered if Lord Alder wanted his borrowed clothes back. Then she dragged me by the hand, giggling and stumbling up the stairs and along the hallway to the guest room. Inside, four candles created a soft light as they filled the air with the smell of honey. Rose petals littered the silk sheets, and sheepskin covered pillows were piled at the end of the bed.

"How sweet of them," Miranda said before she pushed me down.

I fell back onto the bed and watched as the beautiful woman before me undressed. She peeled herself like a grape and then offered herself to me. Pulling the ruined shirt over my head, I was ready by the time she joined me. It was everything I hoped it would be and it seemed to go on for hours. By the time we finished, we were both exhausted and covered in a thin film of sweat. We kissed before drifting off to sleep.

Later we woke and crawled under the sleeping skins and blankets. I was cold and glad of our shared warmth. Miranda wasn't happy with just cuddling, and we made love again. We then slept until a knock at our door woke us sometime in the late morning.

Teal burst into the room, carrying a tray of freshly cooked bread and bacon. She beamed, totally unconcerned we were both naked under the silk sheets.

"You two were so noisy last night, I'm surprised if the staff got any sleep," she said.

"You could hear us?" Miranda asked.

Teal laughed. "Of course not. We were making plenty of our own noise, but it was fun to see the expressions on your faces."

Miranda smiled and then kissed me hard. The sheet slipped down, and I could see her ripe body.

"Don't start again with me here. My days of 'Three in the Bed' are over," Teal said.

"I don't plan on sharing," Miranda said.

"Well I suggest you eat first, but there is no hurry to get up. Tylin has gone down to the merchant area on business and won't be back until later. He also asked me to tell you, Ash, to stop calling him Lord Alder. It seems a bit formal considering what you are now doing under his roof."

I said I would do my best. Then with a twirl of her skirt, she was gone. Miranda and I ate ravenously with her wiping butter from my chin before spreading some on herself. She smiled at me and invited me to clean her. We passed the rest of the afternoon in the guest room, and I didn't get back to the woolshed until it was almost dark.

The walk down the winding roads of the slope past the merchant's houses and the inns of Wind Street took longer than I thought it would. The stone buildings of the upper slopes gave way to timber and daub buildings the lower I descended, though there were many gaps where burnt ruins stood. Carts rattled past me on the cobblestone streets, taking food and goods to the upper markets or directly to the doors of a noble mansion. Empty wagons went the other way, down the steep roads with their wooden brakes grinding occasionally as they sought to control the vehicle's momentum. People glared at me as I passed, and I felt that the tension in Hope lay just beneath the surface. The Watch had set up a number of checkpoints on the wider streets, and small groups of knights patrolled the city.

A passing taxi cart offered to take me the rest of the way to the

Warehouse District, but I decided I needed the exercise, as yesterday's bout with Lord Alder had shown me just how out of condition I was; besides, the journey was all downhill. I started to think of what I was going to say to Kedria. It would be necessary to move out of the small hidden room and find some lodgings at one of the inns that sat on the flanks of the mountain. I was anticipating an uncomfortable discussion, but my mind was set. After ending the relationship, I would continue the investigation by myself and discover the missing Crown's location. Then I could find my sister.

As soon as I arrived at the woolshed I knew something was wrong. One of the upper windows had been opened, and a rope ran from the frame down to the ground. When I reached the main doorway, I found it ajar. The thin alarm wire linked to a number of small bells had been neatly cut, and the swinging bag of rocks had been disconnected from the pressure plate Sabella had previously rigged on the upper walkway. I only carried daggers, one of which I held by the blade ready to throw, the second stayed tucked into the top of my boot. The door to the hidden room had been kicked open and the room itself torn apart. The bed stood on its side, and both chairs were smashed. There was a small amount of ripped clothing on the floor as well as spots of blood. Kedria was missing. One of her crossbow bolts pierced the wall, and her sword lay near the trap door. All her possessions were scattered across the floor except for her cape and high boots. Searching the room frantically, I threw open the trapdoor to the sewers. I could see no sign it had been opened and the flour I had sprinkled on the rungs remained untouched. It appeared as though a group had assaulted the room and snatched the dark elf woman. I looked for some sign of who it might have been but found nothing to begin with.

Then I spotted a small amount of clay smeared on the floor with red seeds embedded in it. These seeds were often found in the rushes which were used to cover the floors of some of the taverns on the edge of Docklands, and the clay was prevalent in the lower city and not on the Peaks. The rushes grew on the riverbanks close to town but weren't used by any except the cheapest boarding houses, as they gave off an odour that reminded one of pig manure. There were other inns on the southern slopes of Hope that covered their floors with them, but most of the time they tended to use sawdust from the timber mills.

Guilt coursed through me, followed by a surge of dizziness. I controlled my breathing, and the sensation subsided. There were tea leaves in a pouch on my hip, but I decided to control the symptoms of the potion by forcing myself to relax. There were three possible groups that could have snatched Kedria and one of those I dismissed almost immediately. Grandfather would have no reason to take the dark elf woman as she had nothing he wanted, and I felt that the old man wanted to distance himself from anything to do with the Crown now he had sold it. Two groups remained suspects in my mind—the Fist of the Snow Leopard and McRobb's men. The Fist didn't appreciate Kedria working with me, and McRobb's men might think she had information on the location of the Crown. Whoever grabbed her, I was determined to get her back. I owed Kedria that much.

11

THE FIST

It was necessary to ask Golden and Kat for assistance. Darkness fell before I located them at the Red Duck Inn. I would not be able to fight five or more highly trained warriors in order to free Kedria by myself. My strength was still returning, and I had yet to control the full effects of the withdrawal potion. Golden was willing to help, but it took some time to convince Kat.

"I don't understand how they found her and why the Fist would bother is beyond me. So she is with you, and they don't like it. She is not interfering with their work, is she?" Kat asked.

"They may have been after me, and Kedria was the only one home," I said.

"Then why didn't they just back away when they discovered their mistake, or warn her off?"

"Maybe it was too late by then or perhaps this is the message. I don't know. It could be that McRobb's men took her."

"Then how did they find her?"

Kat's questions were annoying me.

"I don't know, but she didn't kidnap herself. Is this because she is a dark elf?"

Kat's eyes narrow. "How dare you! Throughout our friendship, when has there ever been a sign that I ever considered your race?"

"You are out of line, Ash," Golden agreed, standing by the elf's side.

I took a step backward. "Alright, that wasn't fair. There are still a number of unanswered questions, but I can't do this alone."

Kat looked at Golden who shrugged. "I'll help, but I still find this very strange."

"Thank you," I said. "I'll find the location of the group and from there come up with a plan."

"If you're seen, they will disappear," Kat said.

"I won't be seen."

After convincing both of them to assist me, I left the inn through the side door. Golden caught me in the alley before I went very far.

"Don't blame yourself for this," he said.

"Why would I do that?"

Golden drew a line in the dust of the alley with his feet and didn't meet my eyes.

"Because you were with Miranda last night, and knowing you, probably believe that if you hadn't been with her, this kidnapping would never have happened."

I shrugged. "It probably wouldn't have."

"Stop trying to guess the future. What happens can't be undone. Just get on with fixing what you can."

I smiled. "I wish I could think more like you. No regrets, no looking back."

"Oh, I have regrets. There are plenty of things I wish I had done differently, but I don't think about them for too long. What's the point?"

I scratched my head and looked at my tall friend with the different-coloured eyes.

"Well, I'll try and concentrate on fixing the problem part and put my feelings to one side."

"Don't let it spoil your first night with Miranda. How was it anyway? Everything you expected?"

"Everything and more, but I'll give you the details later. I want to get to Docklands and check the Rat and Mouse. The inn has a bad reputation and plenty of room in the upper floors for people to stay. It also uses the red rushes."

"Don't forget Ginger's Place. It's a flea pit and will take just about anyone."

I sent a messenger to Miranda with a quickly scribbled note explaining what happened. Then I paid a boy enough for a cart ride up the hill and gave him a silver coin for himself.

"If this message doesn't get delivered I'll come looking for you," I said.

"This is how I make me pennies, Owl. It wouldn't do to give meself a bad reputation," the thin teenage boy said.

Docklands was the only area of Hope that suffered little damage on the night of the riots. Even though the mob had gathered around the edges of the gambling dens, dance halls, and brothels that were controlled by Grandfather, they hadn't attacked any of his property. The usual bustle and energy of the district continued to be well below that which I would expect, but it was still early. As the night deepened, more people would arrive looking for the release that Grandfather's establishments offered. I was interested in the older and more run-down inns that marked the boundary of the Dockland's area.

Ginger's place was the first establishment I watched. A group of men came and went from the inn, but most were either drunk or too unfit to belong to the Fist. Next, I went to the Brown Fox, and though the boarding house was small, I had been told it had extensive cellars where people with little coin could stay. I watched it until the last bell of the day without success. I thought of approaching Stella and Aneeta to see if they had heard any rumours of men moving into lodgings in the area, but I knew this would probably be their busiest part of the night. Besides, time was important. If McRobb's men had Kedria they might be torturing her for information.

The Rat and Mouse was a storey higher than the buildings surrounding it. The wooden structure seemed to lean over the street, creating a dark area around its entrance. A little light leaked through the shuttered front windows, but the illumination only created deeper shadows. The sign itself by the front door showed a rat and a mouse dressed in pants dancing together with foaming mugs in their free hands. Both had their heads thrown back and seemed to be laughing. The reputation of the establishment was out of step with that gaily coloured board. The inn served thin, watered-down ale and cheap wine, but it was known for the potato spirits which were brewed in the sheds to the rear of the building.

A window in the attic room was open. It faced the roof of the adjacent building where the two structures touched along the line of the gutter, as did most of the houses in this street. A thin alley ran at a slight angle to the front door where I settled in to watch. Water lay in deep puddles amongst broken wooden boxes and discarded clay jugs. The smell of excrement was strong, and I discovered people often used the area as a toilet. I wrinkled my nose and ignored the odour, concentrating on the Rat and Mouse on the other side of the road. The weather was cool, but I wore my fur-lined cape as well as rabbit skin boots. The orange moon, Tantarless, was almost full, and by its light, I could clearly see most of the street.

Three cloaked figures approached quickly from the direction of the Peaks and disappeared into the inn after glancing around. One of them peered into the alley in which I stood huddled in the shadows, and I froze. The figure moved away after a soft call from one of his companions. I couldn't understand what was said, but it was the language of the Original Men, I knew that much. I watched as the group went inside, noting the speed at which they walked and the confidence their bodies radiated as they moved. These men were fit and strong and were probably members of the Fist of the Snow Leopard. I hurried back to the woolshed where Kat and Golden waited for me. Spike had joined them and bounded forward to greet me, bumping me with his nose and licking my hand. I scratched the dire wolf's neck before collecting the Cold Blade and the handheld crossbow.

"You've found them?"

"They are at the Rat and Mouse. There were three of them, but I expect more. I thought about what we should do and decided that rather than taking them all on at the same time, maybe we could snatch one of them and then propose a trade," I said.

"We can take them, Ash," Golden said.

"I'm not so sure. Even though my strength is improving, I could undergo the side effects of the potion as we attack. We must also consider that the Fist of the Snow Leopard is made up of some of the best warriors this side of the Great Forest."

"Do you know where they are in the building?" Kat asked.

"I suspect they're on the top floor, or even perhaps in the attic. There were lights up there, and the rooftop does give them an avenue of escape."

"So you're not even sure of their location?" Kat said.

"Be reasonable, a dark elf can observe unseen but cannot go into a crowded common room and remain unnoticed. I'm sure even you would struggle to do that."

Kat grunted and continued to sharpen her shortsword.

"How do you suggest we grab one of them?" Golden asked.

"I think they are most active at night due to the city's hostility to outsiders at the moment. We wait at the front door until a small group leaves, then we get ahead of them, set an ambush."

"It could work," Kat said. "The trouble might be taking our prey alive."

"We need someone to offer in exchange for Kedria," I said.

"If it goes wrong we can hide the bodies and have another try later," Golden said.

I wasn't sure we would get a second chance, but I kept my mouth closed.

It didn't take long to get back to the Rat and Mouse, and we set up in the same alley again, though Golden grumbled about the smell. We moved some of the rubbish and gave Spike the command to be silent. Then we waited. Unfortunately, my belief that the Fist would be most active during the night proved to be wrong. Golden wanted to give up after the first bell had started to ring, but I made him wait. The early tinges of light had crept into the sky, and I had just agreed to call off the operation when a curly-haired woman carrying a bag over her shoulder approached the front door of the inn. Her hair had been dyed and her skin powdered to lighten it, but she limped. I recognised the woman who had been wounded by the crossbow bolt in front of the McRobb mansion.

"She is a member of the Fist," I said.

"But she is going into the inn, not heading away," Kat said.

"I don't care. She is alone and slowed by her wound. I say we take her and run."

"I'm up for it," Golden said.

Kat rolled her eyes and then scanned the street. "Alright, but we better move fast while there is nobody around."

The woman was only twenty paces from the front of the inn and approached our position from the west. As we stepped out of the alley, she saw us immediately and reached for something around her neck. Before she could remove the object, a charge from Golden's ring hit her. A whistle flew from her hand as she was lifted off her feet and thrown backward onto the cobblestones. In a heartbeat Spike was in front of her, growling.

"Don't move and he might not rip your throat out," Kat said.

I ran to the wolf's side and pointed my crossbow at her head.

"You traitor," she hissed as she snatched up the whistle and blew.

As the piercing sound echoed through the street, I kicked her hard. She flipped backward and lay still, but I knew the brief noise would have been heard. A head stuck out of the attic window and called out a name before quickly disappearing.

"Pick her up, Golden. We are going to have to run," Kat said.

"The Rat's Maze is our best chance to lose them. Outsiders take forever to learn the hidden paths of the slums," I said.

My tall friend picked up the woman and threw her over his shoulder with a grunt.

"Why do I always have to do the carrying?" he whined.

"Stop complaining. It's because you're the strongest and the dumbest," Kat said.

"Just the strongest will do," he mumbled as he started jogging.

We made it to the end of the alley when an arrow slammed into a wall across the street. Kat swore and grabbed at her ear. It was a great shot. Shooting a bow down an alley at moving targets in the dark was extremely difficult. I fired one of my bolts from the handheld crossbow in the direction of our assailants with no intention of hitting anything. The aim was to give them a reason to pause, but these were well trained and motivated warriors. The return fire passed just above my right shoulder. I threw myself out of the alley and around the corner into the next street. Golden, Spike, and Kat had pulled ahead of me. I sprinted to catch up to them. In my temples, a slow throbbing began, warning me of greater pain to come. I cursed the need to take the magician's potion but knew it was my own fault. Trying to calm my mind, I slowed my breathing, which is difficult when you're being chased by men shooting arrows at you.

Temple Street curved toward the Peaks before straightening again as it approached the edge of the Rat's Maze. The bend in the road prevented the men following from getting a clear shot, but as our group ran, we began to attract attention. There was still very little light, but it was growing, and more people were now up and about, starting the business of the day. Kat sprinted, passed a man leading a donkey pulling a cart. We all waved at the puzzled milkman as we sprinted on, Golden with the unconscious girl on his shoulder. A pair of older women pushing a handcart loaded with freshly baked bread came out of a side street, and Kat almost crashed into them. We all apologised and kept running.

The long straight stretch of road that stopped at the Rat's Maze opened out before us. It ended at the ruined temple of Gorsander, the long-forgotten god of rivers and lakes. My head started to pound, but I made myself run faster. This was the best chance the members of the Fist would have of putting an arrow in us. Golden was puffing next to me as the woman bounced up and down on his shoulder. I would have told him city living was making him slow if I wasn't so tired myself. Kat and Spike were well ahead of us. The wolf's tongue was out, and ears stood upright as he bounded around the elf. An arrow landed just beyond me and snapped as it hit the stones. The second brushed my cheek, and I jumped sideways in fright. I wondered why they weren't shooting at Golden until I realised they didn't want to risk hitting their companion. Then I saw Kat take aim from next to the columns of the ruined temple. She held her crossbow up to her eye and pulled the trigger. The bolt flashed over my head and behind me. It was followed by a yelp of pain. We reached the temple just as two bolts flew our way. Both went high and skipped off the stonework of the old structure. I turned and could see one man helping another to cover near a side street, and two more individuals further away reloading crossbows. A black bow lay on the road near a couple of arrows, forgotten for the moment.

"Through the back of the temple and we're in the Maze," Golden said.

We followed him past the broken statue of the fallen River God and the ruins of carved reliefs and shattered mosaics. There were gaps in the rear walls where people had removed large blocks of stone for their own purpose. We squeezed through and into the first alley. The streets here were all narrow and ran in different directions. The buildings were so close together that it was difficult to tell how high the sun had climbed in the sky. A little water trickled down the middle of these cavernous streets, and thin light shone through the odd open window. We startled a cat sleeping in a doorway and scared ourselves in the process. Golden changed direction and took us along an even narrower street that ran at a sharp angle up the edge of the Peak, before turning again down an alley which was so steep that steps had been built into it.

Though we glimpsed a few shadowy faces, none barred our path or called after us. The Rat's Maze was a place where people didn't ask questions. The area was old and probably dated back to the beginnings of the city. Most of the buildings were stone, tall and narrow. Dockworkers, thieves, and poor artisans lived in the area, and even Grandfather's organisation had little control over what went on there. Only the slums of the southern slopes rivalled the area for the mantle of the most dangerous area of the city. As soon as people saw Spike, they shrank away and barred their doors.

Golden led us further into the heart of the maze through streets so narrow that we could touch the buildings on either side by simply stretching out our hands. There had been no sign of pursuit, but we wanted to make sure we weren't being followed at a distance.

"I grew up in here," Golden said. "This is where we lived when my father reached his lowest ebb."

I could now make out a grey autumn sky in thin strips between the buildings. There were even people on the street selling small amounts of food from shops built into the front of homes. Our captive was starting to wake up, so Golden took us down a short dead-end alley and placed her against the wall. Kat quickly tied the woman's hands and feet and shoved a gag in her mouth.

"Where to now?" Golden asked.

There was only one place I could think of, and it was some distance from where we now stood.

"I can't go back to the hidden room above the woolshed. The Fist knows of its location. The only place I can think of is Miranda's barn."

"What about Lord Alder's?" Golden asked.

"I don't know how he will feel about kidnapping, even if it is for a good cause," I said.

"And you think Miranda will be alright with it?" Kat said.

"No, but she will come around to the idea if I explain."

The elf snorted and tightened the ropes on our captive's feet. "Yes, she will love you having a captive in her barn that you mean to exchange for your ex-lover."

I ignored the sarcasm.

"There is also Sir Petar to consider," Golden said.

"We won't tell him. He never goes to the barn anyway. Look, this is short term, hopefully for no more than two days. I'll send a messenger with our terms to the Fist as soon as we get her there."

"Alright, I'll hire a wagon," Kat said. "Bring her to the old fountain at the edge of the Rat's Maze and we can throw her under some canvas and take her up the hill."

Our captive glared at us with dark eyes and muttering into her gag before Golden lifted her. Suddenly my tall friend yelled and dropped her.

"She bit me!" he yelped.

The woman squirmed around on the ground but stilled when Spike stood over her and growled. Her eyes went wide at the sight of his teeth, and she tried to crawl away.

"Carry her with her head down toward your backside, and she'll be so dizzy she won't be able to do anything," Kat said.

Golden followed the suggestion, and soon the woman's face turned red. Occasionally she snapped at his back, but the bouncing made any attempt to get a purchase on his skin with her teeth impossible.

It wasn't difficult to find a cart and some canvas tarps to put the woman under, but she kicked them off her three times before Kat threatened to knock her unconscious if she didn't behave. We trundled up the winding road into the noble district, dodging the roadblocks manned by the Watch by taking the lesser travelled paths. As we drove the cart down the driveway towards Sir Petar's barn, I wondered how I would explain this to Miranda. The new phase of our relationship had just started, and already I was taking enormous liberties. The problem was I really had no idea where else I could take the female member of the Fist.

We drove the cart straight into the barn, then tied the woman to one of the beams in an empty horse stall and removed her gag. Later Kat took the horse and cart back to its owner.

"And now?" Golden asked.

"We have to keep her here until I make contact with the Fist. Then we'll work out a trade."

"They'll find me and then kill you, traitor. My people are resourceful, and it won't take them long."

"They'll never trace you here, and besides, I hope you will be back with your companions once the swap is done."

The woman looked at me and her brow furrowed. "What swap?"

"You for Kedria."

"We don't have her."

Golden spun around and glared at me. His attention had been on the entrance to the barn, but now it was fully focused on the conversation.

"What do you mean you don't have her?" he snarled.

"Exactly that. We haven't taken the Sunspear woman, and I have no idea where she is."

"Liar. You took Kedria yesterday because she has been working with me to find the Crown," I yelled.

The woman started to laugh. She doubled over as far as her bonds would allow and tears rolled down her face. Golden and I exchanged glances. I felt my headache starting to return. Something was wrong.

"The Sunspear woman's purpose in Hope is to stop the return of the Crown to the Snow Leopard, not to find it. We thought you were working with her for that express purpose, and to assist your sister, but as the two of you didn't seem to be interfering in our work we gave you space," the woman said.

"But Kedria was helping me find my sister so she could recover the Crown," I said.

The woman started to laugh again, and this time I had to repress the urge to hit her. My temples began to throb, and I rubbed them with my thumbs.

"What is your name?" Golden asked. His voice was quiet, and the colour had drained from his cheeks.

I didn't think the woman was going to answer, but then she whispered, "Shafali."

"Well, Shafali, I think you need to tell us why you believe Kedria Sunspear is a traitor to her people," I said.

12

BETRAYAL

"The Sunspear family have never supported the Snow Leopard. They jealously guard their independence and have taken the attitude they can live in their mountain spur and ignore what is happening to the rest of their people. Their clan opposed helping the dark elves who live in the Golden Hills and did their best to undermine the alliance between the Original Men and the Snow Leopard," Shafali said.

"So why did they send an agent to Hope?" Golden asked.

"To prevent anyone from recovering the Crown. Without it, the Snow Leopard can't be king."

Recalling Kedria's fall as we approached the hidden room where my sister was hiding, it started to make sense. Then there had been that mysterious dark elf woman on the Peaks the day Shafali had been shot. I thought the assailant was my sister but perhaps I was wrong. If Kedria was a traitor, then she wouldn't have wanted me becoming friendly with the Fist of the Snow Leopard.

"She was sabotaging my efforts," I muttered.

"Yes," Shafali said. "And she was also poisoning trust in your family. As it is, we have sent messages to the Snow Leopard warning him of your family's disloyalty."

"What? You have put my father in danger!" I shouted.

"A situation that can be rectified when you set me free, and I talk to my commander."

I was instantly on guard. There was only this woman's word that Kedria was a traitor, yet a lot of what she said seemed to fill in missing pieces of the puzzle. Golden pulled a knife from his belt and walked toward the ropes that held Shafali in place.

"Wait!" I said.

"What for?" Golden said. "Everything she says fits and I must admit I always had a weird feeling around Kedria. Kat never trusted her, and Spike didn't like her."

"Then who took Kedria? Even if she is a traitor, half of what we have been told would be motive for the Fist to grab her."

"We don't have Kedria," Shafali said.

"I believe her, and even if she was lying, I don't see why you would want to rescue her now," Golden said.

"It would be wrong to let anyone torture her."

"The Sunspear woman is not with my group. If you want to find her, then you are wasting your time."

Golden cut through Shafali's bonds, and the woman rubbed her wrists.

"We will return you to your hotel, though I must say your choice in accommodation leaves a lot to be desired," my tall friend said.

The corner of Shafali's mouth turned up. "I can't say I disagree. How did you trace us there? One of the reasons we chose the Rat and Mouse was because it seemed to be the type of place where we could lie low."

"It was the red seeds from the rushes and the river clay I found in the hidden room," I mumbled. I was feeling foolish and angry at what I had learned about Kedria. She had played me for an idiot, and I had been blind to her subterfuge.

"Then we were set up. Someone who knew where we were left signs which pointed you in our direction."

"Whoever took Kedria must have discovered your hideout," Golden said.

"We will need to relocate," Shafali said.

I sat down heavily on a bale of hay and tried to clear my head. Kedria was a traitor, and she was gone; I had lost any idea about where my sister was, and my father was probably in a cell deep beneath the peaks that surrounded the high plateau of the dark elves.

"What is going on in my barn?" a voice called.

Turning, I saw Miranda standing in the doorway with hands on hips. I climbed wearily to my feet and walked toward her.

"If you'll allow me to brew a pot of tea in your kitchen I'll explain."

I sipped my tea while Shafali and Golden munched on some fresh brown bread. It was still early, and Sir Petar had not yet risen. Miranda was up though, organising the small household for the day ahead.

"I'm surprised you missed all the indicators that this woman could not to be trusted," Miranda said sharply.

"He was distracted," Golden said.

"I don't want to know what it was that clouded his mind."

Her voice was severe, and she moved quickly around the room wiping and cleaning spotless surfaces. I knew I was in dangerous territory. It was Shafali who came to my rescue.

"The Sunspears are known for their ability to manipulate the unsuspecting, but that is no longer relevant. The question is how we renew the hunt for the Crown."

"So we're allies now?" I asked.

"It would make sense if we worked together. It would prove your loyalty to the Snow Leopard, and we could share information."

"They could help us track down the meeting place near the Fens," Golden said.

I glared at him.

"You said yourself it would be a dangerous journey in winter."

"I'm not a subject of the Snow Leopard, and I want to see my sister come out of this alive. The Fist has made it clear Shade's safety is not very high on their priority list."

"We can work around those issues," Shafali said.

"I don't think we can."

Shafali shook her head. "Then I'll take my leave. Thank you, Lady, for the bread, and I apologise for my unexpected visit."

"There is no need for you to say sorry for the actions of others," Miranda said.

She gave me a hard look as she spoke, and I felt my head shrink down into my shoulders like a tortoise withdrawing from danger.

"He thought he was doing what was right," Shafali said glancing in my direction.

I found the woman's forgiveness unnerving.

"I'll find you a ride," Golden said.

When we were alone, Miranda turned to me. "I didn't realise how important this dark elf was to you."

I sighed deeply. At least my headache was receding thanks to the tea Miranda had brewed.

"I never felt about her the way I do about you. I was going to end the relationship the night she disappeared and don't even know how it started. It wasn't my idea."

Miranda nodded. "If she wanted to manipulate you, then getting you into bed would have been a good way of doing so."

"I didn't know what was going to happen with you, and I felt very alone."

The excuses were poor, but Miranda's face softened.

She stepped close and stroked my cheek. "I can't blame you. I had married and left, so what could I expect? This woman stepped into your life and decided to exploit the situation."

"I do feel incredibly stupid."

"Don't worry. It probably won't be the last time a woman makes a fool out of you."

She smiled, her gentle teasing cheering her mood. I took her in my arms and kissed her. We became more passionate until the back door banged. Miranda leapt backward and smoothed her hair. I stepped away from her and turned slightly before sipping my tea. Arnold, the one-legged gardener, carried some timber into the room and dropped it in the wood box. He glanced at the two of us but kept his face expressionless.

"I'll be chopping kindling by the back shed, my lady, unless you need anything," Arnold said.

"No, I'm fine, thank you."

"Beatrice will be here to cook for the master soon," he added with a quick look at me.

"Good, good," Miranda said. She blushed.

He left, and Miranda turned to me. "We need to be careful. I don't want to flaunt our relationship. Petar deserves better than that."

I wasn't sure how I felt about her statement but could see we needed to be discrete. However, protecting Sir Petar's feelings was not a reason that concerned me greatly.

"You have to decide what the next move is. Your sister is gone, and your chances of finding Kedria are slim."

"I have no trail to follow except the note about where Sabella is to meet her mysterious buyer."

"Then, much as it pains me to say it, that is the lead you must follow. I know it will take you away from Hope, but you will not settle until you find your sister and set this right. I know that much about you."

Miranda was correct. I wouldn't be able to rest until I found Shade and returned the Crown to its rightful owner. The Fist of the Snow Leopard would also be heading in that direction with the information Golden gave Shafali. And if Kedria had spoken to her captors about the information I gathered on Sabella's past; then they would be travelling northeast too. I wondered why Golden had given the information to the Fist. He was prone to speaking first and thinking later, but what he had said went beyond a rush of blood. Maybe he wanted the Fist to finish this job and wasn't concerned about the fate of my sister, or perhaps he was protecting me.

"I will need to move fast, as it will be a race to reach the Fens and the lands that surround them."

Miranda's eyes began to fill with tears. "Meet me tonight at the Mermaid. Stella can fix us up with somewhere quiet."

I nodded and felt moisture gather at the edge of my eyes. This would be our last night together for some time.

Golden stood out in front of the burnt bookshop. He talked to Lord Alder, but as I approached both stopped and turned to me.

"What are you doing here?" I asked.

"Just remembering old times," Golden said, looking away.

What love about Golden is that he lies badly, but I didn't have time to pursue his evasive answer at the moment.

"I've got to go northeast and see if I can find Sabella and Shade," I said.

"Can't you let the Fist handle it?" Golden said.

"They will kill my sister."

"From everything I've heard about her I'm not sure if she deserves saving," Golden said.

"Did you have the same attitude towards your father?" I snarled.

Golden took a step backward, and his eyes grew wide. He looked away, and I saw a dozen different expressions streak across his face.

"You can't save the world," Lord Alder said.

"But I might be able to save her."

"Then go to Henry's Clothing and equip yourself at my expense. You must do what you think is right."

I thanked my noble friend and stared at Golden.

"That was a low blow about my father," he mumbled.

"I know, and I'm sorry."

"But you're right. I would have done everything I could to save him. I'll be coming with you and so will Spike. As for Kat, I'm not so sure. Tearwyn is up that way somewhere, though. Maybe we could get a message to him."

"I'll handle that," Lord Alder said.

Before I went to see Miranda, I had a lot to do. There were only a few boats moving on the river as the first chunks of ice had started to form, but I found a two-masted lantern which was heading to the edge of the Eastern Woods. The master's home port was the lumber town of Raven's Bluff, and he wanted to return there to spend the winter with his family. I had to buy all the warm clothing that would be needed to survive the colder climate. Lord Alder's generosity smoothed that path, and soon I had a sheepskin-lined cloak with a wolverine fur hood and thick woollen pants and shirts. Golden was still an adventurer and had all of his own gear, and Spike would be able to survive all but the very worst weather. Later I bought food before heading to the inn where Golden and Kat were staying. I had to see the elf myself and ask if she would come. It wouldn't be fair to leave the task to Golden.

It was clear they had been arguing when I sat down with them at the corner booth. Neither looked at the other, and Kat's eyes glowed like coals. Golden's face was pale, and his fingers interlaced together.

"Are you going to lead the man I love to his death?" she hissed at me.

I could see she was not going to hold back, but I forced myself to remain calm.

"That is not my intention."

"How far will you pull him in the name of your friendship? Hasn't he already done enough for you?"

"We don't keep a tally, Kat. I have already told you that," Golden said.

The elf's blue eyes focused on my friend, and I saw him wilt before their heat.

"You have done enough for him. It is time you think about us and our future. We have plans, remember? You said one more season, and we could retire, then we spent all that gold on the magician to cure him." She pointed at me with a slim finger. "Now you are going to follow Ash into a northern winter."

"He can't do this without me," Golden muttered.

I had pushed this too far and if it went any further, the friendship would break.

"I can and I will, Golden. Kat is right. I have taken you for granted and have no right to expect you to come with me."

"But there are too many forces lined up against you, not the least being the weather."

"I have survived worse. She is my sister, not yours, and I will not put what you and Kat have at risk."

With that, I stood and left. Walking to the Mermaid, I felt pretty good about myself but wondered how I was going to achieve my goal without Golden's assistance. My only hope was to find Tearwyn and convince him to help me, but I wasn't even sure his whereabouts in the north.

The Mermaid was crowded, but Stella spotted me almost as soon as I stepped through the door. She was wearing very little as usual but didn't flirt or encourage my attention as she once did. It was as though I was off-limits, which I suppose I was, however, I never thought Stella believed in concepts such as fidelity or monogamy. She took me to a stall near the rear wall and promised to return with red wine. Stella remembered my favourite drink, which made me smile. Miranda had her hair up and was wrapped in a long cape. She sipped her drink, and her eyes met mine.

"Why don't you take these upstairs," Stella said as she arrived with my drink. "I've booked you the best room in the place. It's the most tastefully decorated and away from the others."

Miranda nodded, and Stella took us through the revellers and dancers to a set of stairs. We followed her to a room that hugged the chimney at the back of the building. I saw men being led into different rooms by some of the dancers and wished we were somewhere else.

"I'm so glad you two found each other finally," Stella said as she opened the door.

She then kissed both of us gently on the lips before closing the door. The room was warm, as heat radiated off the bricks of the chimney. I walked to the bed and sat down, never taking my eyes off Miranda. She unfastened the cloak, dropping it to the floor. Underneath she was naked. I'll never forget that evening.

We spent the night there even though others wanted the room. Stella chased the patrons away and made sure we were fed and supplied with wine. I don't know how she managed it, as rooms at the Mermaid were always in high demand. It was hard to part in the morning, but I had a boat to catch, and Miranda would need to return home, so Sir Petar wouldn't worry at her prolonged absence. We said goodbye to

Stella, and she promised to visit Miranda at home. Then we cried and clung to each other for a while. In the end, I tore myself away and strode towards the port. I quickly collected my gear on the way and hoped that the boat hadn't left without me.

Golden and Kat stood at the end of the pier frantically waving at me. I sprinted toward them, and they hauled me on to the boat as the sailors cast off the stern line.

"The master of the Pixie said he wasn't going to wait, but I explained what was holding you up and the old guy seems to be a bit of a romantic."

Golden was smiling at me, and Spike rubbed his flank along my hip. Kat's mouth was twisted as though she didn't know whether to grin or frown.

"I said you didn't need to come."

"Don't look at me," Golden said. "It wasn't my idea."

I gazed at Kat, and the elf stared down at the deck. The breeze grabbed her pale hair and spread it behind her like a flag.

"Yeah, well, your little speech impressed me, and I thought maybe you're not the selfish weasel I thought you were," Kat said.

"Thanks, I think."

"You can't do this alone, but as it seems as though you were willing to try and do it by yourself, I thought I'd give you a chance. After all, friendship and loyalty are our glue."

"Don't blow this," whispered Golden loudly in my ear. "She doesn't give many."

The elf gave her partner a flat look, and he grinned at her.

Looking away from them, I examined the ship. I had travelled on a few and immediately could see this one was well run. The rigging was tight, but there wasn't too much sail up. Ropes were neatly coiled and the masts well maintained. Every sailor I could see was working at a steady but not frantic speed, and the ship was moving on a smooth course out into the middle of the Sigh River.

"The master says we should make Rinport by nightfall. He has asked one of us help spot for floating ice. He won't sail at night because he doesn't want to hit any hidden obstacles," Golden said.

We moved quickly that day, driven by a fresh breeze from the southeast. The weather was mild for this time of year, though we were told it had been a lot colder upstream. Watching from the bow for most of the day, I was happy to be alone with my thoughts about Miranda. I resented my sister for creating the necessity to leave when my mind was so close to finding peace. My ideas of what to do when we found Shade revolved around hitting her over the head and taking her back to stand trial. She would probably face the death sentence, but I was sure my family could convince the elders to change that to a long prison term.

River dolphins rode the bow wave of the Pixie as we approached the small port in fading light. The breeze fell away, and the sun was hidden by clouds to the west. I felt content now we were moved toward a goal. Sailors tied the ship up at the docks, and Master Jamison reported to the town officials. The captain was a tall man but painfully thin with an extremely bushy beard. He had only spoken to me briefly early in the day and thanked me for my diligence at spotting ice flows.

"It is known your people have sharp eyes, so I'm glad to have some in my service," he said.

I wanted to tell him the only advantage my eyes had over his would be at night. It also annoyed me that he referred to my race, but I let it all slide. He didn't mean any harm, and taking offence would only create an unnecessary confrontation.

"Tomorrow the wind will really pick up, and we'll fly along, but the river starts to twist and turn from here, and I believe you are in a hurry. So is the crew. It's a race to beat the weather from this point on," Master Jamison said.

It was a race indeed, and one that I didn't know if I could win.

13

THE NORTH

Enormous black clouds piled on top of each other to the north of the river, slowly converging on our ship. The Sigh had narrowed to half the width of the previous day, but it was still seven hundred paces from one bank to the other. The north wind was strong, and I could taste the ice it brought with it. The temperature dropped, but it had a lot further to go yet.

"The Master says he will push into this storm unless the visibility falls below the length of the ship. He'll run with a storm jib and sail on until he reaches the forest, which he thinks will be tomorrow night. Of course, we will have to stop when it gets dark," Golden said.

"He looks worried," Kat said. "I think he's concerned that the Sigh will freeze quickly and leave him short of Raven's Bluff."

"The river usually takes a few days to freeze when the weather changes," I said.

"That's near the coast where the Sigh is wider, and saltwater slows the process. Up here it can happen quickly and the narrower the river is, the faster it happens," Kat said.

The storm hit with a wall of ice. The master had stripped the rigging to a bare minimum, but the storm jib still moved the ship through the water faster than I thought was safe. There was a double watch for ice at the front of the Pixie, and I joined them with a pike. It was so dark now that my night vision did prove valuable. The snow blew at right angles across the low hills, rattling the rigging and shrieking around the mast. Waves the height of a short man formed on the river but the Pixie sliced through them as she charged forward. Occasionally the captain had to tack as the riverbank loomed up before him, and on more than one occasion he almost left it too late. We couldn't see the approaching bank until we were almost on it and then only a frantic yell warned him he needed to spin the wheel. This is where my vision helped as I spotted the danger before anyone else. It was exhausting work, as I needed to squint into the storm to see obstacles of different varieties. Chunks of ice were now frequent, and we had to fend them off with pikes and spears. Occasionally we would miss one of the smaller ones, and it would thump into the hull. Luckily none of them were big enough to do any damage.

The cold seeped into my fingers and nose. I had wrapped myself in the new cape, and even though it kept me warm, it wasn't waterproof. The waves threw spray over the deck, drenching everything, and soon my cloak began to freeze. Only the wolverine fur stayed clear of ice.

"You need to go below and change," one of the sailors yelled over the storm.

"You need my eyes," I called back.

"We do, but you're no use to us frozen. There's waterproof clothing in the master's room. Just roll the pants up."

I did as he said and returned to the bow quickly. If anything, the temperature had dropped even further. There was more ice floating downstream, and a rim of frozen water had formed close to each bank. I don't know how long I stared into that storm, but eventually, I saw lights in the distance. By the time we pulled into Raven's Bluff, the Pixie was cutting through a thin layer of ice that coated the surface of the river. Out toward the middle of the river in the open water, chunks of ice were floating quickly downstream grinding against each other and setting my teeth on edge. The jetty was protected by a breakwater which stuck fifty paces out into the river, creating an area free of waves. The river's width had halved again, making the frequent changing of direction late in the day an exhausting affair. Everyone was relieved and drained when the Pixie was finally tied to the jetty.

"Well the last run was profitable, but I cut my return a little too fine. I think I'll be more cautious next year," Master Jamison said as we paid him our fare.

"We are lucky you did wait," I said. "You've cut our journey by a third."

The thin master shook his head. "I think you're taking a terrible risk pushing so far north this late in the season."

"I agree, but we have little choice."

We asked for instructions on where we could stay in town and the best place to purchase ponies. Later, Kat, Golden, Spike, and I pushed through the storm to the inn of the Dancing Bear. Inside it was warm and smelled of roast meat. Spike immediately started bumping against us, reminding all that it was a while since he had been fed.

"Keep your pet close, hunter, and he can stay inside. If he so much as growls at a patron he's out in the storm," a bald, thickset man who stood behind the bar said.

Everyone in the room stopped and stared at us as we approached the counter.

"I'm sure you've all seen adventurers before," Golden said mildly.

People turned away, and the low buzz of conversation resumed.

"It's just that they've seen their fair share of Owls lately," the bartender said. "Not that it bothers me. As long as everyone pays, I don't care where they come from, but with the war, to the southwest, some folk are a bit jumpy about the dark elves who moved through the area recently."

"Dark elf adventurers are not unheard of. Many of them take to hunting for treasure in the east," Golden said.

"I agree," the bald man said. "But seven got off the Red Shrike yesterday and rode into the forest. They're probably stuck at the village of Yalton or Grund. If they pushed past either of those hamlets, they'd freeze in this weather."

"Can you describe them?" Kat asked.

"White hair, skinny, I find it hard to tell them apart."

I frowned. "What about armour and weapons or house colours and banners?"

"They were well equipped with bows, swords and armour. There were a mixture of females and males. They moved out of town quickly before the mayor could send them on their way."

"I wonder if they were from the Sunspear family?" I mused. "On their way to pay off my sister."

"Well I don't know about any of that," the barman said. "But if your sister travelled with a feisty blond woman and they too were heading north as a pair, then I have definitely met them."

"When did they pass through?" Golden asked.

The barman leaned back and scratched his bald head. "All this talking is giving me a thirst."

I exchanged a glance with my tall friend. "Of course, what would you like to drink?"

"Dwarven malt and an ale chaser."

It was the most expensive selection he could have chosen, but it probably cost us less than a straight bribe. After he had poured himself the drinks and fixed us up with some warm mead, he sat on a stool.

"They came through about four days ago. I remember them because they were both stunning. One of the boys from the Shining Moon band of adventurers tried to buy them drinks and the dark elf woman was willing to accept, but the blonde wasn't. Tal Green Hand was the adventurer, one of the more experienced hunters who used to pass through here. Anyway, words were exchanged, and blows resulted. I had to chase them outside where the trouble continued. Those that saw it say the blonde killed Tal in less time than it takes to fry an egg. The two women moved off pretty quick after that. I suppose they didn't want any trouble with the town guard."

"Were they on horseback or travelling with a merchant caravan?" I asked.

"They'd missed the last caravan by a few days, so they bought some horses and rode off toward the forest. Everyone seems to be heading northeast, which is a bit strange as most of the traffic is in the other direction at this time o' year, except for those late ones headin' home to winter with their families."

I nodded to the bartender, and we ordered meals and rooms for the night. The information was valuable, and now we knew how far ahead each of the two groups were. Outside the storm rattled the shutters on the inn and occasionally blew the smoke back down the chimney. We ate venison and boiled vegetables and sipped our mulled wine while the noise built to a crescendo. Later, as I lay on the straw-filled mattress and pulled the blanket tight around me, I wondered how we would catch up now that the forest trails would be deep in snow. The only thought that gave me hope was whatever challenges we faced with the weather our opponents would face them too.

It took some time to find the ponies we needed the following day. Even though Raven's Bluff was on the main trade route north, it still only numbered just under a thousand souls and those who had gone before us had bought most of the available horses. We trudged through the snow-filled streets for most of the morning before we found what we were after near the eastern gates of the town. The horses weren't cheap, and Golden frowned at the price, almost refusing to pay. It was only the inclusion of some old saddles that clinched the deal. We bought extra blankets and bags of high-quality feed for the animals. Well-fed ponies move faster and were less likely to freeze during the night.

We rode out of the town's gate just as the snow stopped falling; ahead stretched a white forest. The woodlands continued north and east. At this point, the trees were a mixture of rowans, larch and maples, with the odd northern oak thrown in. As we moved north, they changed, and pine became the prevalent species. It was difficult to tell any of the trees apart as a thick layer of snow covered them. Spike enjoyed the freedom of the trail and rolled in the drifts. The dire wolf sprinted ahead, startling an odd squirrel that had left its hole. The ponies neighed nervously and danced away from Spike as he approached. The path itself was only knee-deep in snow as the wind had piled deeper drifts in the hollows underneath the trees but it was still slow going and we had to rest the animals frequently.

The temperature hovered below freezing all day, and the only way we could keep our water supply from going solid was to keep it close to our bodies. We wrapped woollen scarves around the ponies' legs to help keep them warm and fed them oats mixed with honey as darkness closed in. Our group would have to sleep in the open because of our late departure from Raven's Bluff prevented us from making Yalton by dark. Later, when we stopped, the animals were covered with extra blankets and tied close to the fire.

Golden cooked strips of cured meat wound around sticks over the fire while Kat sawed through a loaf of black bread with a dagger. It took me back to the campfires I had shared with adventurers and hunters in the past as we moved through these same woods searching for forgotten tombs or ruined cities. The camaraderie of those bands had cheered me in the past, but too many of those I had travelled with were either dead or maimed for life. A few were fabulously wealthy, but they were the lucky ones.

The temperature dropped, and we piled extra wood on the fire to keep the ponies warm and then went to bed. We built ourselves a snow shelter and slept close to share our warmth. Spike curled up near my feet, and I was glad of the extra heat. Later we woke to the sound of timber wolves howling in the forest. I could hear the ponies stamping and neighing and became worried they might break free. Spike raised his head and sniffed before padding outside. A little later, I heard a much deeper howl. Spike was answering his smaller brethren. Then there was silence. The dire wolf appeared in the doorway and curled up against my back.

"Good boy, Spike," Golden mumbled before he resumed snoring.

The following day was grey and still. As we travelled the occasional thud sounded as snow slid from branches and landed on the ground. Spotted deer crossed our path mid-morning, and Spike disappeared soon afterwards. Kat looked quizzically at Golden from the back of her pony.

"He'll catch up later. Always does, and probably with a fuller belly than we'll have," Golden said.

The trees were taller now and the road narrower. Low light in the forest made it appear as if it were a twilight world of dim colour and shadow. My eyes adjusted quickly, and I saw everything. A lynx watched us pass from its resting place under the boughs of a snow-covered tree, and a sleepy owl raised its head as we rode through its domain. Otherwise, all was quiet.

Spike joined us just outside Yalton. His muzzle red and stomach round.

The gate into Yalton was still open, and I wondered if we would catch the travelling band of dark elves here. Two men watched us ride in. Both were carrying bows and swords and stopped us a little way inside the walled village.

"What's your business in Yalton?" the taller of the two men asked. Other people appeared from houses, some carrying weapons.

"Just hunters travelling through. We will pay for a roof for the night if one's going," Golden said.

The man grunted. "There's a small inn with a stable. Keep your wolf close, and there'll be no trouble."

"Have there been any problems lately? You seem to be very cautious for a village only a day into the woods," Kat said.

"Some of his type came through," the smaller man said, pointing a gloved finger at me. "They galloped in one gate and out the other, knocking a child down. Didn't even stop to see if Dora was okay. Just kept ridin' like the fires of Hell were behind them."

"Is the child alright?" Golden asked.

"She has a broken leg, but she'll be okay," the taller man said. "But so many dark elves together gave everybody a scare. I mean we've seen plenty of Owls in adventuring groups, but nothing like this."

"Was this before or after the storm?" I asked.

"Just after it finished. It must have caught them in the forest. One was riding double, and they looked in a bad way."

"Did you count how many there were?"

"You got a lot of interest in a group of Owls. They mean something to you?" the man asked.

I didn't answer.

"Well it's none of my business, but I saw six of 'em," the shorter man said.

"They lost one in the storm," Kat said.

"And at least two of their horses," Golden said.

"That will slow them down," I said.

"We don't want no trouble," the tall man said.

"There won't be any," Kat said. "This group of renegades is heading east, and we are tracking them. They are probably deep in the forest now."

"Be that as it may, you can stay here the night, but in the morning we expect you to be gone."

Kat nodded, and we rode slowly to the inn.

The following day we left before sunrise and pushed the ponies hard. They had spent a warm night in the barn and were well fed. We reached the hamlet of Grund before dark. The wooden gates of the tiny village were shut, and warriors stood on the walls of the palisade. Golden rode forward alone, and I pulled my hood over my head to hide my features. I had a feeling that dark elves had also passed through here recently and perhaps made the same poor impression as they had at Yalton.

"What do you want, hunter?" a voice from the wall yelled.

"Food, and maybe a place to shelter for the night," Golden said.

"The gates are closed. You'll need to camp in the forest."

"We have silver. Hamlets such as this will have seen my type before. You would know that adventurers pay well," Golden continued.

There was a moment of silence, and I could see heads close together on the battlements. To say that Grund is fortified is an exaggeration. The palisade is only twice my height. Golden would have been able to reach the top of it and haul himself over if he wanted to. The gate was built from pine boards that had bowed with age, and it looked as if it might be possible to squeeze between it and the wall to gain access to the hamlet.

"We were attacked the other day. Owls came through and stole horses and food. Some people were killed and a house burnt in the fight. We ain't taking any chance letting anyone else in."

I wasn't worried. We could ride around the village and the weather, though still hovering around freezing, wasn't threatening. It would have been pleasant to sleep in a warm bed and eat a home-cooked dinner, but we would be alright in the open.

"Did you kill any of the Owls?" Golden asked.

"Wish we had," the voice said. "But they caught us by surprise and wore armour. We were lucky more of us didn't die."

We skirted the hamlet and led our ponies across the fast-flowing stream on the other side. The water was frozen near the banks but moved too quickly in the middle to solidify. It only came up to the ponies' fetlocks and didn't slow us except for drying the animals' legs on the other side.

I was disappointed the dark elves were fully mounted again but glad we were still on their trail. They might even have a few spare animals so they would be able to change them as the horses grew tired. I was now convinced that these dark elves were from the Sunspear clan and they were riding north to meet Sabella and Shade. If we could catch them before they reached the Fens and then tail them to the meeting with my sister, perhaps we could recover the Crown and capture her. I wondered how far behind me the Fist of the Snow Leopard would be. They wouldn't have been able to get as far upriver as we had before the storm froze the river, but they might have made it as far as Darlton. From there, they would have been able to purchase all they needed to follow us. The snow on the open plains before the forest might still prove difficult to traverse, but I knew that the Fist would be out there somewhere struggling to catch up.

It took another two days to reach Red's Place. This single inn was built like a castle in the middle of the forest and serviced traffic crossing the woodlands on the Middle Track. There were also northern and southern paths that crossed the woodland. A less used road headed north and south from Red's, linking all three tracks. I had been at this inn before and knew the proprietor well. Ginny was not much older than Golden and had taken over management when her husband died seven years ago. Nobody had thought a young woman would be able to run an inn located deep in the wilderness, but she succeeded. The food had a reputation of being delicious and the ale never watered. Ginny also managed the twelve guards provided by the towns of the north with a firm hand. She managed in holding on to her staff despite the temptations of the outside world with good salaries and a charming demeanour. I wondered how Golden would handle the meeting.

We rode in through a solid gatehouse past the stone walls and then let our mounts be taken by a tall blond boy. The young man's eyes grew large when Golden flipped him a silver piece. Only two people sat in the taproom, both men wearing leather armour. Crossbows and swords hung on their chairs. Behind the bar, a tall redheaded woman beamed and ran toward Golden. She wrapped him in a bear hug and kissed him solidly on the lips.

"Now this is the sort of surprise that brightens up a winter," the woman said.

"Hello, Ginny," Golden said.

Kat frowned and dropped her saddlebag in the doorway, glaring at the entangled couple. Golden detached himself from the tall woman and made introductions. The elf's eyes remained hard, and Ginny met her stare with one that didn't flinch.

"You're with the elf, then?" Ginny asked.

"Yes," Golden said.

"Well, you're welcome, Kat of the Blue Eagle Clan, and know that I respect Golden's choice."

It impressed me that Ginny had seen the small brooch on Kat's shoulder. I often forgot that all elves came from tribes sprinkled through the different woodlands and grasslands of the Far East. Kat's expression softened slightly until she met Golden's nervous glance. Then it blazed.

"You should have told her, you idiot."

I had forgotten how blunt Ginny could be. My tall friend shuffled from foot to foot, failing to meet anyone's eyes.

"Is this why we always take the other trails when we head east?" Kat asked.

I decided to intervene.

"Hello, Ginny. Is it alright if we book a couple of rooms for the night? We are chasing a group of dark elves and need a little rest."

The tall woman turned and regarded me. "Ash, it has been an age.

Of course, you can stay. As for dark elves, none have been through my doors except for a single woman and her blonde companion, but that was six days ago."

"Have any of your scouts seen anything in the last few days?" I asked.

She put her finger to her lip. "The scouts found horse tracks yesterday, and I wondered why travellers avoided my inn in this weather."

"There were eight horses, but not all of them carried riders," said one of the men sitting at the table.

The half-elf had a pointy brown beard and grey eyes. His gaze swept us, taking in our equipment and armour.

"Karlen Theiolin holds a Cold Blade just as you both do. He has agreed to scout around the inn until spring," Ginny said.

I should have noted the longsword when had entered the room. Once I would have spotted someone of the half elf's skills almost immediately.

"I know of Karlen," Golden said. "You took down the hobgoblin bandit prince last summer, didn't you?"

The half-elf nodded once, but his expression didn't change.

"I followed the tracks and came upon a camp of Owls. One was wrapped in furs and blankets and lay near a fire. That one seemed ill or wounded. The others were skinning a deer. A female commanded them."

"And they didn't see you?" Kat said.

"I was wearing the fur of the white bear, and I'm never seen."

The half elf's arrogance was annoying, but I had a suspicion it was well deserved.

"Did you see a device or a family symbol?" I asked.

The half-elf reached into a pouch tucked into his leather armour and pulled out a gold brooch. It was a vertical spear set on top of a rising sun.

"I took this from a saddlebag along with a little coin," Karlen said.

"I don't like stealing," Ginny said.

The half-elf shrugged. "I'll never take from clients, and the group looked as though they had something to hide."

He picked up the pendant and put it away again.

"You're right, there," I muttered.

It was now confirmed, the Sunspear Clan travelled north to take possession of the Crown, and I suspected I knew who was leading them.

14

HARSH JUDGEMENT

The stay at Ginny's was short and yet comfortable. The tension between Golden and Kat, however, made me wish we could hurry on our way. I spent most of the evening with Karlen who described the dark elf party to me in detail. He gave me a very good idea of their equipment and personnel. A magician travelled with the group, and that complicated any plan to regain the Crown. The thought I might have to fight and kill my own people made me uncomfortable. This clan had become an enemy of the Snow Leopard, but that didn't soothe my conscience as I felt no allegiance to the distant war leader either. I tried to appease my concerns with the idea that fighting the Sunspears would help free my father and clear my family's name.

The half-elf began telling stories of his adventure in the far north. It was known the dwarves had once built cities in the mountains which ran to the Great Ice Sheet. Legends said they lived there, mining the rich seams of gold and living off their high-country cattle and goats until the ice crept south. The Troll Fens prevented adventurers and hunters exploring these lost cities until now.

"There are supposed to be books which describe the dwarven caverns," Karlen said. "I would love to get my hands on such manuscripts, as the tunnels go on forever and it's easy to get lost down there. I've already found two solid gold shields and a silver dagger at a shrine to some old God. You should come with me, Ash. We could make our fortune. My group could use someone with your abilities."

He sounded like Golden, though the discovery of the caverns meant that he was closer to becoming richer than most adventurers dreamed of. Even though he impressed me with his confidence and calm demeanour, I still suspected he would die in these underground cities. There were nameless monsters in the deep that killed without pity. The ancients summoned creatures of unspeakable horror, and these beasts now roamed the edges of the civilized world. Many of them resided in caves, grottos and abandoned cities.

"I think my days as a hunter are done, though you should talk to Kat and Golden. They might be interested."

I never suspected at the time what damage that suggestion would cause.

The wind picked up flurries of snow and sent them skidding across the track as we rode east. The sun hadn't made an appearance, and it remained bitterly cold. Even Spike looked as though he would prefer to go back inside.

"There has been talk of hobgoblin raiders on the roads north of the forest, so stay alert," Ginny said as she waved us goodbye.

She was wrapped so tightly in a rabbit skin cloak that I could only see her eyes. I saw her speak briefly to Kat and noted the small smile on the elf's face as they parted. Golden didn't receive a kiss goodbye and had to make do with a wave. Ginny showed more affection to the dire wolf, giving his ears a good scratch.

"You are always welcome," she whispered to me as her lips brushed my cheek.

"I like her," Kat said as we rode through the forest. "She has a direct way of speaking."

"She is one tough lady," I said.

Golden didn't speak and kept his eyes firmly on the track in front of him.

"Of course if you ever go there without me, my love, I'll cut your balls off."

My tall friend slumped down into his saddle and pulled his cloak a little tighter around his body.

Wheelon is bigger than Raven's Bluff but only by a few hundred souls. It sits on a river, but nothing as large as the Sigh. The walled city is a day's ride from the forest and surrounds a broad hill which runs alongside the waterway for a thousand paces. A keep resides on the highest ground overlooking the long bend in the river. From the town, the road runs either east to the Stony Ground of the hobgoblins, or north to the Troll Fens. The land consists of rolling hills cut by wide fertile valleys. Remnant woodlands dot the area and wild animals are frequently seen. The town is the largest settlement of people from across the western sea east of the Great Forest, and as such was frequently attacked by the different groups of humanoids. Wheelon was therefore well defended. The town mayor had been appointed for life by the nobility and made responsible for defence and keeping the peace. Adventurers were a common sight but not always welcome, as they sometimes fought pitched battles with other groups in the streets.

We rode in through the massive outer gatehouse into the town just before midday, not that we could see the sun. It was snowing again.

"The ponies need a good feed of oats and hay. They are almost exhausted," Kat said.

"As am I," Golden said.

I was tired too but somehow exhilarated. The effects of the potion rarely affected me during the journey, and when I controlled my breathing and calmed my thoughts, I quickly banished any symptoms. Our little group now believed we were close to our quarry. Every time we had questioned people as we travelled, they had spoken of the Sunspear Clan as being only a day in front of us, sometimes even closer. I was positive we would catch them before they reached Snote.

We found an inn on one of the roads that led to the mayor's keep and made sure the ponies were well fed and kept warm. There were plenty of adventurers around, and we saw them in the streets and at various armourers and smithies having their equipment repaired. Once, Golden and I had chosen to winter at Wheelon as it was closer to the tombs and ruins we plundered. The close confines of the small town and the number of hunters which stayed there over winter led to conflict. Somehow Golden always ended up in a fight, and we would be told to leave. That was how we ended up staying at the Red Tavern in the middle of the forest. Asking around, we found a group of dark elves seemed to have left Wheelon that very morning.

"One day's hard riding, and we could catch them," Golden said.

"That's been the situation since we entered the forest," Kat said.

"If we bought a few more horses then we could make better time," I said. "The ponies have been great, but they never get a rest, and if we could change mounts, we would close the gap even further."

We agreed to purchase three extra horses that evening and leave first thing the following morning. Golden set out to find the animals while Kat and I bought food and more blankets. Later we met at the inn and ate a meal of root vegetables and roast meat.

"I only managed to get two animals," Golden said. "Both of them are older than I would like, but they seem well enough."

"It's better than nothing, and will allow the ponies some rest," Kat said.

I wished we had bought three horses, but Golden had done the best he could. Soon after dinner, I went to check the animals before settling for the night. When I reached the stalls where the horses should have been, I found them empty. I thought perhaps I had come to the wrong part of the stables but after a quick check realised I hadn't made a mistake. The ponies were gone, and so were their saddles. Running back inside, I told the others before confronting the owner of the inn. We found him in the kitchen, helping the cook. He was a small, round-faced man with bushy eyebrows.

"The stable boy Finny is supposed to watch the animals! If he has abandoned his post I'll skin him alive," the proprietor said.

"That's all very well, but what about our ponies?" Golden said.

"You can buy more," the little man said.

"The horses I just bought cost a fortune, and I only found two of them," my tall friend yelled.

"Can we have some of the other horses in the stables?" Kat asked.

"They belong to customers, not me."

"We need to find Finny and see what he knows," I said.

The stables were dark, but the lantern the proprietor carried was like a small sun. Our two newer horses were still there as were three others and a donkey. We found Finny sleeping in one of the stalls, and Golden tried to shake him awake. The young boy just kept snoring, his head rolling around on his shoulders as my friend shook his body back and forth.

"It's not a natural sleep," Kat said. "You might as well put him down."

Golden dropped the boy, and he hit the ground hard but still kept snoring softly.

"A magician did this?" the proprietor said.

"It looks like it," I answered.

"But why only take your ponies and leave the others?"

"Because it is possible for an individual to take three horses but difficult to handle more," Kat said.

"This theft is meant to inconvenience us," I added. "No one else."

"Well, I will need to call the town guards. Magic has been used illegally and property stolen," the small man said.

"You do what you have to, but we need some compensation," Golden said.

"I'm not responsible for this," the owner squawked.

Golden loomed over the man, and I thought I might have to step between them.

"You can have the donkey and freeboard for the night, but that's all."

My tall friend took a step backward and stroked his chin. He seemed to ponder the issue for a moment.

"That is acceptable," Golden said.

"I'm not riding north on a donkey," Kat said.

"We will get another horse in the morning, and the donkey can carry our gear," Golden said.

As a precaution, our little group slept in the barn that night, and it was lucky we did. Just before dawn during my shift on watch when I heard wood splintering and a yell. A dark shape dropped from the roof of the inn into a snow drift before rolling to its feet and sprinting off down the street. I shouted to Golden before running outside. The figure had already exited the courtyard between the stables and the main building and charged away. Running after the shape, I followed as it veered into a small orchard that stood between two single-storey houses. The trees were bare, and the snow lay deep beneath their twisted branches, but this didn't bother the figure. It threw forward a gloved hand and shouted a single word, and the snow parted as though a sword had cleaved it. When I reached the area, the spell had faded, and I waded beneath the trees. Then Spike appeared. He bounded ahead, carving a path for me to follow.

We reached a narrow lane on the far side of the orchard and ran along it, finding ourselves in a small square with a well in the middle. A robed figure stepped from behind the brickwork of the structure and gestured at Spike and me with both hands. I just had time to fling myself sideways before a wall of force hit. My legs were caught in the blast, and I was flipped sideways onto the snow, landing on my back. Spike wasn't so fortunate and was thrown into the wall. The dire wolf hit hard and lay still. I rolled onto my back and fired one of the bolts from my handheld crossbow. Sparks flew from the brickwork of the well, and then a figure cursed in a familiar language. My opponent was a dark elf as well as a magician. The figure turned and ran off down a steep side street while I staggered over to check Spike. The dire wolf continued to breathe, and no limbs were pointing in unnatural directions, so I was confident Spike would be alright. In the meantime, the dark elf had made his escape.

Golden and Kat joined me after a short time, both well-armed and panting.

"We followed your tracks through the snow," Kat said.

I quickly filled them in on what had happened.

Golden checked the wolf and then waved a small potion under the animal's nose. Spike shuddered and then sprang to his feet before falling back onto his haunches.

"He's okay, just a bit shaky," Golden said. "He has a hard head, like his master."

"Can we keep following the dark elf?" Kat asked.

I shook my head. "He will have found some bare rock or a snow-free stretch of cobblestoned street by now. Or he will have used some magic to have blown away his tracks."

"The dark elf will be tired, though. He used two spells close together and another earlier in the day. Spending that much of his power will leave him weak. If he casts again he will be exhausted," Golden said.

I agreed. Magicians take time to gather their power, and when they use their spells, it tends to leave them flat like an empty waterskin. Only the greatest practitioners of the art could cast more than four spells in a day, and they tended to stand by the side of kings and emperors. Only dragons can cast more.

"We are probably safe enough for now, but the Sunspear Clan will soon know that our group is right behind them," I said.

"How did this mage figure out we were a threat?" Golden asked.

"They would have our description from Kedria, and we are hard to miss, especially with Spike by our side."

It took us until just before high sun to purchase another pair of horses, but at least this time we got our money's worth. During the night, two adventurers duelled over a woman and some spilt wine. They managed to kill each other, though one of them took a little longer to die than the other. The first adventurer owned a sturdy quarter horse and a cold-weather animal blanket. The other had ridden a woolly pony which must have been taken from the northern hobgoblins. Both animals were relatively inexpensive and well-rested. Golden complained about being on one of the older draft horses, but they could best take his weight.

The wind picked up ice crystals and threw them sideways across the road. We wrapped scarves around the horses' ears and eyes and rested them in sheltered areas as often as we could. Later that day, we found a dead pony by the side of the track. It was stiff and cold, but Golden said it hadn't been there for very long. I guessed the Sunspear clan had pushed their mounts a little too hard and were now down one animal. Perhaps they had driven the pony to exhaustion after the magician had informed them of our presence in Wheelon. It was all conjecture, but it fitted together nicely as a plausible theory.

We stayed at an isolated farmhouse on the edge of a small village for the night. The owners were happy enough for us to sleep in their barn for a silver piece, and we were pleased to be out of the weather. The strong stone walls that surrounded the compound gave us a sense of protection. All farmhouses were fortified east of the Great Forest.

The wind dropped, and we rode into a world dominated by grey and white. Only the small village in front of us showed the boundary between sky and ground. Golden urged us to push the animals a little harder as they seemed fresh after a night indoors, and he guessed the dark elves would not ask for the hospitality of farmers. It was later that day we found out how desperate they had been. The building was still smouldering as we approached and in front of it lay three bodies under colourful blankets. The reds and oranges seemed cheerful against the snow-covered ground. One of the bodies looked smaller than the other, and I saw the small foot of a child protruding from one corner. Men with weapons had gathered, and they glared in my direction as we approached.

"I don't like the look of this," Golden muttered from my side. "Be ready to ride."

The local folk carried spears, pitchforks, and the odd axe.

"That one's a Dark Owl. We should string him up," a man in a sheepskin jacket said.

There was a hiss from the crowd, and they took a few steps toward us. I readied myself to dig my heels into the pony and follow Golden's advice.

"There has been enough murder today," a man on horseback said.

The figure rode between the two groups and drew his sword. He wore chainmail under a breastplate of polished steel. A wolverine-lined cloak hung from his shoulders, and the symbol of the griffon stood out on his small shield.

"You asked the Northern Knights to handle this, so let me do my job," the man said.

He was young with a long chin and deep grey eyes. I couldn't see his hair, but he sported a blond beard.

"We have just arrived in the area, Sir Knight, and know nothing of this atrocity," Kat said.

The knight tilted his head and then signalled to the man in the sheepskin.

"Bring the girl and let her look at the Owl," the knight said.

I sat nervously on my pony still ready to ride for my life as I had been mistaken for other dark elves before. A girl, no older than twelve summers, was brought before me. She had been wrapped in a woollen blanket, and dirt decorated her face.

"Lincy, we need you to look at this dark elf carefully and tell us if he was with those that attacked your family," the knight said. "Take your time and be careful. These people do not all look the same."

I thanked the Twelve Gods this knight was more intelligent than most. The young girl looked at me with big brown eyes. She stared, and her mouth made a small circle, and then she frowned.

"Not him, Sir Knight," the girl said.

"Are you sure?" the warrior asked.

"She just said it wasn't him," Golden growled.

The knight turned his head and gave my tall friend a flat stare.

"His face is wrong," the girl said. "And those that attacked Pa had longer hair. Also, he is missing a finger, and they weren't."

The knight nodded. "Thank you, Lincy. You may take her, Goodman Wellows."

The man in the sheepskin jacket didn't move. "He's still an Owl, and blood will pay for blood."

"Much as I sympathise, Goodman, I do recall you asking for justice to be served. Killing this dark elf is only about sating your desire for revenge. I will not allow such an act, as then we will be no better than those who slaughtered most of this family."

The man in the sheepskin jacket glared at the knight and then me before walking away with the girl.

"What happened here, Sir Knight?" Kat asked softly.

The man sighed and sheathed his sword. "A band of dark elves burst in on the family last night. They came over the wall and forced their way inside. The father and eldest son tried to stop them and were cut down. A small girl got caught up in the fight and was hit by a crossbow bolt. The dark elves then stayed the night and left in the morning after taking the horses. One of them set the place on fire as he left. The woman who we believe was their leader yelled at the man who set the blaze, according to Lincy, but it was too late. Even the barn went up in the end."

"A bad business," Kat said.

"I have sent messages to other outposts along the road, but in this weather, my organisation will be hard-pressed to cut them off," the knight said.

He looked us over. "I would like to know what a group of adventurers is doing on the road in this weather. Usually, your lot stay in warm inns until the spring. My captain says you are like hibernating bears at this time of year, and best not prodded until the weather warms."

I smiled at the description, as it was apt. The knight sat on his mount and waited for my response, and Golden glanced at me. I decided to tell part of the story.

"We pursue the dark elves to retrieve something that was stolen," I said.

The knight patted the neck of his stallion and then glanced at me.

"It seems to me they are heading the wrong way if they want to reach safety," he said.

"They go to meet those that stole the object," I continued. "I think they want to be as far from prying eyes as possible."

"Ah," the knight said.

"We are from Hope, and are associated with Lord Alder," I said.

It wasn't really a lie, but I said it to try and create some sympathy with this man. It is well known the nobility clumped together like bees in a hive, and I couldn't tell him I was recovering an ancient relic for the war leader of my people.

"A name I have heard before. I wish I could help you in your quest, but all I can do is scribble a quick note. It will take little time."

The knight dismounted behind the wall of the barn and cleared some snow off the top of a barrel. He then took a candle and some writing tools from his saddlebag. The wall gave him some shelter from the wind, but the process still took longer than I would have liked. I was anxious to move away from the angry farmers and the bodies. Eventually, the armoured man returned and handed me a rolled parchment sealed with blue wax.

"I thank you, Sir Knight."

The man nodded and then pulled himself up onto his stallion. We urged our mounts into a canter and rode north.

"They are taking risks," Kat said.

"I think the Sunspear clan is becoming desperate. My people are not worried by the cold as we experience it often on the High Plains, but I wonder if this group was equipped with this kind of journey in mind."

"Well, they took another two horses from the farmer, so they are fully mounted again," Golden said.

"The woman who leads them is Kedria," I said.

Golden and Kat both turned to stare at me.

"She staged the kidnapping to throw me off her trail and perhaps get me killed taking on the Fist of the Snow Leopard, but that didn't happen. I know she is a spy and a traitor to her people, but she is doing what her clan has ordered her to do. Kedria wouldn't have been pleased at the death of the child, and we know she was unhappy when one of her warriors set the farm on fire. Believe it or not, she's not all bad."

Kat frowned. "If you are right then when we meet Kedria you cannot hesitate, and if she gets in your path show no mercy."

I looked at my pony's mane and tried to sort through my feelings.

"Kat's got a point. If you hold back, then one of us might pay the price. If Kedria comes before me with a sword in her hand, I will strike her down," Golden said.

I imagined my old lover lying naked and smiling at me with her arms outstretched, and I tried to visualise her with a blade in her hand. I pictured her slamming a sword into Golden's back.

"If she draws a weapon against us, I shall kill her," I said.

15

BLOOD ON THE SNOW

It wasn't as cold as it had been previously, but the sky was grey and threatening. The wind fell to a gentle breeze, and the air had a bite to it that could leave human flesh blue in a few heartbeats. We saw deer during the day and heard wolves howling in the distance. Spike had answered those calls, and they fell silent. The dire wolf had a way of dominating his smaller brethren. There was nobody on the road, and the few farmhouses we passed were locked up tightly. Occasionally we saw a man with a bow standing guard on the low towers farmers built at the four corners of their compounds. You could sense we travelled on the edge of settled lands.

"It's hard living this side of the forest. Hobgoblins and giants raid often," Golden said.

"Maybe the pale humans should have been happy with the land they acquired on the other side of the woods," Kat grunted.

"What is it with those from across the sea that they are never content with what they have?" I asked.

"Don't ask me," Golden growled. He pulled his hood up over his head and settled his large horse into an unsteady trot.

"That probably wasn't fair," I said. "He's not responsible for the actions of his race."

"Golden's a big boy," Kat said, then she shrugged. "I suppose you're right, but it doesn't hurt him to understand how the other races feel about the loss of their lands. Many elf tribes have lost country to his people as have dwarves, giants, and hobgoblins. Hell, even your people and the Original Men are under pressure."

"Hence the Southern War," I whispered.

"But do you think the western men see that?"

"Some are starting to," I answered.

"I don't know, Ash. With the exception of a few good men, most of the pale skins I have met are greedy and concerned only with their own betterment. They have a great sense of self but a poor sense of community."

I couldn't help but agree with Kat. Long ago, family and clan meant everything to me. When that had been torn away, I had lost my sense of identity. It was only the comradeship I had found with adventuring groups and Golden's enduring friendship that kept me sane.

We had been engrossed in our conversation and were completely taken by surprise when the bolt of power struck Golden's mount. The horse shrieked as it was hurled back up the road and my tall friend tumbled to the snow. Spike started to run to his side but collapsed in an untidy tangle of legs and fur.

"Ambush!" Kat screamed as she hurled herself from the quarter horse.

Three bolts hit her mount with meaty smacks and the animal charged for the woods. It collapsed before it had gone a dozen paces, pumping bright gouts of blood onto the ground. The donkey and the other draft horse were also hit and squealed in pain. I jumped off my shaggy pony, dragging my Cold Blade clear of its scabbard as I twisted through the air. My animal bolted into the forest unscathed. Glancing sideways, saw Kat rolling behind a snow-covered log. I felt too exposed and ran toward a large oak tree. A bolt streaked toward me, so I rolled my shoulders, letting it pass harmlessly by my chest. Another shaft slammed into the wood near my hand.

"That magician will have maybe one spell left," Kat yelled.

"Perhaps not even that," I said under my breath.

I tried to make out where the shots had come from and decided the magician and at least two with crossbows were to our front. There appeared to be at least one bolt in the side of both the donkey and quarter horse, so there were more archers to our left. Golden wasn't moving, but his mount took most of the force from the bolt of power. I didn't think he was dead but wasn't sure what had happened to Spike.

We were in trouble, though I had been in worse situations. Only one came to mind, however, and that scenario included an angry dragon. I tried to think of a solution as I loaded two bolts into my handheld crossbow. Kat managed to string a shortbow and held arrows in her left hand. For the moment, the initiative rested with our opponents, and I didn't like that. Up ahead, I could hear running water, and I could see a depression in the land and a line of trees. We were close to Rylan's Ford, but that wouldn't help us. The crossing point was usually unguarded at this time of year as the water would be frozen and the ferry unused by travellers.

Only one of the wounded animals still lived, and it was fading quickly. The donkey lay on its side and thrashed its back legs around before lying still and moaning. Blood had made a lake around its body coating its flank and the side of its face. I watched the woodland carefully for movement and saw two figures wading in the deep snow between the trees to my right. If they could find a good position, then we would be in a crossfire with little hope of surviving. Kat came to her knees and took a shot at one of the figures. He didn't see the shaft coming and wailed when it hit him in the upper part of the arm. It was an impossibly good shot through the foliage and one that shouldn't have had any chance of success. I marvelled at Kat's combat ability and thanked the Twelve Gods she was on my side. The dark elves went to ground, and the wounded man cursed and swore as he sought to remove the arrow from his flesh.

Everything went quiet. I scanned the trees and shrubs with their bare branches. There were small mounds behind which a body could wait in ambush, and I only knew the approximate location of the dark elves to my right.

"Why won't you just leave this alone?" a female voice called.

Even though I understood Kedria was leading the Sunspear contingent, the sound of her voice was a shock.

"You betrayed me and what we had," I yelled back.

The voice laughed, but there was no mirth in the sound. "We never loved each other, though I did have a growing affection for you. Your heart was fixed on the human woman."

She had me there.

"You lied to me and deceived me," I yelled.

"Grow up, Ash. That's what spies do. My loyalty is to my clan, and they have decided not to bow to a self-appointed dark elf king."

"Be that as it may, my father lies in prison, and my family is in disgrace because of your manoeuvres. I will stop you, Kedria."

"And I thought you had forgotten about loyalty to family and clan. It's a pity my actions have instilled in you the trait I most admire, as it now becomes the reason why I have to kill you."

"Ash, the dark elves are on the move again. They're coming in from the left, and the woods are too thick on that side for me to get a shot," Kat said.

I saw Golden twitch on the roadside, but he was not going to be able to help any time soon. Transferring the crossbow to my left hand, I took a firm grip on the Cold Blade.

Then I heard the barking of dogs. Sleds pulling humans clad in fur approached at speed from the west. They pulled into the forest, and people jumped off and took up positions behind the trees. The two dark elves to my left were caught out in the open as they had forest at their front but none behind them. Both fell as arrows punched through their chainmail. Kedria yelled for the dark elves to fall back to their mounts, but she was too late. Sword clashed with sword and screams echoed through the forest as more humans hit our enemy to my right. They must have crept into position before giving a prearranged signal to those on the sleds. A curly-haired woman took aim at a running figure near the river. She fired, and a bolt flashed from Shafali's crossbow, and the magician who had stolen our horses in Wheelon fell with a grunt. The Fist of the Snow Leopard had arrived, and they weren't taking prisoners.

Another dark elf ran west along the riverbank, and I took off after her. I recognised it was a woman by the shape of the legs and realised it must be Kedria. The Fist were still busy killing the last of the dark elves and Kat had run straight to Golden, so I was alone. I pounded through the soft snow next to the river, desperately trying to keep my feet on the slippery surface. Next to me, the river had frozen over, but the water moved under the ice. Kedria stopped and fired a bolt from her handheld weapon in my direction, but the snow had made my gait uneven, and the shaft whistled over my head as I struggled to stay upright. I felt a headache begin and immediately started to use the mind technique to control the pain. Stopping, I fired a shot from my weapon at Kedria's legs, but my hand was unsteady, and the bolt whizzed past her flank. She quickly changed direction and headed for a tree which had fallen across the river. Kedria jumped onto the trunk and ran through the snow that coated it. I closed the gap and screamed at her.

"Don't make me shoot!"

She seemed to run faster, and I dropped to my knee and took aim. It was possible I could hit her, but something stopped me from pulling the trigger. Though I remembered the promise to Kat and Golden when it came to actually killing my old lover, I couldn't do it. I tried to aim in front of her to scare her into stopping, and the bolt flew past her chest. She skidded to avoid the shaft and lost her balance. Kedria yelled and hit the ice and then I heard the crack as it broke. Her arm and face slid through the hole into the water. The white of Kedria's eyes seemed unnaturally large as her hands clawed the hard surface of the river. Then she was gone.

Running onto the ice, it cracked and groaned under me, so I threw myself flat in order to spread my weight. I slid across to the hole beneath the fallen trunk, but the current had taken Kedria and pulled her downstream by at least ten paces. Using my dagger as a pick, I tried to pull myself to her new position and hammer a new crack in the ice to reach her, but the water kept pulling her away. Her hair spread like a cape, and I glimpsed her dark face as she pounded against the hard layer above. It was like looking through frosted glass. The cold of the ice seeped through my skin, and I could only guess at the shock Kedria's body was experiencing. Sliding along, I tried to smash holes, but she drifted farther from me. Screaming for help, an answer came back. I hated what Kedria had done and wanted her to answer for her betrayal, but not like this. Finally, she stopped moving at a rock that stuck up through the ice in the middle of the river. I slid above her and peered downward. I couldn't see Kedria's face anymore. Her arms floated by her side, and she had stopped struggling. I started to chip through the ice, and then I heard Kat yell from the riverbank.

"Kedria is under the ice. I'm trying to get her out," I yelled.

"Leave her there," Kat said.

"No, no-one deserves this. Throw me a rope."

One of the members of the Fist of the Snow Leopard threw a long length of hemp. It had taken me some time to chip through the ice and more to pull Kedria from the water. The cold was numbing, and I felt it in my fingers and hands. I tried to clear the liquid from her lungs and force air between her blue lips from my own mouth, but Kedria remained still. Her eyes stared at the grey sky, but they didn't blink, and her fingers hooked like claws. Two men pulled her from the ice to the snow that lay thick on the ground. I crawled after her sliding body.

"How is Golden?" I asked.

"He'll live, and Spike is already sitting up. That wolf has the strength of three men. I don't think anything can kill him," Kat said.

A slim woman with curly hair guided a dog team toward us. Lying amongst the equipment on the sled was Golden. He waved one hand slightly before slumping backward.

The sled stopped next to us, and the woman pointed at the body. "That is all of them then. I don't know if you were brave or stupid going out on the ice after this one."

"I believe the latter is more plausible," Kat said.

"I had to try," I whispered.

Shafali shook her head. "It is done. We don't have time to bury the bodies, but you may return it to the water if you wish."

"We normally burn our dead."

"I know," Shafali said. "But that is not an option, and if you leave her where she is wild dogs, ravens, and crows will tear her apart."

"It is what she deserves," Kat said.

"No, it isn't. She served her clan, and even though that made her our enemy, Kedria believed she served her people," I said.

"The Sunspears are traitors to the Snow Leopard. When the army returns home, they will be dealt with," said Shafali.

"They don't want a king, and I can understand their position. The current war leader may be a genius. He may be just and wise, but what about his son or daughter? The dark elves have lived as a loose alliance of families and clans for centuries. Our warrior societies bound us together and protected our people, and it worked," I said.

"You are a fool," Shafali said. "Our ways were similar, but when the pale men came from the west, the old ways didn't protect us. We were forced deeper into the jungle, and your people lost their most fertile lands. It was only a matter of time before we became serfs for the men in armour."

Kat rolled her eyes. "This is not the time or place to discuss the politics of the south. Ash, are you going to dump the body in the water or not? It's time to go."

I glared at the two women before pulling Kedria's corpse to the edge of the river. Then I borrowed an axe from the sled and smashed a hole in the ice. Gently, I pushed the body into the water. As it sank, I recited the Chant of the Dead. It felt better thinking that at least some of the rites of my people were observed.

When I turned, the sleigh was already moving. The members of the Fist who had thrown me the rope trudged away in their snowshoes earlier and only Kat waited for me. Her dark blue eyes met mine, and she leaned wearily on her bow.

"Put it behind you now, Ash. This chapter is closed, but the search for your sister and the Crown remains."

"And now we have more companions, but I wonder if that will make the task easier?" I said.

The leader of the Fist and the other six members of the group stood around their sleds and dogs, near the ferry that crossed the Vebrim River. A short man dressed in old furs crouched near them. I watched as a tall figure stepped forward and hit the man.

"You will take us across now, and there will be no delays."

"The ice is too thin. I told the Owls the same story. It's no good now until the ice is hard enough to walk on. Then I'll string some ropes across to help people."

"We will smash a path, and you will take us over. There will be no discussion."

The small man cringed and nodded.

"We will still pay you your usual fee. Do not try and cheat us and all will be well," Shafali said in a softer voice.

The tall man glared at his companion before issuing a series of orders in his own language. Four men moved on to the front of the large square ferry and started to smash the ice with axes and hammers. They had soon cleared a path around the craft, and the ferryman fed a rope through a large pulley on our bank of the river. I noticed the tall individual who had been giving the orders walk toward Kat and me.

"You have two choices, come with us and follow my orders or turn back to the city. I only take you with us as this is dangerous country to travel through in winter and the wolf may be needed to track your sister. We have some items with her scent on them."

Kat shrugged and looked away. I stared at the Leader of the Fist.

"I want my sister taken alive."

"That is not your choice. If she surrenders, then we will take her for trial. If she fights, then we will kill her."

I couldn't really argue with that, but something about this man made me believe it wouldn't take much to push him into violence.

"My friend may need treatment for his wounds."

"Tasha has seen to him and tells me that he will be ready to ride in a day, and able to fight in two."

A woman with long dark hair lifted her head at the sound of her name and nodded in my direction. My heart jumped when I saw her; if it wasn't for the different hair colour, she would have been Cassie's twin.

We crossed the river after the ice had been broken up and Shafali paid the ferry master. The man looked at us fearfully as he accepted the money and then returned to his shack amongst the trees, slamming the door to the modest dwelling behind him.

Shafali joined me on the bank and stared over at the broken-down house.

"I can't blame him for being frightened. Aslim is not a man to be kept from his path. He was chosen for this role because he is known for finishing what he starts and is fiercely loyal to the Snow Leopard. He would die for our war leader without hesitation," Shafali said.

"Why? I know he has helped your people, but he is not one of you," I said.

"Aslim is of the Wretched; a class of people in our society who one may not touch without fear of displeasing family and friends. The Snow Leopard has lifted this group higher. He has given them dangerous missions and rewarded them when they have succeeded. The tribal leaders have been forced to accept this, and now some of the Wretched hold positions of power within the Snow Leopard's army, though never over their own people – except in the Fists," Shafali said.

"Because the Fists answer to the Snow Leopard, not the chiefs."

"Exactly," Shafali answered. "And Aslim is one of the best, though he was not my original leader. Vental and I are survivors of the Twelfth Fist. The rest of my group were casualties in Hope."

I stayed quiet, thinking I was responsible for at least one of those deaths. Shafali probably knew this but didn't seem to hold a grudge.

That night we camped in a hollow amongst the trees where our fire could not be seen. The scent of the smoke would give away our location to those who wandered close, but at least raiders wouldn't be able to spot us from the other side of the shallow valley. Golden walked around and tried to help with the cooking before being chased away by Tasha, and Spike harassed the sleigh dogs by marking his scent nearby. The animals dared not respond as the dire wolf bared his teeth at the leader of the team who cowered and curled his tail under his belly.

"Control your wolf," Sharhon snarled, the largest of the Original Men.

Golden brought Spike to his side and scolded him briefly before scratching his ears.

"You are too soft on your pet," Aslim said.

"He is not a pet," Golden said.

"Then, what is he? Your lover?" Sharhon asked.

Golden stood slowly and reached for the Cold Blade that hung on his back.

"Apologise, Sharhon," Aslim said quietly.

The big man looked at his leader then glanced away. "I'm sorry. I was trying to make a joke, but it was in poor taste."

Golden held the other man's eyes for an instant before nodding once and sitting down near the fire.

"The wolf needs to stay clear of the dog teams. They have work to do, and I will not have them distracted," Aslim said.

Golden didn't respond to the comment and ruffled the wolf's coat. Spike slumped down next to him and dropped his head onto my friend's lap. For a brief instant, I had a vision of other campfires where I had seen the same scene. The warmth that the recollection brought was out of place. Cold eyes appraised us in the flickering light, and I wished we were somewhere else.

"You both carry Cold Blades?" Tasha asked.

She smiled at me as she sat on a log close by. The straight white teeth and thick lips reminded me again of Cassie, and I looked away.

"Yes, that is a long story."

"I'm not in a hurry."

Glancing at Golden, he shrugged at me. I could see he was tired and not in the mood to tell the tale himself. He was still recovering from the magician's bolt of power.

"Well, my bright friend here found the lair of a dragon. Some hobgoblins swapped the information for their freedom, and Golden talked me into stealing from the beast. We would sneak in and grab what we could and then flee. The rest of the group were all in favour of the idea, but I was hesitant for obvious reasons. The few dragons that survive have a fearsome reputation. Anyway, they convinced me, and we snuck into the lair through a low tunnel. It was hands and knees all the way until we reached the larger shafts. That was where I found the shortsword in the hands of a long-dead dwarf. He was all bones, his armour rusted as he lay on a thin scattering of silver coins. One of his arms was missing, and that should have been a clue for us to leave; the money filled our coin pouches, but it was gold our little team was after."

"Gems and artefacts would have done nicely as well," Golden added.

"We moved into a larger cavern, and our jaws hit the ground. There were piles of silver and gold coins as well as chests of gems, rolls of silk and even some ivory tusks. I remember picking up a couple of handfuls of gems and gold coins when we heard the soft tinkle of metal falling. Then the dragon struck."

"I'll never forget that sight," Golden said. "The head was as big as a cart, and its teeth were like shortswords. It was covered in red and gold scales, and I thought it was the most beautiful creature I'd ever seen."

"It spat a ball of fire at Meller, and he just evaporated," I said.

"He still had time to scream," Golden said, shaking his head.

"Indeed, and then we ran – at least Golden and I did."

"I saw at least three arrows or bolts bounce off the dragon's scales, but it didn't seem to like the wizard's bolt."

"The magician's spell didn't slow it, and he was the next to die," I said.

I remembered the dragon's jaws snapping shut around Milandy's waist and how the legs stood on their own after the body disappeared.

"I thought we were going to die," Golden mumbled. "I just ran into the darkness."

"The dragon didn't kill everyone else immediately. It looked at Felicity, and its eyes changed. I had stopped just inside the entrance to a side cavern and turned to call the survivors of our group to me. She just stood there staring at the creature, her hands by her side. The dragon slowly brought its claw up to her throat, and then it pushed her down onto her knees. It must have sensed me at that stage because it turned, and the eyes changed again. I dived into the cavern as the bolt of power sheared off part of the roof."

"It could cast spells?" Tasha asked.

"Yes, and they were more powerful than anything a human could create," I said.

"What happened to the woman?" she asked.

"We don't know," Golden said. "We never saw her again."

"At the next corner, I tripped over Golden. He was tangled in the bones of a man."

"I think it was an elf," Golden said.

"Well, whatever it had been it carried another Cold Blade, and now we had two. It was by the dull light of the second weapon that I guided us through a maze of low tunnels back out onto the mountainside."

I could still see the wall of ice Golden created behind us with his new sword and hear the hiss of steam as the dragon fire washed against it, but I didn't mention that part of the tale. We had never understood how the weapon managed to do that. Many of the abilities of the two weapons were still a mystery to us.

"And then you were safe?" Shafali asked.

"No! You don't steal from a dragon and think it will forget you. It burnt down most of the forest that clung to the mountain slope while Golden and I huddled under the overhang of a large boulder. We had to wait for two days before I thought it safe enough to head south."

"And where is this dragon now?" Sharhon asked. "Every knight north of the Great River would have wanted to kill it and take its treasure after you told that story."

"It moved. You are correct. Others decided to destroy the beast," Golden said. "But dragons are smart and realised it wouldn't be safe to stay put."

"There aren't many of them left, though some say there are more of the creatures living in the northern wastes of the hobgoblins and in the deep mountains of the far east," I said.

"It is madness to anger a dragon," Golden whispered. "I was crazy to lead us into its cave and we were lucky to come out alive.

"Well it is fortunate then that we chase a dark elf and a human," Aslim said.

The dream was vivid; the colours and smells very real in my mind. I stared through the ice at a face. It was blurred at first, but slowly the features materialised and I could see Kedria below the surface, bubbles pouring from her mouth. The cold made my fingers tingle. I pounded the ice with my fists, trying to smash a way to her. Kedria's eyes became dark pits, and her hands became claws. They broke through the ice and sank into the flesh of my forearms. The nails ripped into the skin and blood poured from the wounds. I fought her as she tried to pull me below the water, but she had immense strength, and the ice was slick. Sliding under the ice, she kissed me, stealing my breath away. Beating at her with one hand, I drew my shortsword and reached for the cold breath of a clear winter's morning. The sword turned white, and the temperature dropped. The water froze around Kedria, sealing her inside a tomb of ice. I swam for the surface, but the water continued to freeze. Looking down, I saw my legs trapped, and I let go of my sword as I started to sink, but the river continued to freeze. I felt the water around me go solid, and I screamed. Then I was awake.

"Bad dream?" Kat asked.

She sat by the glowing embers of the fire, and the light washed her in shades of orange and red.

"Kedria was in the river, but I went down with her."

The elf nodded and prodded the coals with a stick. A small flame rewarded her efforts. "She deserved to die."

"Why? She wasn't cruel or malicious; she was just doing what her clan asked her to do."

Kat sighed. "No, she was our enemy who used murder and betrayal to reach her goals."

"It's more complicated than that."

"Is it? Sometimes things are only as complicated as you want to make them. Granted, our big lump of a friend tends to oversimplify issues, but you do the opposite. Kedria was your enemy pure and simple, and she would have killed you in a heartbeat if it furthered her goals. You shouldn't shed any tears for her."

16

THE FRONTIER

It was getting colder. In the morning, we had to shake the ice crystals from our sleeping skins, and Aslim suggested tonight we build a shelter to keep the horses and ourselves from freezing. Only the dog team and the wolf looked unaffected by the cold. The members of the Fist tried to hide their discomfort at the icy weather, but I saw them jumping about trying to keep warm and heard their softly muttered complaints. Winters on the high plateau had prepared me for the cold north, but the Original Men were people who lived in the tropical rainforest to the south. No amount of training could have prepared them for the bitter weather that closed in on the north.

"There are few villages between here and Wheelon, and only scattered homesteads near the road. We will pay for lodgings in the barns of the frontiersmen and ask if they have seen Shade and her human companion," Aslim said.

He looked at me and frowned. "Best you stay hidden. No need to frighten the locals."

"I don't know what sort of welcome your people will get either, Aslim," Golden said. "People around here can be suspicious of strangers, though they do tolerate hunters and adventurers."

That wasn't completely accurate. It depended what reputation the group had as to whether they would be welcome inside one of the fortified households that bordered the wilderness.

We didn't need to build shelters as the gold the Fist carried smoothed our path and enabled us to stay in the stone barns of the farmers. We kept clear of the larger households, and I stayed hooded as Aslim had asked. I caught glimpses of the heads of families as they negotiated with the Fist. They were hard men and women who knew how to wield the spear and axe. All the homesteads were heavily fortified, and everyone carried a bow of some variety. Stone walls twice the height of a man surrounded main houses and barns, with sheds and storage areas contained within. In every central courtyard there sat a well and a small grain silo. I had usually passed along these roads in summer and remembered south-facing fields of golden grain swaying in the wind. At the moment those days seemed to be a dream, but I had heard the seasons had been kind and the silos were full. That would create a different problem for raiders who liked to swoop down on the farms for food during the darkness of winter.

Shafali was cooking flatbread in a pan, and I was warming some bacon on the same fire. Spike stared at me. The barn held only a few animals as many had already been slaughtered and salted for winter, so the dire wolf's presence wasn't a problem.

"You've been fed, you monster," I said.

"He is always hungry," Golden said.

"I understand now why you pamper him," Sharhon said emerging from the stall where the dog team had been bedded down. "I have listened to some of your stories, and I realise he is more than half your reputation."

Golden snorted and scratched the wolf behind the ears. Spike, however, fixed his stare on the biggest member of the Fist.

"I mean, the Cold Blade and the wolf are really what makes you feared, aren't they? Without them, who knows what type of warrior you would be."

Golden tensed, and Spike let out a soft growl. I looked around for Aslim but couldn't see him.

"You're not going to let him pull you into this are you?" Kat hissed.

The tightness around my tall friend's eyes disappeared, and his fist unclenched.

"Sharhon, do you always have to prove you are the best?" Shafali said.

"I know I'm better than this warrior. He even lets the women do the talking for him while he hides behind his wolf."

Kat groaned, and Shafali moved away from the fire with the bread. I watched as the Cold Blade left its scabbard in a shower of frost.

"I don't need a magical blade," Sharhon said.

"Aslim won't like this," Arale said. The thin man had been sitting near the barn door sharpening his daggers but stood and walked into the light from the fire.

"He is not here, and I won't kill the pretty man. I'll just mark him a little."

Golden threw down his bastard sword. "You, archer, can I use your longsword to strike down this yapping dog?"

Raserman had also been observing from the shadows. I watched as he shrugged and limped across to the barn floor. The arrow wound Kat had given him back in Hope still hurt, and he had little trust in my friends.

"Stop him," Kat whispered. She moved next to me and clutched at my sleeve. "He's still recovering from the wizard's bolt and now is using an unfamiliar weapon."

Golden had used a longsword in the past but that had been before he came into possession of the Cold Blade. The hand and a half blade was heavy and needed to be wielded with two hands, making it different to use than the lighter weapon.

Leaving the bacon, I stepped between the two men. I felt some apprehension as both warriors were powerful and fast, and I didn't want to be in the middle if they started trying to stab each other. Drawing my Cold Blade, I quickly placed it against Sharhon's weapon while summoning the power of the storm. I was aware the man was wearing gloves and hoped I wouldn't permanently damage his hands. My shortsword turned white, and the cold radiated from it dimming even the flames of the fire. Sharhon screamed and dropped his sword on the ground. I heard a hiss as Raserman reached for his bow and Arale drew his daggers.

"Stop it, everyone, now!" Shafali shouted.

Everyone stood with their weapons drawn, looking around the room. Spike growled, but Kat gestured for the wolf to hold his ground. The barn door opened and Aslim, Tasha, and Vental stepped through the door. The leader of the Fist took in the situation at a glance.

"Stand down," he commanded.

Arale put his daggers away, and Raserman lowered his bow. Kat kept her shortsword ready, but the muscles in her arm relaxed. I kept my sword in the guard position.

"Your big warrior provoked Golden into a duel, but I thought it best if the show of strength waited until after our mission has been completed," I said.

"Your attack was unfair, dark elf," Sharhon said. "It broke the rules of a duel."

"I wasn't in a duel, and I fight to win," I snarled.

"Ash has a better grasp of our task than you do, Sharhon. We are in the north for one reason, and that is to retrieve the Crown for our leader. If anyone puts the mission at risk, then I will kill them, even if it is one in my command. Is that understood?"

Aslim didn't shout, but his words were ground out between lips that barely moved.

"Tasha, see to the fool's wound and make sure he can still fight. If he can't, then he will head home alone," Aslim said.

The small woman took the warrior into one of the side stalls and tended his wounds by the light of a lantern.

The members of the Fist lapsed into silence and busied themselves with small tasks.

Golden glared and moved next to me.

"You shouldn't have interfered," he hissed.

"Yes, he should have," Kat growled. "I tried to warn you, but no, you had to prove what a man you could be. What annoys me the most was how the comment about women speaking for you provoked you to fight. Are you an idiot? What does it matter if the women are the only ones that talk sense! You could have spoken up for yourself, but perhaps it's easier to wave a sword around rather than think of an appropriate reply to a man who is obviously nearly as stupid as you are. And did you think that maybe a few days after being hit by a bolt of power was perhaps not the best time to duel with an extremely well-trained warrior?"

Golden looked at his feet and shuffled away toward the fire. I caught Shafali's smile and couldn't help grinning myself.

"I will store away some of those words to use at a later time," she said.

The corner of Kat's lip turned up, but then she flicked the expression away.

"Without us, all the men would be dead," the elf said.

Sharhon's hand was blistered, but Tasha announced that he could hold a blade, but it would hurt. Aslim said the pain would remind him the mission came first and his ego was less than nothing. Golden remained quiet and stole the occasional glance at Kat, who ignored him. I rode with Shafali and Tasha as I wanted to get to know more about the Snow Leopard, and they seemed the most approachable members of the Fist to speak with.

"He is not even your race, and yet thousands of your people follow him as though he is a god," I said.

"Some say he is," Shafali said.

"He has never lost a battle, and he treats our people with great respect," Tasha whispered.

"Yet he challenges your taboos, such as giving responsibility to the Wretched."

"He didn't do that straight away and is careful how he does it. The Snow Leopard changes the way we do things, but without directly challenging the chiefs," Shafali said.

"He won them over first. To begin with, it was weapons and gifts that brought our leaders to his side, but then his command of our language and understanding of our ways strengthened their loyalty to him. Of course, the Snow Leopard's ability to win every battle and fill the chiefs' coffers with war booty helped," Tasha said.

The healer's horse was riding so close to me that I felt her leg brush mine. She looked at me and smiled. I averted my eyes but felt the heat rise on my face.

"Those who joined the Fists first were on the edge of our clans, but when others saw the esteem in which our small bands were held, then many more tried to enrol," Tasha said.

"The selection process is tough, and the final candidates are chosen by the Snow Leopard himself. It is a great honour," Shafali said.

Sharhon signalled Tasha to ride to his side, waving his bandaged hand in the air and grimacing. The woman sighed and urged her mount forward at a trot to reach the warrior's side.

"That young woman would have you share her sleeping skins," Shafali said.

Looking down at the neck of my pony, I imagined Miranda curled next to me. I could remember her smell and the way she breathed when asleep.

"I'm with another."

"But she isn't here. I know the dark elves and the humans from over the Great Water believe you bond with one partner for life. Even some of our people who live amongst you come to think the same way, but all I saw in Hope was jealousy and men visiting the dancers and working women of Docklands."

"I don't want to be with anyone else," I said.

"Really? I hear Tasha is very talented, and I don't think you would regret it."

I didn't answer but knew she was wrong. Now that I was with Miranda, I could not see myself with anyone else. Lying with another woman would feel like a betrayal.

Three days later we reached a small fortified farm. It sat on a rise of land that overlooked a frozen stream. The countryside was dotted with patches of mixed woodland, and to the west, we could just make out the dark outline of the Great Forest. Aslim negotiated our lodgings and handed an older woman wearing a sheepskin coat a pouch of coins. We took our dogsled and horses into the barn which lay across the courtyard from the house. Almost every building was made from granite blocks which were held together with cement. The roofs were covered in wooden shingles, with only some of the walls of the sheds made from wood and covered in thatch.

"Mistress Arlon says she will give us the flour we need to make bread, and if we want to buy more salted meat she has some for sale," Aslim said.

"Good," Shafali said. "We are low on meat, and could do with some more dried fruit as well."

The bearded leader grunted. "We will have to make do. She wasn't prepared to sell us very much, but at least she has agreed to feed the dogs."

The group ate without conversation as darkness closed in. Outside, the wind picked up, but the sky remained clear.

"Tomorrow will be fun to travel," Arale grumbled. "The stinging ice will be particularly pleasant."

No one answered, but even I had to agree with his gloomy assessment.

I awoke to the sound of raised voices and the smell of smoke. Golden and Spike were by the door to the barn, and the Cold Blade glowed softly with frost. Looking outside, I could see flames flickering from the thatch that covered the sheds near the wall. The Fist were moving and gathering their weapons. I pulled a thick woollen jumper over my shirt and put my boots on. The Cold Blade was quickly in my hand.

"What's happening, Golden?" Kat asked.

The elf strung her shortbow and nocked an arrow.

"The farm is under attack," Golden said.

With that my tall friend and Spike ran out of the barn. I took my small handheld crossbow but only loaded the upper chamber with a bolt. Kat and the entire Fist had now left, and I could hear fighting and screaming outside. Running to the door, I looked out onto the courtyard. My eyes adjusted to the flickering light from the flames. Figures fought by the well, blades clashing. To my left, men and women fired bows over the wall, but to the right, hobgoblins jumped from the ramparts to reinforce their companions fighting near the silo. Grappling hooks caught on the narrow brickwork of the walls, and one of the humanoids aimed a hunting bow at a farmer on the far side of the compound. I brought up my crossbow and fired, and though the range was beyond what was considered favourable for the weapon, the bolt hit him in the shoulder. The hobgoblin slumped forward and grabbed at the wound. I saw Kat shoot at the figures flooding over the wall from her position behind a small wagon. A hobgoblin pitched forward, grasping at the arrow in its throat, clawing the air as it fell. Everywhere there were shapes fighting, but Golden and Spike grabbed my attention. The pair carved their way through a group of hobgoblins near the door to the house scattering the humanoids with the ferocity of their attack. A young man had been trying to hold the raiders at the opening using a spear. His shield arm hung, and it was clear he was wounded, but Golden cleaved a path to his side and with Spike, leaving a trail of corpses in their wake.

Raserman joined Kat at the wagon, and the two of them picked off more of the humanoids as they came over the wall, while Vental and Shafali fought back to back. Sharhon was engaged with a well-armoured hobgoblin, and Aslim stood over the body of another briefly before running toward the wall where the grappling hooks were embedded. Tasha fought with a shortsword and hand axe near the clay silos, but she was hard-pressed by two hobgoblins. One slashed at her with a longsword while another threatened her flank with a spear. I was at her side in ten strides with the Cold Blade in my hand. The warrior with the spear sensed my approach and turned. He thrust at my chest, but I swayed away from the point of the weapon. I grabbed the wood of the handle just beyond the metal tip and pulled with all of my strength. The hobgoblin lurched forward off-balance, and I plunged the shortsword into his neck. Tasha killed the other warrior and stood panting over its body.

A horn blew, and the remaining hobgoblins turned to flee. Aslim was on the wall cutting the ropes attached to the grappling hooks and blocked the humanoid's line of retreat. He killed them as they ran up the internal stairway, attempting to get back over the wall. Sharhon pressed the raiders from the rear, and Kat and Vental shot them from the stairs as they clustered together in confusion. The hobgoblins didn't surrender, knowing the farmers would not show them any mercy. They were cut to pieces as they crowded together trying to escape. Soon the only sound was the moaning of the wounded and the crackle of flames. We grabbed buckets and helped form a line with the farmers to throw water from the well onto the burning thatch. Others picked up spades and proceeded to shovel snow onto the fire. It didn't take long to soak the thatch and put the blaze out. I glanced around the courtyard and guessed at least twelve bodies lay in pools of blood. Sharhon turned over the corpse of the armoured hobgoblin and picked up the dead warrior's longsword.

"This one knew a little about swordcraft," he said.

"But mainly they were unskilled," Aslim said.

The older woman who had negotiated with the leader of the Fist on our arrival limped over to us from the northern wall. Blood dripped from a bandaged wound on her thigh.

"We thank you for your assistance. Without it, we would probably have been overwhelmed. This band is from the Black Bear tribe, and much larger than raiding parties we have known in the past. Another four are lying beyond the wall with arrows in their flesh."

"It was lucky we were here. I presume they attacked for the grain," Aslim said.

"For the food and what slaves they could gather. They also collect the weapons and horses. You are welcome to take what you need for the rest of your journey free of charge. It is the least we can do."

Aslim grunted and nodded.

"Thank you for your generosity," Shafali said, glancing at her leader from the corner of her eyes.

"We have wounded, so I must leave you."

Tasha glanced at me and smiled before gesturing at the young man holding his flank.

"I have some skill in this area, so I will help," she said.

The rest of us piled the dead hobgoblins onto the wagon. A few arrows stuck from the woodwork and I pulled one out. The arrowhead was poorly fitted and the fletching made from duck feathers.

"We will take the bodies to the edge of the woods and leave them for the scavengers after we strip them of their armour," an older man dressed in a squirrel skin cloak said, "Though most of it is not worth keeping."

Looking at the rusted pieces of metal stitched to some of the ragged leather clothes, I couldn't help but agree.

The shallow valleys of the north once all belonged to the hobgoblin people. Now they had been pushed back into Stony Hills and moors further east. The face of the armoured hobgoblin stared up at me. Brown eyes were open but empty. The grey skin and prominent lower canines were clearly visible as was the pronounced ridge above the eyes. The soft fur that lined the neck and shoulders of the humanoid were covered in blood and the damage to the throat raw and exposed. I turned away and frowned.

"The sight of the dead disturbs you, dark elf. I am surprised," Sharhon said.

"Actually, I was just thinking how the hobgoblins are not so different to us."

The big warrior snorted. "These creatures are little more than savage beasts."

"That is how some of the humans from the west describe my people. We are supposed to dine on human babies and slaughter indiscriminately. It is all an excuse to take our lands for themselves, and isn't that what has happened to the hobgoblins? This was their country once. It was their best land, and so the westerners pushed past the Great Forest and took it. I feel some sympathy for their plight."

"Yet you live amongst those that came from over the wide ocean," Sharhon said.

I nodded. "Yes, life is complicated sometimes."

It was late when I returned to the barn, and everyone seemed to be sleeping. I had washed the blood from my hands and face in warm water the farmers had heated and then eaten a little bread. A voice whispered to me from some sleeping furs, and I wandered over to see who was awake. Tasha flipped back the bearskin under which she lay, exposing a smooth, sleek body. Her eyes smouldered as they met mine, and she smiled.

"You came to my aid tonight, and I would like to thank you," she said, gesturing at the empty space.

My pulse quickened, and my eyes travelled up and down her body as though they had a will of their own, but I shook my head.

"I'm tempted. Yet as I look at you, my mind goes to the face of the woman I love."

Tasha left herself exposed. "Are you sure? I don't mind if you imagine her while you are with me. I'm not offering love, just release."

It was a very appealing proposition, yet I knew later I would torture myself with guilt and self-loathing and then would start to blame Tasha, and I liked the woman. I didn't want that to happen, so I shook my head and turned away. Placing my sleeping skins near Kat and Golden, I tried not to think of that firm body which lay only a few paces from where I tried to sleep.

When everyone started moving the following day, I felt as though my eyes had just closed.

Tasha brought me some bread and cheese and smiled at me. "Didn't you sleep well? I did. Just remember the offer is still open."

Golden glanced sideways at me and grinned. I knew as she walked away, swaying her hips that I probably wouldn't sleep tonight either.

17

SISTER

It wasn't long before Golden found me alone and offered his solution to my predicament.

"What happens on the road stays on the road, you know that," he said.

"So Kat would be okay if the situation was reversed and it was you who had the open invitation to share another woman's sleeping skins?" I asked.

"Well, no, but I'd keep it a secret, and it wouldn't change the way I feel about her."

I shook my head and smiled. "She would kill you for even thinking that way."

"That is why we are having this little talk away from her. The Original Men have a different attitude to staying with one partner so there would be no problem on that front, and it wouldn't change the way you feel about Miranda."

"No, it would just change the way I look at myself."

"I don't get you. Tasha is a beautiful woman who in many ways reminds me of Cassie."

"I wondered if you had noticed the resemblance, and that is just another factor which makes me certain I am making the correct decision."

"But she is not Cassie if anything she is even more appealing."

"Golden!"

"Well, I am only speaking from the point of view of someone who is looking but not buying. You are being offered a free sample, and yet you say no."

"Much as I appreciate the trading of metaphors, for me, the price would be too high."

Kat brought her pony up next the two of us and eyed Golden suspiciously.

"What are you two so engrossed in conversation about?" she said arching an eyebrow.

Golden's cheeks developed two bright pink spots, and I was tempted to throw him under the wagon, but years of friendship kicked in, and I decided not to tell Kat her lover's opinion on fidelity.

"My blonde friend was just encouraging me to hold firm in my decision not to take Tasha up on her offer to join her for an evening under the bearskin."

Kat looked at her partner, and her eyes narrowed. "Perhaps that is because he has spotted the resemblance to an old lover of his, and he doesn't want you going near her."

My eyes widened, for I hadn't seen that coming. Golden sat upright and blinked rapidly. Kat's expression changed at our reaction, and she rubbed her chin.

"Alright, I got that wrong, but I find it difficult to believe Golden is counselling you to stay out of a woman's bed, but I truly hope he is. My only addition to the debate is to ask how you would feel if the situation was reversed and Miranda received an offer too good to refuse."

"You make an excellent argument Kat, wouldn't you agree Golden? I mean, how would we feel if it were our partners who gave into temptation?"

Golden nodded quickly. "It was going to be my next point."

Kat continued to stroke her chin then she flicked the reins and trotted away to join Shafali, who rode in front of the dog team.

"Thanks," Golden muttered.

"She's right, you know. If Kat lay with another man you would be furious."

My friend watched the elf as she slowed her pony and reached Shafali's side.

"Yes, I know," he said.

We reached Wallington just before the blizzard hit. The town sat around a tall keep inside a high wall of granite. The land on which the houses sat was flat, but the keep perched on the top of a small yet steep hill. The surrounding countryside was covered with a thick layer of snow, burying the fields and cloaking the nearby patches of forest. We couldn't see the Fens from the town but knew they lay only a short ride to the north. Our group found a modest inn which sat at the base of the hill and I shed my winter clothing. The fire bathed the room in glowing warmth as the group ate roast potatoes and pork.

"Your sister and her lover will be either here or at the village of Snote," Aslim said. He held out his hands to the flames. "I don't know why anybody would live this far north."

"Timber and fish," Golden said. "The streams that flow into the Fens are full of red back trout in spring and summer, and the silver bark oak grows just to the north of here. It's the only hardwood that grows straight and tall, not like the southern oaks."

"Well that explains the log wagons sitting by some of the homesteads we have passed recently," Shafali said.

"Yes, they use bullocks to pull the timber to the bigger rivers, then float the logs all the way to the coast or the larger towns like Wheelon," Golden added.

"I bet the trolls don't like the westerners cutting down the forest," Vental said.

"They like eating them, but no, they don't like sharing their country. In the past, they used to fight occasionally with the hobgoblins, but that has all changed, and they have withdrawn into their swamp," I said.

"Another victim of the western expansion of the pale skins," Shafali said.

"Yes, but I find it a lot harder to feel any sympathy for them. They are brutes that have always killed with little reason. Their only loyalty is too small family groups, and they are as likely to murder each other as anyone else," I said.

"That is changing," Kat said. "Over the last two seasons larger groups of trolls have worked together and the lumber camps to the north of the swamp have been destroyed."

Shafali nodded. "So even the Trolls band together to fight back."

It was a frightening thought. Even though trolls were smaller than giants, they were faster and their skins like leather. A giant was powerful but cumbersome. You could see their blows coming and move aside. The club or spear of a troll would strike quickly and with more power than any human could deliver, and they were cunning and unpredictable.

"We will have to watch out for them, as hunger might bring them out of the Fens and I don't want to be on their menu," Golden said.

"Battle axes and heavy weapons are the best way to kill them. Shortswords and sabres don't do enough damage," I said.

Aslim nodded and said he would buy some, whilst I decided to get something heavier for myself. The handheld crossbow I carried would be useless against the large creatures, so I needed a heavy crossbow or longbow as well.

There were only three inns in town as the population inside the walls only just numbered over seven hundred souls. We were lucky enough to be staying at the one my sister had used. The innkeeper spotted my dark skin immediately and made a comment.

"Two of your race in the last few days, that can't be a coincidence," the man said. He had a red beard and thick hands which looked like they could crush the wooden mug he cleaned.

I decided not to lie as this man's eyes twinkled with intelligence. "That would be my sister, and I'm trying to catch up to her."

"Not sure your sister and her companion wanted finding. They were trying to keep a low profile to start with, but the Dark Owl took a liking to the wine on the second night, and her dancing attracted a lot of admirers. The blonde woman didn't look very happy with her."

That certainly sounded like my sister. She always loved to be the centre of attention, and if alcohol was present, then her behaviour would tend toward the uninhibited.

"When did they leave?" Aslim asked.

"Two days ago, heading for Snote, though I don't know why anyone would want to go there at this time of year. Except for the central stockade, the place will be almost deserted until spring."

We were close. There wouldn't be many places to hide in an empty village, and the group of dark elves Shade thought she would be meeting, with their chest full of silver, was no longer on the way. That money was safely under Aslim's chair and had travelled with us since the battle at the ferry. Those funds would now help finance the Snow Leopard's army and the rest of our journey.

It was easy to purchase battle axes and longswords, and I found a serviceable blade with a worn wooden hilt, but I had no luck buying a crossbow. Kat bought a longbow with funds given to her by Aslim and gave her shortbow to me, but I knew it lacked the hitting power to seriously hurt a troll. We sharpened our weapons and waited for the blizzard to blow itself out, glad we had shelter and fire. The conversation was minimal as people dozed in chairs or sipped large mugs of ale.

I tried to rest but was aware of Tasha's presence. Occasionally she would brush up against me or smile in my direction, but I never received the overt invitation to share her bed as I had in the barn the night of the hobgoblin attack. Golden noted my predicament but said little. He seemed to think differently about the situation since Kat had spoken to us on the trail north. I was still determined to stay true to Miranda, but the close confines and warmth of the inn were sapping my willpower. Outside the wind howled down the narrow streets and the shutters rattled. We only ventured outside to buy new weapons and then quickly retreated to our sanctuary before frostbite set in.

Spike slept in front of the fire and occasionally scratched on the door to be let out, but he was always back quickly. It seemed the storm was even too much for him.

Aslim woke while it was still dark. "The sky is clear, and the wind has dropped. Be ready to move by sunup."

I dressed in winter furs and strapped on my weapons, feeling a surge of relief. Realising how close I was to knocking on Tasha's door, I now believed the crisis had been averted. It was harder to give in to temptation in a barn where my friends were only sleeping a few paces away. I realised my sister may now be close by and I tried to think about how to capture her and convince the Fist to keep Shade alive so she could be taken south and put on trial. I also wanted to save Sabella, but that would prove an even tougher proposition.

"We will need to leave the horses and walk using snowshoes," Arale said, sticking his head into the room. "The snow is too deep for horses, and there are too many of us for the dog team."

I grunted and wondered where we would stay tonight. Walking would make us sweat, and when we stopped moving, that would become an issue unless we could find some shelter at the end of the day. Our damp skins and wet clothes would make us freeze on a clear night. Snote was close enough to reach by sunset as long as nothing delayed us and I hoped we would find refuge there.

The sky was clear, and at first, the glare from the snow troubled me. The whole world was a blinding white that held a beauty all its own. The shapes the snow made as it lay draped over trees and houses softened everything, but as the sun rose in the sky, the brightness intensified. I was glad when high cloud started to roll in from the east, and the world took on its familiar winter grey.

Snote appeared in the distance as the light faded. Wading across the top of the snow in the oversized shoes was more tiring and slower than I remembered. The distant village looked like so many small lumps on a flat plain. Over the trees, a tangle of low snow covered the pines and bushes which marked the edge of the Fens, but the swamp was frozen and invisible. A trickle of smoke came from three of four buildings inside a high palisade which surrounded the centre of the village. One of the log cabins outside the fortified walls also had a fire burning.

"That's where they will be," Raserman said from the back of the dogsled. Because of his wounded leg, he had driven the team all day.

"Vental, check it out and report back. We will wait near the old mill," Aslim said.

A plan to save my sister still eluded me. I hoped she wouldn't put up a fight, and surprise would see us through. After all, Shade was expecting Kedria and her team to show up, not us.

We took the dog team around to the rear of the stone structure. A channel had been built from a nearby creek to a water wheel that now lay broken. Inside the narrow building, I took off my snowshoes and climbed a stone set of stairs to the second floor. From the window, I saw a shape moving slowly from one patch of cover to another as Vental made his way toward the log cabin. The light faded, but I had no trouble following his path. A body leaned on my shoulder, and a voice whispered into my ear.

"Can you see him?"

The warmth of Tasha's breath tickled my neck, but I didn't object. "Yes. He is by the pines near the small hill."

I pointed and felt Tasha put more of her weight on me, and I turned slightly. She smiled into my eyes and my resolve snapped. Her mouth opened slightly, and I leant forward to kiss her.

"What can you see?" Kat snapped.

We jumped apart like startled rabbits.

"He's near the house," I stuttered.

The elf's face was blank, and she nodded and joined us at the window. I watched as she peered out into the gathering darkness.

"Golden wants you downstairs," Kat muttered.

I found my snowshoes and wandered around to where my friend helped to unfasten the dogs from the sled.

"You wanted me?"

Golden stood back and looked at me curiously. "No."

"But Kat said…"

I realised that the elf must have seen Tasha follow me up the stairs, and as I stood there, an intervention was taking place in the mill tower.

My temptress was being warned to keep her distance. I wondered if Miranda would ever find out about the debt she now owed the fierce elf.

It was completely dark before we started to move toward the log cabin. Vental had seen my sister through the window sitting on a chair near the fire, but he had not spotted Sabella. We broke into two groups with Golden, Kat, Spike, and I heading with Arale and Shafali toward the rear of the single-roomed cabin. Vental informed us there were two horses in a small barn attached to the northern wall of the structure, and the area had been crisscrossed by wires attached to bells and other implements. These early warning devices had been rendered useless as they were mostly buried under deep snow, and we knew where the effective ones were.

We were supposed to wait at the rear door and catch anyone who tried to flee, but I had a different plan. When we got to our assigned position, I checked to see if there was any sign that our quarry had heard us, but there was no indication we had given the alarm to the occupants of the cabin. A single lamp shone near the shutters and smoke came from the chimney. I went straight for the rear door and kicked it open. Sabella had been sitting in a chair near the fire and moved faster than I thought possible; she drew her Black Blade and leapt toward me so quickly I hardly had time to block the downward sweep of her sword. I was pinned in the doorway as my sister sprang from the bed. The Cold Blade shone with frost, and I thought of the blizzard of the previous day, but as I willed the cold into Sabella's blade, I saw the magic fade and die. Shade stared at me in shock for an instant before grabbing a small sack and a bearskin cloak. She ran for the door, scooping up her boots on the way.

"Help me hold them," Sabella shouted, but my sister was already outside and running. She stepped into the path of Aslim, who appeared out of the darkness. He hit her with the flat of his blade and Shade crumpled sideways, and then the rest of the Fist swarmed into the room.

"Drop your weapon, Sabella, it's over," I said.

The tall blonde stared at my sister's body lying in a shaft of light just outside the doorway. Her sword arm had dropped, and I could have killed her, but I felt sympathy. My sister had abandoned her, leaving Sabella to be killed or captured.

"She is not worth dying for," I whispered.

The rest of the Fist had surrounded Sabella, and her life hung by a thread. I stepped between her and the archers, trying to buy some time. "She is my sister and has done this before. You are not the first person to be betrayed by her."

Blue eyes clouded with pain, and she dropped to her knees, the Black Blade slid from her fingers. Sharhon took a stride toward her and raised his sword. Kat picked up the magical blade and slid it into her belt.

"No," I barked. "She has done nothing to deserve death."

"The woman has assisted in the theft of one of the most important artefacts of your people," Aslim growled.

"She didn't steal it from the Snow Leopard but took it from McRobb's men. In a way, she has helped you get it back, as it would have been almost impossible to retrieve from the crusading army."

Aslim hesitated, his eyes locked with mine.

"This woman is as much a victim of my sister as the Snow Leopard. She has been seduced into actions she would never have undertaken normally."

The leader of the Fist nodded and then turned to Arale. "Bind her and Shade. They are coming with us. The Snow Leopard can decide their fate."

We decided to stay in the cabin for the night as it provided shelter and warmth. Aslim said we would move quickly in the morning as the trolls in the Fens would have probably noted the smoke coming from the isolated dwelling. I found out from Sabella that she had planned to move with my sister inside the stockade the following day for the same reason.

Shafali retrieved the Crown from the sack which had fallen to the ground when my sister had been knocked out. It was a plain thing made of iron rather than steel and if it wasn't for the flat fist-sized opal worked into the metal above the nasal bar it would have looked like any of the other helms my people had worn into battle a thousand years ago. The opal was of outstanding quality and glimmered with the colours of the rainbow when held before the fire. It was said to be magical and to protect the kings of our people. I stood there staring at the artefact in my hand, wondering if it had been worth all the lives it had cost.

"You can see why I wanted it then, brother," Shade said.

I turned and put the Crown down before facing my sister. The cold fury that rose within me had seen many of my foes to an early grave, and I had to work hard not to walk over to her bound form and cut her throat. A headache started to build for the first time in many days, and I wondered briefly where my tea was. I took a deep breath and slowed my heart rate.

"No, Shade, I was thinking of how many lives had been lost trying to retrieve it for the Snow Leopard."

"It was never his in the first place. Kedria explained to me the dark elves used to select their kings. They didn't choose themselves. Anyway, our people haven't been led by a royal family in over six hundred years."

"That is not why you took it. You like gold and luxury and thought this would be a way of becoming rich. Maybe the Sunspear Clan drew you in, but I doubt they would have had to try very hard."

My sister hung her head and tears started to well up in the corners of her eyes.

"You know how weak I am! I see a pretty gem and must have it. It is a force that drives me."

It was probably true, and I felt a spark of compassion growing, but then I remembered the dead boys on the boat. Those young teenagers were butchered so my sister could escape. I smothered my feelings, and my mouth became a grim line.

"Too often, you have used the excuse that you are weak or can't control your urges. I have also felt needs I couldn't control, and luckily I had friends who saved me, but your choices have almost destroyed our family, and now the only way father's and the clan's honour can be regained is with you in prison."

Shade started to sob and wail. I had watched this performance before, but I saw Golden look at me in surprise as I stood unmoved.

"She does this when faced with her crimes. I have seen it many times, but it will have no effect on her future choices."

"You should understand. They turned on you as well for a crime you didn't commit. I know you didn't lead your command into those caves. Someone else did, but you took the blame," Shade snarled.

Everyone stopped what they were doing and stared at me.

"About time that one came out," Golden muttered.

"Shut up, both of you," I growled.

"You covered for your lover!" Shade yelled. Her eyes were red and the tears had stopped but her fists were curled into balls.

"Something you would never be accused of doing," Sabella said.

The blonde woman listened to the exchange with my sister with her head hanging down and hair obscuring her features. Now she sat upright, and a single blue eye shone from behind the locks, burning into Shade. I was grateful for the distraction.

"I do love you, but I was frightened."

"But I just heard your brother say how you have done this before."

"He is a liar!" Shade hissed. "He has always hated me and poisoned others against me."

"Really? Who was it that begged father not to disown you, and who was it that swore to your good character when the Brotherhood of the Wolf accused you of theft?"

Shade stared at the wall.

"She killed your friend, Wink, with Kedria's help," Sabella said. "At the time she told me the Sunspear woman insisted it was necessary, but now I'm not so sure."

My sister's eyes didn't move, but they became cold. Her hands clenched and unclenched and I could see her straining against her bonds.

"I never loved you, Sabella. You were good at pleasing me, but there have been plenty of others who have done that before. I needed a sword arm and someone who could get to the Crown, that was all."

"I have spent the time-bound here on the floor coming to the same conclusion, but I will survive. I've been betrayed before, and given the chance I will have vengeance."

"You are both going before the Snow Leopard," Aslim said.

Meeting the blonde woman's stare, I gave her the tiniest of nods. I would speak with the leader of the Fist and see if I could change his mind. Sabella might be willing to give me the information I need about the Grandfather's operations back in Hope, and I would pass the evidence along to Captain Waldheigheim. Then the old man would be made to squirm.

18

TROLLS

Eventually, I slept, though it was a night filled with dark dreams. I could see the large red eyes of the demon and the bodies of the dark elves scattered before it. Flickering torchlight lit the cavern, and the stench of sulphur made my eyes sting. My lover Zenta crawled just beyond the circle of magical ruins that held the beast in the cave. Her leg lay near the stone chair on which the beast sat.

"Do you want her back?" a voice that rumbled like thunder asked. "Her friends were tasty, but it is so long since I have eaten anything other than animal flesh. Sentient bodies are much more enjoyable."

"You cannot pass beyond the runes." My voice quivered despite my effort to keep it under control.

"I know that, fool! I killed the magician who made them but still they bind me. Nevertheless, your little friend has yet to crawl past them. Shall I help her?"

My head pounded with the power of the voice. I wanted to run and drag Zenta the final pace to safety, yet I stood still.

The Demon left the throne, throwing a gnawed arm aside. Its skin shone blood red as it stretched to full height. Two horns of black almost touched the roof, which was three times that of a dark elf. It took a few paces and picked up Zenta in a clawed fist. She moaned as it squeezed her and blood ran from the stump below the knee.

"I don't think she will live very long," the Demon said. "Something inside is broken. Oh well…"

It threw her casually across the cavern onto the rocks near the entrance, twenty paces from the runes cut into the ground. She landed with a wet smack before sliding outside, leaving a red smear behind her.

"Yes, definitely not alive now," the creature rumbled. The Demon then wandered over to another body and dragged it toward the rear of the cavern.

Waking with a start, I looked around the room. It had been a long time since that dream had troubled me. I had never told my sister what had happened that day. The only person I shared the truth with had been Golden. Shade suspected I hadn't told her the whole story, but how she had pieced the facts together remained a mystery to me. My sister was curled up on her side near the far wall; long white hair covering her neck and shoulders. I remembered her sleeping like that when we had travelled as a family across the high plateau to watch riders from our clan participate in the annual race around Tear Drop Lake. We were both been young then, and I had often protected Shade from the wrath of my father when her antics created harmless mayhem. She made me laugh when few others could, and we had shared food taken from the Pavilions of other families, most of it expensive and imported. Mangoes and bananas always seemed to taste better when Shade stole them from the table of a rival clan.

Smiling, I tried to picture her riding next to me before she became a young adult and started to steal important items. A little twinge of guilt surged through me. I had encouraged her antics as a youth, but then I imagined Golden wagging his finger at me telling me no one can see the future. Now I hoped she would be locked in a southern prison where inmates were forced to work producing food and building items such as wagons and carts. I really want to believe she could change and in time reunite with the family.

"Can't sleep?" Tasha asked.

I looked over at the woman who kept watch through a slightly opened shutter. "Just thinking about the past," I said.

"Must be hard seeing your sister like this."

"It is. The only thing that makes it a little easier is that we didn't kill her."

"She is not out of danger yet. The Snow Leopard may still have her thrown from the Black Cliff."

"I hope to convince him to do otherwise," I said.

"Does that mean you will travel south with us to your homeland?"

I wanted to return to Hope and Miranda's arms, but this task needed to be seen through to the end.

"There is no choice if I'm going to try and save her life."

Tasha looked thoughtful. "Will the elf come as well?"

I laughed. "She warned you off, didn't she? Well, I can't say for certain, but I doubt it. Kat and Golden will probably turn back toward Hope at some point."

"Then I will wait for my chance," Tasha said with a smile.

"The moment has passed," I said without much conviction.

"Really? I don't think so."

Her confidence scared me, and I wondered if I should try and convince Kat and Golden to accompany us to the homeland of my people.

Arale stood and stretched. "You should leave him be, Tasha."

The dark-eyed woman gave the man a flat stare, and he shrugged before picking up his coat and walking to the door.

"Back soon," he muttered.

Spike opened an eye and growled low in his throat. As Arale opened the door, a wave of cold air rolled into the room. The dire wolf stood and looked toward the opening. We heard a grunt and Arale staggered sideways. A crude spear stuck from his chest, and blood poured from the hole in his back. He toppled forward as Tasha, and I screamed out warnings. A creature filled the doorway and thrust inside with an axe tied to a long pole. The improvised halberd swung sideways and caught Tasha with a wicked blow to the chest. If she hadn't been wearing her breastplate, it would have been a death blow. As it was, her body was thrown into the wall, and she fell on top of Shafali. I pulled out my Cold Blade and touched the shaft of the troll's weapon willing the power of a chilly winter's night into the creature's weapon. It screamed and dropped the halberd, stepping backward. Another larger troll took its place. It tore the door from its hinges before reaching inside with a long arm. Golden was first to move, shearing the limb off above the elbow with a powerful blow from his blade. The creature screamed as the arm dropped onto the ground.

The back door exploded inward as it was hit by a large piece of firewood. Other logs which had been cut for winter fuel followed it through the gap, and Vental was caught a glancing blow. He landed near Shade, who looked into the darkness with wild eyes.

"Give me a blade," Sabella yelled.

I was tempted to free her and hand the blonde woman some type of weapon, but everything happened too quickly. Raserman strung his longbow and fired out into the darkness. He must have seen movement because a grunt of pain came back. A troll then ducked into the room and attacked Aslim with a large axe. The leader of the Fist danced aside, and the blade smashed into the packed earthen floor. Another creature ripped off some of the roof and threw logs as quickly as it could. Everyone dodged the missiles, but they bounced from the walls and tables, showering us with splinters. Sharhon jumped forward and swung his longsword with two hands into the exposed rib area of the troll inside the room. It protected its face from the flying splinters and had not seen the warrior step toward it. With a howl, it fell to its knees. Aslim chopped down onto the troll's head, shattering the skull and killing the creature. More of the roof was ripped away, and spears were launched from the darkness, landing inside the log cabin. Sabella followed Spike under the table as the point of one of the weapons buried itself in the woodwork above her head.

"Take the fight to them," Aslim roared as he dived out into the snow through the shattered doorway.

Those remaining upright from the Fist followed him as did Golden and Spike. I had to wait until the entrance cleared, and then heard a hiss of pain behind me. Turning, I saw Kat holding her side. Blood poured from between her fingers, and her eyes grew wide. Shade disappeared through the other doorway with the Crown in one hand and a heavy cloak in the other. I screamed for Golden and took off after my sister. She was struggling through the snow toward the small barn. I hadn't picked up my crossbow. If I had, I'm sure I would have shot her without hesitation. Fury exploded within me, and I fell to my knees. The headache hit me like a sledgehammer, and my senses blurred. I forced myself to be calm and felt some control return. Staggering after her, I used the path she ploughed before me to ease my passage. Shade reached the small barn and looked over her shoulder. I saw her hesitate and then pull the barn door open. She could see as well as I could in the dark and had probably spotted my pursuit. I was almost at the barn when a pony charged through carrying a slender rider. Slashing as it passed, I felt the blade jar in my hand as it sliced through tissue and into bone. The animal staggered and fell, spilling Shade to the ground. The sound of combat stopped, but I heard bodies moving in the snow. My sister stood holding a shortsword and a dagger and looked around wildly. I moved in front of her with the Cold Blade gleaming with frost in my right hand.

"Just give me a reason, sister," I hissed.

"You are my brother. Let me go, and we can split the money. Better still, come with me, and we can both be rich. You know how much I have missed you."

A promise of riches and emotional manipulation all in a few short sentences. I stepped into her and hit her across the face with the back of my hand as hard as I could. She spun with the blow but then came back at me, feinting with the dagger before chopping at my neck with the sword. I blocked both blows in quick succession before smashing my left fist into her jaw. Her combat skills were rusty and no match for mine. Shade fell and started to cry.

"I hate you, I hate you all! Why couldn't you just leave me be, and everything would have been alright."

She screamed and wailed until Raserman tied her hands behind her back, and Shafali gagged her.

"Can't put up with any more of the noise," the curly-haired woman said as she dragged my sister back inside.

Kat lay on the table where Sabella and Golden endeavoured to save her life.

"Mop the blood up quickly so I can get a good look inside the wound," the blonde woman said.

Tasha and Vental were still unconscious, but both would live. Sabella had been released because she knew how to treat battle wounds. Her hands were red, and she held the lantern close to the wound, peering intently as Golden quickly wiped as much blood away as he could. Spike whined as he looked at Kat before rubbing against me. I was too distracted to respond.

"Shade may have nicked an internal organ, but I can't do anything about that. Some major blood vessels have been cut, but I think I can close them off with some stitches. Get me Tasha's pack and mine."

Aslim signalled to Shafali, and she hurried to obey. Sabella took a curved needle and some thread and signalled Golden to clear away as much blood as he could. I took one of the elf's arms, and the rest of the Fist pinned her down. Raserman went to the door and watched in case any of the surviving trolls decided to return.

Kat moaned as Sabella worked. Despite the missing doors and holes in the roof, the blonde woman had sweat on her brow. Golden was as pale as the snow, and his eyes were filled with fear. The needle worked its way in and out of the flesh of the elf and she groaned every time the thread was pulled tight.

"Almost there," Sabella whispered.

Eventually, she stood back and sighed. "The internal blood vessels are closed, and I didn't notice any damage to the liver. Of course, there was still a lot of blood, and it was difficult to see, but the flow has almost stopped, so that is a good sign. I'll close up the outer skin and then you all better pray to any god you believe in. Keep her warm and hope that blood loss or shock doesn't kill her."

Golden took Sabella's shoulders in his hands and looked into her eyes. "Thank you."

"I feel bad about not seeing Shade slip her bonds," the blonde woman mumbled.

She looked uncomfortable at my friend's attention and excused herself to wash her hands. Aslim nodded at Shafali, and she moved to watch Sabella.

Golden turned and stared at my sister. His face tightened, and the different-coloured eyes grew hard.

"We should hang her and leave her for the crows," he said.

I didn't argue. Kat was important to me, and the wound she carried might still kill her. My sympathies lay with Golden, and I wondered why I tried so hard all my life to rescue my sister from the havoc she created.

"She was captured alive, and the law requires us to deliver her to the Snow Leopard for judgement," Aslim said.

"If Kat dies tonight then Shade will not leave this room alive," Golden growled.

My sister started to make gasping noises beneath her gag until Shafali gave her a cuff to the side of the head.

Aslim nodded and put his hand on Golden's shoulder. "We will wait and see what happens. Hopefully, your friend will live."

That night Golden and I didn't sleep. We patched up the doors and roof as best we could and watched the surrounding fields for any sign the trolls were returning. Mostly though, we watched Kat. The elf moaned occasionally but didn't move from where she lay covered by woollen blankets and a bearskin cape. Sabella also sat with us.

"There is a good chance she'll make it. She is tough and fit, and I'm almost sure the internal organs weren't cut. It's just the blood loss that worries me and the cold."

"Can we do anything else to help?" Golden asked.

Sabella put her finger to her lip. "You could get in there with her. Your body heat may help warm her, but be careful not to bump the wound."

Golden gently slipped under the bearskin and eased into Kat's undamaged flank. Spike watched and then slipped under the table before curling up and falling asleep.

I nodded to Sabella, and we were quiet for a while, alone with our own thoughts.

"I'm supposed to take you back to the Captain," I said.

Sabella turned slightly to face me and then ran her long fingers through her hair.

"If you do that, Grandfather will kill me as soon as I step out of the watchhouse."

I rubbed my chin. "You could tell me what you know and then travel east. I believe some western settlers have even settled on the edge of the far ocean."

"I heard that too. It took them two seasons to get there."

"Probably out of Grandfather's reach."

Sabella stretched her shoulders and then glanced at Golden before looking back at me.

"His resources are many, but I don't think he has any contacts on the other side of the continent, and I do know where most of his people are."

"Then, just tell me, and maybe the Captain will bring him down. At the very least the Watch may cause him so many problems he will be too busy to discover who provided the information," I said.

Sabella snorted. "The Watch is half of the problem."

I knew what she meant. Corruption was rife amongst the members of the police force of Hope, as salaries were low and temptation for other income considerable.

"The Captain won't take bribes. I tried once when I first met him, and he almost threw me out of the watchhouse."

"He is not in Grandfather's pay, though plenty of others are," Sabella said.

She gave me a list of names that I had trouble remembering. In the end, I got some charcoal from the fire and wrote them down. Sabella told me of Grandfather's connections to the nobles of Hope. I knew of his association with the Snowfelds, but some of the other names were a surprise. The Armborfelds were supposed to be an incorruptible house with lineage back to the early settlers, and yet Sabella told me they had become heavily involved with smuggling since the departure of the Dance Master. They now worked closely with Grandfather to bring ale and spirits into the city in a variety of ways that avoided the city's taxes.

It took Sabella most of the night to tell me what she knew, and I had to commit some of it to memory as charcoal is not the best writing tool.

Then I glanced at her. "Why come all this way to exchange the crown?" I asked.

Sabella chewed her lip. "The theory was to be as far removed from any prying eyes or interference as possible. Shade didn't want to travel this far, but Kedria insisted. She didn't want anyone to know that dark elves had the crown. The McRobbs were supposed to keep it, but Shade told me to steal it back. She wanted more money. Kedria wasn't pleased at your sister taking it again but in the end, agreed it was probably for the best. She didn't think humans could be trusted to hang on to it."

"I will try to convince Aslim to let you go before we reach the Great Forest," I said.

The woman shrugged. "I know you will do your best."

I glanced over at my sister. "What about her?"

Sabella's eyes glinted. "We are through. Your sister is seductive and made me feel wanted, but now I can see it was all an act. Sometimes I suspected everything wasn't right. As we travelled, her mask slipped when she was tired or frightened, and I would get a glimpse of a different person. Then she would hold me and tell me how much she wanted me, and I would forget what I had briefly seen." She shook her head. "What will happen to her?"

"I don't know. I was going to ask – no, beg – for leniency, and thought if I returned the Crown with the Fist, then the Snow Leopard might show mercy. Now, after she has almost killed Kat, I'm not sure if I want to try and save her," I said.

"She is still your sister, I suppose."

"Shade will always be that, but I'm not sure it is reason enough to keep trying to save her."

In the morning, Kat still lived, and a little colour returned to her cheeks. We gently moved her to the sled using one of the broken doors as a stretcher. Then the dog team took her slowly across the snow to the open gates of Snote. The heavily armed guards let us inside and directed us to the only inn in the village. It was a low stone building with a chimney at either end of the structure. Both sent smoke into the grey sky and melted the snow near the walls into muddy slush. The rest of the village consisted of thirty or so dwellings and a lumber yard. Some of them now stood empty, but a small fort inside the walls held twenty armed men commanded by one of the Northern Knights. Some of the poorer timber workers had also stayed, and they turned and stared as we carried Kat into the inn on the stretcher.

A large man with a thick beard and a battle axe strapped to his back turned from the bar and stared at us.

"By all the gods, where have you all been? I've been looking for you since I received Lord Alder's message."

Tearwyn carried a mug of ale in each hand. He put both drinks back on the bar before wrapping me in a bear hug. He did the same to Golden and gave Spike a scratch. When he saw Kat on the stretcher, his brow creased and he stroked her pale hair.

"What happened?" he asked.

Golden grimaced and helped move Kat to one of the rooms while I told Tearwyn our story.

"The guards said trolls were about last night, and we knew a couple of fools had set up outside the wall. Gandern, the head knight, believed that if people wanted to kill themselves by living outside the walls at this time of year, it wasn't our business."

"This Knight Commander must have a healer with him," I said.

"I haven't seen one," Tearwyn said. "You have to understand, Snote is at the arse end of the world. The Northern Knights only patrol the area so they can warn the towns further south if trouble comes spilling out of the Fens. They're short of everything except salted fish, ale, and lumber. The military order's presence here is not much more than a tripwire."

"We need someone to care for Kat."

Tearwyn shrugged and then spotted my sister being bundled into the room with her hands tied behind her back. The Fist manacled her feet so that she could only take small, shuffling steps.

"This is the one that caused all the trouble? Your sister?"

I nodded while Tearwyn stared at her. She met his eyes and then mine before being dragged to the far side of the room.

"She certainly got the looks in your family."

"Thanks," I said drily.

I told Aslim there wasn't a healer in Snote and Tasha should stay with Kat.

"We need our healer, and she isn't in the greatest shape herself," he said.

"All the more reason for her to stay here."

The leader of the Fist shook his head. "She is under my command and will follow her comrades south."

"I could look after Kat," Sabella said.

Sabella was still bound, but her legs were free. She was leaning against the wall listening to our conversation. I turned and raised an eyebrow at Aslim. He took off his thick coat and threw it on the large wooden table before answering.

"I don't think the Snow Leopard needs to see her, so she can stay, but if she runs and abandons your friend, it will be on your head."

"I won't run," Sabella said.

"If you decide to trust a thief, then you are a fool," Aslim said.

"She has saved Kat's life already. I don't think she will leave her."

Sabella gave me a nod and then held her hands toward me. I sliced through her bonds with a dagger, and she massaged her wrists before heading to the small room where Kat lay.

It was dark when Golden approached me by the fire. The dire wolf lay next to the bed where the elf slept. He was pale and haggard. Slumping into the chair next to me, he started nervously tapping with his fingers on the furniture.

"I'm not coming with you, Ash."

"I didn't think you would," I said.

"Spike can travel south to your homeland if you like, and I'll reunite with him when you get back to Hope."

I shook my head. "You and he are a team. He should stay here."

Golden smiled, but it didn't reach his different-coloured eyes. He leaned over and picked up his mead, sipping the warm drink.

"Thanks for getting Aslim to leave Sabella behind. My skills have never been in healing."

"I know. I'll never forget the job you did stitching up poor Tehana's leg."

Golden chuckled and drank a little more. I sensed there was something he wasn't saying.

"Spit it out," I said.

Golden glanced away and wouldn't meet my eyes. "She's no good, Ash. Shade should face the noose."

"She is my sister. I can't change that."

He turned, and his stare suddenly bored into me. "Don't try and save her. She doesn't deserve it. Shade will do this again to someone else. She'll never change."

What he asked shocked me. He wanted me to stand by and let my sister be executed. Only a day ago, I would have shot her myself, but now my anger had cooled and the blood ties restored. I couldn't answer him, and he must have seen something in my face because he stood and thrust his chair back against the wall.

"If I ever see her again after tomorrow I'll kill her myself," he hissed. He left and returned to Kat's bedside, closing the door behind him.

The Knight Commander paid us a visit after dinner. I didn't speak to him, but he spent some time questioning Aslim about the attack by the trolls. He seemed to accept that the Fist was taking a murderer back to face the judgement of the Snow Leopard. The Northern Knights weren't at war with the dark elves or their allies, so he didn't really care. He was more interested in the weapons and tactics used by the trolls. Some of the soldiers based in the fort also came to the inn that night and attempted to flirt with the female members of the Fist. Shafali wasn't interested in their clumsy attempts at seduction and Tasha was too sore to do anything but nurse her drink and grimace occasionally. She gave me a weak smile across the room later in the evening, but I kept my distance.

Golden didn't say goodbye the next morning, and when I went to find him, Sabella told me he had gone for a walk somewhere in the village. He must have really wanted to avoid me because the temperature was below freezing. I kissed Kat on the cheek, and she stirred slightly, then gave Spike a scratch. The dire wolf licked my hand a few times and flopped down near the fire.

"I will tell her you came when she wakes. For now, I'm using a very small amount of the poppy mixed with some other herbs to keep her asleep. At least this dump has some useful medicine."

"Don't give her too much," I said.

"I know what happened to you, Ash. I'll not let her become addicted."

We stopped on the way and retrieved Arale's body. Sharhon gathered timber with Vental before placing their companion's body on top of the pile. The scout's bandage fluttered in the cold wind as he gathered fuel. Aslim poured oil over the corpse before muttering in a language I didn't understand. Then he put a torch to the kindling. The Fist didn't shed a tear, but their faces were grim.

The dog team led the way over the white expanse which stretched to the horizon. The only indication that trees, houses or buildings existed was an occasional splash of brown or black against the backdrop of snow. Tearwyn came with us on a large horse draped in bearskins. He said he didn't want to stay in Snote for the winter and had always wondered what the high plateau of the dark elves looked like. I warned him he might not be welcome, but Aslim said Tearwyn travelled with them, and as long as he supported the Fist in their mission there wouldn't be a problem.

We were travelling south and approaching Wallington when the sky cleared. The days were warmer, but frost outlined the branches of every tree come morning. That night Tearwyn sat next to me in the fortified barn of one of the frontier farmers and stretched his fingers toward our small fire before scratching at his beard.

"I think I heard the McRobbs were looking for a band of Original Men a while back," he said.

I turned slightly. "And you just thought to tell us this."

"Well, it was before the first storm hit and as this Fist, as you call them, weren't mentioned in Lord Alder's message, I didn't think a lot of it."

Aslim walked over and then sat with us. "Tell me what you have heard, big man."

"Just that the McRobbs would pay coin for any information about the whereabouts of a group of Original Men, and even more for anything which led them to a certain dark elf woman, but as we have her, that's not important."

I tried to stay calm. "Well, it probably is important, as both parties now travel together and have taken no precautions in hiding their location. I would guess the McRobbs haven't stopped looking for us while you were holed up in Snote."

Aslim slapped his thigh and stood. "Big man, you must tell us all you know and not presume anything."

"I'm sorry. I thought this was old news and didn't matter anymore."

"What is done cannot be changed. Just tell us what you have heard, no matter how unimportant you think it may be," Aslim said.

Tearwyn couldn't really add a lot more except that he had heard the story in more than one tavern and been approached by a hedge knight in Wheelon who asked him if he had seen such a group.

"We must avoid Wallington and the bigger population centres," I said.

"If the nights are not too cold we will camp away from habitation," Aslim said.

Inside I shivered at the thought. We were now in the depths of winter, though the one consolation was that we were travelling south.

19

FOR THE SNOW LEOPARD

Our small group skirted Wheelon to the west. Aslim thought we were in more danger of hobgoblins operating from the Flint Hills and the moors than from any group that might appear from the Great Forest. We camped for the night in a hollow not far from another fortress-like house, and Tearwyn told me he could smell the farmer's cooking. The scent never reached my nose, and I thought he was imaging it.

"I'm pretty sure it's pork, Ash. Maybe we could buy some of them."

"You know we are supposed to keep a low profile. The agents of McRobb would have passed our location along to their masters by now, and they could be waiting anywhere on our trip south. They know where we have to take the Crown, and there are only a limited number of routes to my homeland."

"But it's so cold, and porridge doesn't fill a man!"

I had come to appreciate no amount of sustenance ever seemed to satisfy Tearwyn. His appetite ran our little band low on food, and we had been forced to buy salted meat and fish on our travels. Now we were down to oats, and Aslim was rationing our intake.

"Maybe if I go alone. I'll use my own coin and share some of my purchase with you."

"No," I said. "It will have been noted by now you travel with a dark elf and a group of Original Men. We have kept my sister out of sight, but that won't matter as the agents of McRobb know what the rest of us look like."

"Aslim doesn't command me," Tearwyn grumbled, and he went and sat by the fire.

My sister lay bound and chained across from him. She smiled at the big man. I went to join them and turning around, I let my back be warmed by the flames. The Fist were off tending the animals or gathering fuel for the fire as I had done the previous evening.

"Brother, my bonds are too tight. I can't feel my fingers," Shade said.

"That's just the cold," I said.

"No, I really can't feel them. You know how that bitch Tasha likes to tighten them. She wants me to hurt."

"That doesn't sound like her."

Shade snorted and switched to our tongue. *"Of course, you protect her. I can see her eyes following you. And sometimes yours follow her. That little bitch wants you, and you know it, but you are devoted to that doe-eyed cow back in Hope."*

I had forgotten how vicious my sister could be when people weren't cooperating with her.

"You don't know anything about Miranda."

"I know enough. Grandfather told me a little, so I sniffed about, and Sabella dug up more. She married the old man and won't have anything to do with you!"

I laughed. Shade had gone too far, as usual. But her information was old and out of date.

"You need to be very careful, sister. Golden asked me not to intercede for you when you are dragged before the Snow Leopard. He is probably my closest friend, and you almost killed his partner."

Shade went quiet. The fire crackled, and Tearwyn's stomach made loud noises.

"Ash, you won't let them kill me, will you?"

Her voice was that of a frightened child. The problem for me being, I didn't know if it was real or just an act. It remained an issue, trying to see behind her mask. I walked off into the darkness, deciding to help the Fist collect wood.

Wondering how Kat was doing, I regretted not tracking down Golden before I left. His hatred toward my sister was understandable. I had a hard time not agreeing with most of what he said, but she was still my blood, and I didn't want to watch her die. We had played and grown up together. I knew she had a kinder side, one where she could show affection and loyalty, and I hoped one day that aspect would reassert itself. It was impossible for me to do what my friend asked, and I didn't know if he would forgive me. I wanted to tell him everything would be alright; Kat would recover, and my sister would never leave her homeland again, but I couldn't promise anything. I just wanted Golden to be happy next time he saw me and not walk away.

Later I sat and ate my porridge on a log dragged from a copse of trees. Tasha came and sat next to me, and I enjoyed the warmth of her hip against mine. I was too tired to fight my attraction to her. The cold and the journey had worn away my willpower.

"How is your wound?" I asked.

"It is healing. The cut was shallow, but the blow bruised my ribs, and I can't run or do any heavy exercise yet as it causes too much pain. My breastplate is ruined."

That was probably just as well, I thought. Unfortunately, Tasha read my mind.

"So, any attempt at getting you into my bedroll will have to wait."

I laughed. "We could always just take it very slowly."

Tasha's eyes widened. "Flirting! Now there is a step in the right direction." She put a finger to her lip. "No, I don't think that is an option. The first time with you I won't slow down for anything."

The idea that Tasha planned on spending more than one night with me brought heat to my cheeks. I had to shake my head at my own stupidity. This woman was determined, and I found her wicked sense of humour exciting. Desperately I tried to focus on Miranda, but her face was hard to envision while sitting on a snow-covered log at the edge of the wilderness. Then I looked up and saw my sister watching.

Her eyes gleamed like a raven's before it swoops down to eat carrion. Then her lip curled slightly, and she gave me the tiniest of nods. I didn't feel hungry anymore.

In the morning, Shade's bonds had been loosened. She could now move her hands around more freely and manipulated a spoon when eating instead of waiting to be fed.

"Who did that?" I asked, pointing at her hands.

"Someone who cares for me more than you do."

"I'll find out so you might as well tell me."

Shade tried to keep her face free of emotion, but a smile kept creeping to the corner of her lips.

"Tearwyn is a gentleman, and he understood I was suffering. I didn't exactly appreciate the sentiment he expressed as he rebound my hands. What did he say? Ah yes, 'I wouldn't treat a dog like that.' I pointed out I didn't look anything like Spike or any other creature of the four-legged variety, and he said he agreed with me."

I didn't like the sound of the conversation she repeated. Later I asked Aslim if he cared her hands were less restrained, and he pointed at her manacles and then held up the key that hung around his neck – the implication being that she couldn't run anywhere. I had to admit the chains, and attendant lock prevented her sitting on a horse, and that was why she travelled on the sled with Shafali.

We travelled around the bottom of the Great Forest, heading southwest into an area of low hills covered in patches of deciduous forest. Later our group crossed a number of frozen rivers before reaching country where the snow was only the depth of my wrist, and farmers no longer felt the need to build houses like small keeps. The elves had lived here before western men pushed up the river valleys and drove their tribes to the east. Aslim choose a place to camp near an old elven hill fort. The wooden walls had either fallen over or rotted, but some of the hardwood posts carved for the deities of their people stood surrounded by crumpled dwellings.

"We camp here tonight to help us remember why we fight them," the leader of the Fist said.

Tearwyn shuffled his feet and looked at the ground. I approached my big friend and patted his shoulder.

"They don't mean you," I said.

"I think they do, and I probably shouldn't be here, but I wanted to help. Maybe I should leave."

I spread my hands. "That is up to you. No one will make you stay."

He glanced over his shoulder at where my sister was being chained to a heavy log and then rubbed his forehead.

"No, I'll stay for now."

I frowned at Shade, who raised an eyebrow at me.

That night it started raining, and the group brought all the animals into cover under a section of roof that had yet to collapse. We huddled around a smoky fire as the downpour turned into sleet.

"We will need to sell the dogs," Shafali said. "If the weather changes, there will be no snow for the sled to run on."

"Perhaps we could let them go. If we wander into a town and try to sell them we will be recognised," Raserman said.

Aslim scratched at some dirt in his beard. We were all filthy after avoiding inns and other dwellings. It had been almost two ten days since we skirted Wheelon, and I needed a bath.

"Normally I would agree, but if we lose the sled, we will need pack horses. We have no choice."

"I could do it," Tearwyn said.

Everybody looked at him.

"Maybe I wouldn't be recognised. I just thought it would be worth a try."

Aslim looked tired and worn but still alert. "It is a good idea. We will make the swap at the next town. Hopefully, there will be enough snow on the ground to allow the sled to move until then."

The large town of Erinthorpe sat between two small lakes. A round keep of white stone perched on a low curved ridge which separated the two bodies of water. Houses climbed the long hill on both sides, some of them almost touching the walls of the fortification. Boats left from a jetty that ran into the water. People fished with nets and hauled in catches that glinted silver in the sunshine. Farmers brought carts and wagons to the town, entering through a wide gate that pierced a low wall. The population of Erinthorpe had outgrown its fortifications, and dwellings ran along the road both to the north and south.

"Winter doesn't bite so hard here," Tasha said.

"This town is doing well and has grown fat. How far is it from here to the Snow Leopard's army?" I asked.

"At least two ten days, but the people here have nothing to worry about. The Snow Leopard will hug the coast."

"Why?"

Tasha glanced at me from the corner of her eye. "To cut off the men and supplies that come from across the sea."

"There are enough soldiers and weapons here already without needing the Old World to send more."

"The Snow Leopard knows that. The tactic is to weaken morale and force the Dukes to sign a treaty. If the men from the west feel as though they are cut off from the Old World, they are more likely to give in."

I thought that the idea was logical, but what my people and the Original Men didn't understand was the mindset of those from the west. The nobility of the Old World believed it was their right to possess all that they could see. If they failed once they would just try again later. I knew only a great defeat might slow them for a generation. The thought was depressing.

Tearwyn left the forest and took the dog team toward Erinthorpe. We waited for him in a small patch of woodland which crowned a steep hill to the south. The trees were bare and the ground covered with rapidly melting slush. There existed the possibility of more snow, but it seemed unlikely. My big friend returned just on dusk leading three horses. When I asked him how it had gone, his eyes slid away.

"I did the job like I said I would."

"I was only curious," I said.

"Yeah, well, a little trust wouldn't go astray. I know I'm not one of them"– Tearwyn pointed at the members of the Fist –"but I'm not your enemy."

"What are you talking about?"

I was staggered by the harsh words and wondered why he said them. It was true that Aslim remained distant toward Tearwyn, but he wasn't exactly warm and welcoming with me either.

"I got the horses, and it was almost a straight swap so everyone should be happy."

Shaking my head, I walked to the edge of the forest where Tasha joined me. She slipped her arm through mine, and we admired the wide valley between us and the lakes.

"Your big friend is angry with you?" she asked.

"He seems annoyed with the world today. I wonder what happened in town."

"Maybe it was nothing. Perhaps he sees how pleasant Erinthorpe is and wishes to stay."

I thought of the comforts of town, of the inns and feather filled beds and imagined glowing coals in a fireplace and the smell of cooking bacon. My mouth watered.

"I'm sure he bought himself a nice cooked meal, so he is doing better than we are," I said.

Tasha put her head on my shoulder. "Does Ash miss his comforts? I think the poor dark elf needs a bit of distraction."

She turned and kissed me on the lips, and I didn't resist. The kiss grew deeper, and my arms surrounded her.

"It's a pity we both stink," she said when we finally stopped.

I kissed her again and would have continued, but Aslim called, and we broke camp.

Later, when we rested, the guilt hit. I thought of Miranda and how happy I was with her and cursed myself for lacking self-discipline. Sitting away from everyone, I stared into the darkness. My eyes picked out a curious opossum and spotted a weasel stalking it. I threw a rock in their direction, and both animals scampered away.

"I'll never understand the way westerners and dark elves bond for life. It's unnatural," Shafali said.

She was munching on a chicken leg, and I licked my lips.

"Where did you get that?" I asked.

"Your hairy friend brought back cooked meat. You should get some."

I looked over at the camp and caught Tasha's eye. Hurriedly I dropped my gaze.

"This woman of yours is not here, and you will return to her, yes?" Shafali said.

"As soon as I can."

"Then, why the misplaced guilt? You should only feel bad if you mean to leave her."

"I don't think she would see it that way."

"That is strange. When you tell her, why should she object if someone makes you happy when she cannot?"

"I couldn't tell her!"

"But isn't being dishonest to your partner a slur on your honour? If I shared my sleeping skin with you, I would tell my partner if he asked, as I expect would Tasha."

"She has a man waiting for her?" I asked.

"Yes, he is a master bowman and commands all the archers in his tribe. They love each other deeply."

This attitude confused me, but at least it helped me to understand the Original Men had a very different view on fidelity. I remembered that my friend Cassie hadn't wanted to share Golden, but she hadn't been raised amongst her own people.

"Go and sit with her. She thinks she has done something to offend you," Shafali said.

It was not right for me to make Tasha uncomfortable because of my own weakness. I went and sat on the log next to her, smiling as she moved aside for me. Across the fire, my sister stared at me, but this time I met her gaze and didn't drop my eyes. She couldn't lecture me on morality, and at least my feelings for Tasha were real; I just had to sort out how I would manage them. I slept next to her that night but didn't touch her. I just enjoyed the sensation of Tasha's soft breath on my ear.

"There are two of them just inside the woodlands, but they have three horses. I think the third man is probably amongst the rocks on the tree line just a little further along," Vental said.

The small scout knelt on one knee before Aslim, who squatted before him. He held his bow in one hand and spun an arrow in the other as he talked.

"Both carry heavy crossbows. You know, those ones you need a winch to reload. But the taller man also has a bow. They are wearing leather armour and carry well-made swords. I couldn't get close enough to see what the third man carries."

"And they are all men?" Aslim asked.

"The boot marks I found near the riverbank tell me they probably are."

"Well, it doesn't really matter. They are obviously watching the ford so we will have to go around them."

"We could kill them," Sharhon said. "After all, if they are McRobb's men, then they are our enemy."

"When they don't report, our enemies will know we have passed by this way. It is best we avoid fighting and stay hidden," I said.

"Ash is right. We will avoid trouble and move past these men silently," Aslim said.

Shafali pushed a gag into my sister's mouth and wagged a finger in front of her nose, as we were in earshot of McRobb's men. Our group crossed the stream a full two hundred paces south of the ford at a point where the water reached our necks. It was cold and I thought Aslim would let us stop and get dry, but he pushed on until the sun dropped low in the sky. Where my skin touched the pony, I was warm, but above that my body tingled. I shivered and slapped my arms together, but it wasn't until we stopped and I peeled off my shirt and cloak and pulled a bearskin around my shoulders that I became comfortable. Most of the group did the same, and Tearwyn helped my sister. I watched them very closely until Tasha slipped into the bearskin with me.

She kissed me, and I felt her naked skin against my arm.

"You have no clothes on," I said.

"I have some," she said.

She grabbed my hand and put it on her upper thigh. It was encased in rabbit skin.

"They are all I have that is dry," she whispered. "Though I don't think that will be the case for long."

Tasha's wicked behaviour stirred me, but then I saw something in my peripheral vision. My sister was kissing Tearwyn. I cursed the timing and removed my hand.

"Much as I would like to take you to somewhere quiet and spend most of the night exploring new ways to stay warm, there is something I need to stop."

I left the bearskin and strode over to Shade and Tearwyn.

"I know what you're doing, and it won't work this time," I said.

"Why, Ash, you have your fun, and I'll have mine," Shade said in the language of our people.

I stayed in the common tongue of the west. "You will not use this man as you have so many before."

"I can look after myself," Tearwyn said.

"No, you can't," I said.

A bare-chested Aslim walked from the horses and stood by my side. He had been stripping off his wet clothes and noticed the confrontation. He gestured, and Sharhon joined him.

"She is our prisoner, Big Man, and should be put back in her restraints as soon as she has changed into dry clothes. This woman is treacherous, and I will not allow her to escape again. Remember, Shade has already badly wounded a good friend of yours."

"She was trying to save her own life and didn't mean for Kat to get hurt," Tearwyn mumbled.

My sister had obviously been talking to my large friend when the rest of us were occupied. While I had been watching Tasha she had been working on him with soft words and gentle touches. I returned to the bearskin, determined not to become distracted again. I pulled Tasha to me and gave her a hard kiss that lingered for longer than I wanted.

"I can't be with you," I whispered. "I must watch Shade. She is planning something and has already ensnared Tearwyn. There are other reasons why I shouldn't touch you as well. Your way isn't mine, and I struggle with guilt every time I am with you."

She kissed me softly and then pushed me away. "Alright, but you can get your own bearskin."

The side of her mouth curled and her lips glistened slightly. I had to fight hard to walk away. That night I watched Shade, and she noticed my vigilance.

"Come brother, don't let me keep you from the pretty girl."

I said nothing, just laid in my sleeping skins and pulled the furs tightly around my shoulders.

"I'm surprised you are interested in her, as you always went for the women with a bit more roundness to them. This one is more like your lover who died at the Demon Caves. What was her name again? She certainly didn't look that pretty when you brought her back. Zenta! She was as slender as this Tasha. I wonder if they will end up the same way?"

I ignored her and closed my eyes. Aslim had agreed that Shade needed watching and had arranged for someone to take my place later that night. In the meantime, I had to put up with being taunted.

"The women have always liked you, Ash, as I believe, have a few men. Of course, you were never that way inclined. A pity really, you should broaden your horizons. I certainly did."

"Do you really like women, or is that just another act to manipulate others?" I cursed myself for speaking, for engaging with her.

"I don't really mind. One body is as good as another for pleasure, but it is mainly a means of control, and if I was only interested in men, then I would be limiting my options."

"And now you seek to use Tearwyn."

She switched to the language of the dark elves. *"He is vulnerable. I found out all about his sad past and how desperate he is to show everyone he can watch over someone he loves."*

Shade jumped back to the common tongue. "Tearwyn is a good man who needs people to show some faith in him."

"You need to leave him alone. If you don't, I might not speak on your behalf when we get home."

Her lips smiled, but her eyes became hard. "That is a bluff. Your conscience won't let you do nothing. I have been thinking about prison and have decided I don't want to spend the best years of my life shovelling shit and repairing saddles."

"I will not let you escape."

"You will try, Ash, but you will fail."

Our small group only just managed to hide in the tangled bush by the side of the road when the patrol rode past. The leading man was dressed in knee-length chainmail and carried a kite-shaped shield. His equipment showed him to be a poor hedge knight, but the banner that flew from his lance marked him as a member of the Northern Crusade. Three symbols were emblazoned on his yellow pennant: a boar's head, a red snake, and a mountain with two peaks. The serpent indicated the Frenel house had joined the army marching to confront the Snow Leopard. Ten men dressed in leather and scale armour rode behind the knight.

"They search the roads. I suspect that the McRobbs know we are in the area," Aslim said.

Vental took point well ahead of the group while Raserman dropped back to give us early warning if riders approached from behind.

Soon after high sun, the same group rode back in the other direction but at a slower pace. Vental gave us plenty of warning, and we watched from cover.

"It is only a matter of time before they find us," Sharhon said.

The large warrior tightened his grip on the hilt of his sword and grinned. I didn't share his enthusiasm for combat, as we were outnumbered and still more than ten days from the leading elements of the Snow Leopard's army. Between us and safety also sat the army of the Northern Crusade and the remaining forces of the Southern Dukes. We still needed to swing further east to avoid them.

For two days, we managed to dodge roving patrols, and Vental's sharp eyes warned us of men watching from hidden locations. We tracked southeast, but the countryside was becoming more open. It was a little warmer, and the ground was free of snow, making camping easier, but soon we would reach the edge of the elven grasslands. This area was cut by a number of meandering rivers but was otherwise an open expanse of gently undulating hills. For most of the year, it was covered by low grasses grazed by small herds of brown deer and wild ponies. In summer it dried out, and the grazing deteriorated, pushing the animals back toward the central mountains. Wolves, bears, and cave lions hunted here, and the odd tribe of elves could sometimes be spotted camping by a stream, but most of them had moved southeast after being defeated by the Dukes at the battle of Long Lake a generation ago.

"McRobb will know we need to skirt the armies. He will have patrols here too," Aslim said.

"Then there is the problem of the dwarven bridge," Shafali said.

"I haven't forgotten," Aslim said.

My memory of the bridge built by the dwarves centuries ago had faded. They had mined the hills at the edge of the plains for gold and made the bridge so they could communicate with their major dwarven halls to the north. The White Water it crossed was well named. Though not as wide as the great rivers in spring and winter, it was a torrent which carried snowmelt or rainfall from the central mountains.

"We will have to cross it," Vental said. "There is no other way at this time of year to get past the river."

"When we get there, we will see what needs to be done. Until then we remain hidden," Aslim said.

We tried to skirt the edge of the plains, staying in the shadows of the low hills to the west and hiding in the ever-decreasing patches of woodland. At least there were fewer people here. In the evening I watched brown deer cropping grass in the distance. The large animals occasionally lifted their heads and scanned for lions or bears. At night I listened to the wolves howl before making my way back to camp where I settled into the routine of watching my sister and enduring her taunts. I occasionally crossed paths with Tasha, but the constant strain of avoiding patrols and my nightly penance with Shade left me little time for anything more than fleeting smiles.

Tearwyn managed to speak with my sister when everyone was busy setting up camp or while we travelled. When I saw an exchange, I would immediately approach them, and the conversation would stop. I thought of asking Aslim to order him from the group, but I didn't want him to be left in the wilderness by himself. It also remained a possibility that we might need his axe when we were finally confronted by McRobb's forces.

Again a patrol approached from the north. We hid and waited. I was always impressed with how well our group blended into cover. It was no easy task when you had horses with you, but I could barely make out any sign of the Fist amongst the rocks and scrub. I knew if we avoided this patrol, our next obstacle was only over the next low ridge. The white water was visible in the distance, and I could just make out the rumble of its water as it crashed through the gorge.

"We are over here; in the rocks to your left!" Shade screamed.

While Shafali tried to restrain her, Tearwyn stepped up and struck out with his fist and then picked up my sister and ran toward the road.

"Sorry, Ash, but I must save her!" he yelled.

Shafali pulled herself up and spat out a mouthful of blood while I aimed my handheld crossbow at the nearest rider. The patrol was now alert and knew of our presence. The small bolt sped toward the man as he brought his mount to a halt and reached for his sword. The projectile ricocheted from the metal pauldron as he slid from the saddle. A second man was slower to join him, and my other bolt hit him in the base of the throat. I ran toward Tearwyn and my sister, but they stopped just short of the gathering patrol and attempted to undo her chains with a strange key. I knew Aslim had the proper key around his neck and wondered where my friend had found this unusual object.

The lock came open, and Shade pulled the chains from her legs. An arrow snapped against the rocks to her side, and Tearwyn pulled her into a gap which ran up the hill and away from McRobb's men. Tasha leaned against the bark of a fir tree, fitting another arrow to her bow, but her target disappeared, and the next shaft sped at the men running on foot toward me. One of them howled and grabbed his leg. There was no time to think. I dropped my crossbow and drew the Cold Blade and a dagger. The first man to reach me was in too much of a hurry, and as he lifted his sword high above his head, I stepped into him and rammed the Cold Blade through his midsection just below his ribcage. He fell, and then the rest of the patrol was on me. I backed away and probably would have been overwhelmed if it hadn't been for Sharhon. The large warrior appeared next to me with his sword swinging hard from the wrist. Another man fell, and then one grunted as an arrow took him in the side. The patrol was down to six men, and some of them turned and charged toward Tasha's position.

"Two each, Ash, but as you have already taken a man with your crossbow I might steal one from you," Sharhon said.

He would have been a match for Golden in combat, as his moves were fluid and powerful. A short man carrying a war axe died before he could position his weapon defensively. I summoned the power of the Cold Blade and sent a burst of freezing energy down the sword of my enemy into his hands. As he screamed, I jabbed the end of my weapon into his windpipe. It only penetrated to the depth of my finger, but his breath rattled in his throat as he fought for air. The other men turned to run, and in their panic, we cut them down.

Raserman and Tasha came down the gentle slope from the thin line of trees holding bloody swords.

"The one I shot in the foot escaped," Tasha said. "He will bring reinforcements."

"Where are the rest of the Fist?" I asked.

"We did not need them, Ash. They would have just spoiled the fun," Sharhon said.

"I'm more concerned about my sister and Tearwyn," I said.

I ran in the direction Shade, and my big friend had taken. In the distance, I could hear metal striking and the sound of raised voices. Rounding a corner, I saw Shafali rolling on the ground with my sister. Vental crawled to a rock, leaving a trail of blood behind him, and Tearwyn and Aslim circled each other in the middle of the clearing.

"Stop this madness," I yelled.

Aslim took a few paces back from my friend but kept his sword held high.

"I must save her. Last time I failed, but this time will succeed," Tearwyn wailed.

"You put that madness behind you when you were rotting in the cells below the watchhouse. Now drop your weapon."

Instead, Tearwyn stepped over and kicked Shafali in the ribs, forcing her to break her hold on Shade.

"Run my love, I will hold them!"

Tasha and Raserman fired together. One arrow pierced the back of my sister's leg as she tried to flee and the other hit Tearwyn in the shoulder. He yelled in frustration and swung his axe at Aslim repeatedly while Shade screamed like a wounded pig. I called for him to stop, but he kept attacking. The next arrows hit him in the side and back. Tasha circled left and Raserman right, and when Aslim was clear, they fired. Tearwyn slumped to his knees, and blood bubbled out of his mouth onto his beard. He had been shot through the lungs, and there was nothing I could do to save him. Shade continued to whimper, but I ignored her. Dragging my friend to a low rock, I propped him against it.

"I'm drowning in my own blood," Tearwyn said.

"I know," I said.

"It's usually a quick way to go," he said.

I didn't answer.

"I failed her, and now she will die."

I shook my head. "Her fate has always been her own. You are the aggrieved party here. I'm sorry I didn't better protect you from her."

"She is your sister, Ash. You can't let her die."

I wish he hadn't said that, but it probably saved her life.

"Let's kill her now and ride," Shafali said.

"We take her," I said.

I went to her side and took the fletching of the arrow in my hand. It was barbed and needed to be pushed through her flesh.

"This will hurt you more than me," I whispered.

I pushed, and the arrow slid through her calf muscle. She screamed loud and long, and I smiled at her pain. When the tip came through her skin, I cut it off with a hand axe and pulled the wooden shaft free.

I turned back to Tearwyn, who watched me through clouded eyes.

"I will stand for her before the Snow Leopard," I said to him.

Large bubbles of blood appeared on his lips, but he nodded once before his head slumped sideways.

"We must move," Aslim said. "Sharhon, take Vental. He cannot walk with the axe wound to his leg. Ash, you are responsible for your sister. If she can't keep up, I'll kill her myself."

We dragged ourselves back through the bushes and rocks to where our horses waited patiently.

"How will we cross the bridge?" I asked.

"The rider fled north and the bridge lies to the south, so whoever waits there will not have been alerted. I would prefer to attack at night, but we don't know how long we have before more men appear to squeeze us between here and the bridge. We will rush them. Gather the lances of our dead enemy, and then we charge," Aslim said.

It was the longest sentence I ever heard him say, and it filled me with dread. There would be more casualties. You couldn't charge men with missile weapons and not expect a few to fall.

"We should take the McRobb banner," Tasha said. "It might give us a little more time before whoever holds the bridge opens fire."

Aslim nodded his agreement. I hoped it would be enough and prayed the way was barred by a squad, not a company.

The bridge sat across a gorge almost two hundred paces wide. Below it the ground dropped away into a river which tumbled around boulders the size of houses. Two wagons could have driven side by side across the structure. Huge blocks of granite and marble held the bridge together. At either end, carved dwarves, twice the size of Golden stood guard, regarding us with weathered faces.

"We will go slowly and wave. Ash, you and your sister, stay cloaked at the rear. We will ride in ranks of two with me and Sharhon in the lead. The helmets we stole will hide our faces," Aslim said.

The ruse seemed to work. I listened to the click of the metal shod horses on the stonework as we rode slowly forward. On the other side of the bridge, men appeared and waved, and Sharhon returned the gesture. I rode double with Shade to control her, though the arrow wound seemed to have robbed her of any fight.

Our leading horses were halfway across when one of the guards called.

"Did you see anything?"

"Nothing but deer," Aslim said.

I picked the strange accent of the leader of the Fist, and so did the guard. He glanced at our horses and saw me riding double.

"What's the password?" he yelled, swinging the crossbow off his shoulder.

Aslim dug his heels into the flank of his mount, and it jumped forward. We all followed his lead. The first bolt flew above our heads, but more men ran from behind the carved dwarves at their end of the bridge and fired. Vental's pony crashed to the ground, causing me to swerve my animal around it, and then Sharhon's horse fell. The big man flew over the horse's neck. Another mount was also hit, but Shafali kept it going despite blood pouring from its neck. The leader of the Fist reached McRobb's men first and rammed a lance through the guard who had seen through our subterfuge. Shafali was next to him a heartbeat later and killed another man. I didn't like fighting from horseback, so I threw my sister off and sprang into the fight. The man in front of me struggled to reload his crossbow when he looked up. I saw the terror in his eyes as my sword fell. It sheared through his shoulder and into his chest. Any other sword would have become stuck, but the Cold Blade slid free easily.

Sharhon was next to me, swinging his sword into the crossbowmen, blood covering his flattened nose. They died quickly now as Aslim's weapon rose and fell on the demoralised men. I was glad only ten soldiers had guarded the bridge, and they had been armed with crossbows. If they had possessed faster loading bows, we would have suffered far greater losses. Soon all was quiet except the whimpering of the injured.

Behind us on the bridge lay two dead horses and Shafali soon had to put her mount out of its misery too.

"We don't have enough animals for everyone," Shafali said. "The men here only have a cart that was pulled by a bullock."

Vental hobbled closer to us, using a spear as a crutch. "I will need to ride. My leg is completely useless."

I heard noise to the north, and Tasha yelled. "More riders are coming. At least twenty I can make out."

She was shielding her eyes against the sun, but I quickly counted sixteen horses and informed Aslim of my observation.

"We need to hold them," he said.

I helped Shafali push the cart onto the middle of the bridge, but even though we turned it sideways, it still left gaps that could be forced at either end.

"They will not rush us as they know we will be ready for them, but they can wait for more men. If we move, they will follow us," Tasha said.

Aslim stroked his jaw. His brow was furrowed, and I could see him examining the ground, trying to find a way around the problem.

"I will stay and hold them," Vental said.

"No," Aslim said.

"I can't ride, and I'm useless as a scout, but I am almost as good a shot with a bow as Raserman. We need to get the Crown back to the Snow Leopard so he can be king."

Aslim kept scanning the ground to the south before looking back at the riders on the other side of the bridge. One man remounted and galloped away, leaving a trail of dust as he went.

"That soldier has gone to get help," Shafali said.

The leader of the Fist growled and thumped his chest. "I have never left a member before."

"This is for the Snow Leopard. He raised us up and gave our people hope. It is the least I can do for him," Vental said.

We propped him up behind the wagon with forty arrows and his bow. I also loaded a few of the crossbows for him. Tasha did what she could for his leg before kissing him on the cheek. I helped pile some crates and barrels at either end of the overturned wagon and touched his shoulder.

"You know this isn't about your sister. For me, it's about something much bigger. I don't care what happens to her."

I passed him one of my black daggers as a parting gesture and dragged my wounded sibling up onto the saddle with me.

How long Vental held McRobb's men for remains unknown, but it gave us enough time to get a decent break on them. We didn't see any sign of pursuit for the next three days.

20

THE LONG ROAD ENDS

After two days of hard riding, we exhausted the horses and ourselves. Aslim had pushed us hard, and when Shafali complained, he had insisted Vental's sacrifice wouldn't be in vain. We were now travelling southwest and approached the countryside which had recently seen conflict. Some farms were abandoned, and others burnt. Cows bellowed in pain with the weight of unmilked udders and sheep wandered unattended. The plains were now behind us, and we had re-entered the hill country of the Dukes. Occasionally we caught a glimpse of a small castle or keep perched on a patch of high ground. We skirted around these fortifications and watched carefully for any patrols.

Everyone was on edge. I was so tired my muscles ached, and my skin itched with the bites of the lice I carried. Tasha was too exhausted to flirt, and even the iron-willed Aslim was seen to slump in his saddle. To begin with, Shade was very quiet. She seemed to sense it wouldn't have taken much for the Leader of the Fist to kill her, but in the end, her discomfort overcame her caution.

"We need to rest and eat a proper meal," Shade said.

I looked up from my bowl of oats to where I had chained her to a tree. Her hair was greasy, and she had lost weight.

"The Snow Leopard is close, so Aslim pushes us hard," I said.

We were at the fire with Tasha and Raserman.

"Look at yourselves. You can barely walk, you're so tired. If we don't stop, you will make a mistake and fall short of your goal," she said.

"What would you care?" Tasha said. "If we fail then you will be free."

"I don't know how McRobb's army will treat me. Before we got this far south, I thought the patrols sent to find the Crown might look after me, but the common soldiers are as likely to kill me on sight as they are the rest of you. I want to get clean and eat a decent meal."

"We would all like that," I said.

"And I need someone to have a look at my leg. It needs washing and another dressing," Shade said.

"Tasha did that yesterday," Raserman said. "Now stop complaining or I'll gag you."

"Oh, you don't like my logic so you will stop me from speaking. That won't change the facts. You need to slow down, or you'll blunder into the enemy because you are half asleep."

Raserman growled and stood. "I will not listen to this anymore."

He walked off into the darkness carrying his bow with him.

"I have one more dressing, and I'll put it on your leg tomorrow. After that, we will need to leave your wound open to the air. It is healing well, and it is unlikely to become infected," Tasha said.

"Perhaps, but I don't know if you have my best interests at heart. If I get sick, then you would kill me. With me gone, you could have my brother all to yourself."

"Not everyone thinks like you do," Tasha said.

My sister snorted and started to eat her porridge. Her eyes didn't leave us, and I became uncomfortable.

"Why don't you two go for a walk? I know you want each other and now that Tearwyn is gone you don't need to watch me so closely."

"I'm tired, dirty, and not interested," Tasha said. "So save your breath. You will not tempt me from guarding you."

That my sister could casually drop Tearwyn's name into the

conversation infuriated me. She had manipulated him and led him to his death, and already the incident had no importance to her.

"I suppose since your rescuer is no longer with us, you are resigned to your fate. What happened to Tearwyn no longer matters," I said softly.

Shade stopped eating and made eye contact. "In the end, he failed me, just as he failed his little magician friend. Tearwyn is probably one of the dumbest people I have ever met."

"He was a good man who wanted to do the right thing," I said.

Shade switched to the language of the dark elves. *"What is the 'right thing' brother? My needs are different than yours, and then there are the aims of the Fist. I need my freedom, so I do what I can to regain it. Your sense of honour dictates you take me home so father can stand tall and Golden can pat you on the back. Why is what I want so easily dismissed?"*

"Do not compare yourself to your brother. His aims are for others, something that you fail to understand." Tasha spoke our tongue perfectly, with hardly a hint of an accent.

"He does this to build his esteem at home and to make up for his mistakes," Shade said.

"From my consideration of conversations that I've heard you conduct with Ashen, he is not responsible for those errors and took the blame for the decision of his lover. That is the type of man he is. You, on the other hand, have never concerned yourself with the feelings of others. It is my understanding you wander through the journey of life, leaving a trail of destruction as you go. Then you blame others for the wreckage you leave behind or try and say we are all really the same in our desires. That is not true. Your own brother is worth ten of you. The only reason he is here is to try and save your life."

"I can't help the way I am and have tried to change, but it's too hard!" Shade wailed in the common tongue. She started to cry and rocked back and forth, wrapping her arms around her knees.

"You are pathetic. In the end, your actions are your own, and you will be held accountable," Tasha said.

My sister kept crying, but Tasha's words stirred me. I felt a burst of pride that this strong and resourceful woman admired me. I knew that 'doing the right thing' was not always easy and choices could be blurred by life's experiences, but at least I tried as did people like

Aslim and Tasha. My sister never attempted this path and had always taken the option that satisfied her whims. I watched her sob and felt my heart grow hard.

Shade was right about one thing; our exhaustion would cause us to make mistakes. It was midday, and I admired the first glimpse of green buds bursting on peach trees in an orchard. Nearby the burnt skeleton of a house stood framed against a blue sky. There were two freshly dug graves next to the vegetable patch, and I couldn't help wondering who had died here. Our little group rode through a wide valley surrounded by ploughed fields where there was no cover. We rode over a small rise and straight into a group of light horsemen.

Most of them weren't mounted, and they seemed to be trying to light a fire. How we didn't hear their chatter, I'll never know. They turned and looked at us curiously, and then one of them swore and snatched up his bow. We put our heels into the flanks of our horses and galloped through the group, scattering their mounts. Aslim and Sharhon drew their swords and cut down two men who tried to stop us, and then we urged our tired animals up a gentle incline and headed toward a line of trees in the distance. It wasn't long before I heard the sounds of pursuit. The day was still, and the pounding of hooves carried a long way. I looked over my shoulder and noticed the enemy horsemen were rapidly gaining on us. Their animals were obviously a lot fresher than ours.

Aslim changed direction, turning us almost due south, and I wondered what he was doing until I saw a ruined temple in the distance. It sat on a small hill and had a commanding view of the surrounding countryside. I wasn't sure if we would make it to the building before the enemy was upon us. Looking again, I saw the individual features on the faces of the riders. Urging my mount to increase its speed, I felt it lengthen its stride. This pony had been with me since we had left the Great Forest, and it hadn't let me down. We bolted up the gentle slope when the first arrows started to fly. Shooting from a horse at full gallop is never accurate, but some shafts fell uncomfortably close. The crumbled walls of the temple loomed in front of me, and I followed Shafali's mount up a flight of stairs and inside the walls of the temple. We dismounted and turned to the doorway. One rider tried to follow us, but Shafali shot him with her crossbow as he slowed to navigate the narrow doorway. He fell in the opening, and his horse shied and bolted back into the rest of the horsemen, throwing them into confusion for a few precious moments.

A wall as high as two men surrounded the interior of the temple, though in some areas it had crumbled or worn away to half its original size. Large columns stood inside the walls and must have at one time held a roof in place, but now only a frame of large timber beams sat above our heads. In the centre of the temple, there was a small room that would have once been the priest's quarters. There were only two entrances to the structure, but the doors had long since disappeared. Some of the columns of stone were toppled over, and Aslim immediately started to roll one of the pillars toward the opening, outside of which the horsemen were dismounting. He and Sharhon had just manoeuvred it into position when the enemy attacked.

They came in a rush seeking to overwhelm us before we became organised. The Fist were too well disciplined to let that happen. Raserman and Tasha stepped behind the piece of stone and fired two quick volleys before the dismounted horsemen reached the top of the steps. Being light troops, they only had small shields, and two fell before the enemy got to the doorway. Then Aslim and Sharhon took the archers' places. They used shortswords and daggers and thrust at the soldiers, who found it hard to use their longswords and scimitars in the confined space. Another two fell to join the body of the man who had been killed earlier. Shafali ran to the other door as I tied my sister to one of the columns.

"We could go through the back door and give ourselves to McRobb's men. I'll make them listen, and then we could escape with our lives," Shade said.

"I thought you said they were just as likely to kill you as listen," I said.

"It's better than staying here," Shade said.

I thrust her against the stonework and made sure she was tied tightly with rope from a saddlebag, the chains not being long enough to go around the broken column.

"You are a fool, Ash, but I'm not going to die."

I ignored her and started to roll one of the round pieces of the column toward the southern doorway. Behind me, I heard the clash of weapons and hoped the others could hold their position. Shafali crouched behind a square block of cement near the opening, her crossbow loaded and ready. She had her shortsword clenched in her hand. I watched as Shafali forced herself to relax and scan the steps in front of her.

"They will creep along the walls," I said softly so as not to startle her.

"Then we will only get one shot, and it will be blade work."

"I might get two," I said as I loaded my handheld crossbow.

It took some time to get both bolts in place, and just as I finished, Shafali put a finger to her lips and pointed at the wall. Boots scraped on stone, then a blond man sprang around the corner. His face was narrow, and he had a sharp beard. Shafali shot him in the shoulder, and he spun backward down the steps. The next two men followed immediately behind him. I hit the first one between the eyes and the second one in the chest. They were so close there was no time for them to try and move out of the path of the powerful bolts. More soldiers endeavoured to force their way past the bodies, but again our shorter blades gave us an advantage. The Cold Blade did its deadly work, freezing the swords of my opponents and allowing me to kill them with ease. Blood splashed the walls, and I felt it drip from my hand. It was grim work, and soon the way around the broken column was blocked with the bodies of the dead.

Panting heavily, I had to relax to delay a headache. I didn't want the effects of the potion that kept the cravings for opium away to weaken me now. The soldiers surrounded the old temple and sent riders west toward the army of the Northern Crusade. I looked at Shafali and saw that her eyes were wide.

"We did it," she said, smiling.

"They will be back," I said.

We gathered the weapons and rations of the dead. They hadn't carried much in the way of food but the waterskins some had brought with them would allow us to keep our thirst at bay for a while. We piled more stonework in the doorways and threw the bodies down the steps. I glanced over the wall and watched as a knight rode up to the men surrounding us. He wore the latest plate mail, and his helmet was hinged at the cheeks. Such equipment would be expensive. His banner was a yellow boar on a black field, and I realised one of the McRobb commanders had arrived. He had brought a contingent of ten hedge knights with him. They wore a mix of armour, some of them carrying round shields and encased in scale mail, their equipment not being of the same standard as their commanders.

"I count about twenty, maybe a few more with these latest arrivals," I said.

Aslim cursed and kicked pieces of equipment across the tiled floor.

"We were so close. Another two days and we would have reached the inner patrol lines of the Snow Leopard's army. Now we are trapped and can go no further."

"You can surrender and hand over the Crown. Perhaps they will let you go free," Shade said.

Sharhon punched her in the stomach and then gagged her. I could see the shock on my sister's face and the tears in her eyes. The Fist had obviously had enough of her.

"We need to light a fire to try to signal our army. They may be closer than we think. We can use the wood from the roof supports. Also, it should be possible to fortify this place. If we survive long enough, maybe help will arrive," Tasha said.

I smiled at her. Even in the most hopeless situation, she was positive. Her words spurred the group to action, and Sharhon and Aslim started to tear down the timber. Tasha and Raserman dragged heavy stone supports next to the walls. Standing on them, they would be able to shoot at an approaching enemy. They placed a number of them in position, sweating and cursing as they did so.

"Why so many? Only two of you will be firing." I said as I split timber with an enemy's war axe.

"We will need to change position after each shot. Otherwise, enemy archers will target us. If we keep popping up at different places after each shot, we are less likely to get hit," Shafali said.

It was a good idea as long as the force besieging us didn't have too many missile troops. Shafali prepared food and rested. She had taken a nasty cut to her hip in the fighting at the southern doorway that I hadn't noticed, and even though Tasha stitched the wound, the curly-haired woman moved with a pronounced limp. We started a fire as the shadows grew long. Thick ropes of smoke curled up into the clear sky. I was glad of the still conditions and hoped that someone from the Snow Leopard's forces would grow curious and investigate. The doorways were blocked, and soon we could do little except wait for an attack, but the enemy didn't oblige.

As night fell, we ate a little of our rations and gave what comfort we could to our mounts. Sharhon suggested we chase them from the temple complex, but Shafali pointed out that would limit our options to sitting in the temple and waiting for the inevitable. I thought dying in an old temple dedicated to the god Tellonous or while charging through the open countryside didn't make a lot of difference. Aslim said we would keep the animals for now, but if they began to suffer, they would be released. I wondered if the forces of the Northern Crusade would attack during the night, but Aslim thought they wouldn't bother.

"They don't need to take casualties. Their army can just wait until we run short of food and water and when we try and break out, cut us down without the need to mount an assault. I don't think they know who we are yet. If they realise we have the Crown, then all that might change."

"Maybe Shafali's right, and we should make a run for it," I said.

"Most of us wouldn't make it a hundred paces. They will have archers waiting for us, and though I would accept the death of nearly our entire group to get the Crown to the Snow Leopard, I have no way of knowing who would make it. Then there is the condition of our horses; they are tired and need quality food to recover. I will only try and break free if the situation is hopeless. For now, I put my trust in the signal fire."

I resigned myself to an early grave.

Feeding Shade, I waited for her to try and convince me that the best course of action was to betray the Fist. Instead, she surprised me by staying silent. Her eyes burned with fury, and her mouth formed a thin line, but otherwise, she ignored me. I checked her bonds but didn't engage with her. If she was captured during the fighting, the fact she was tied up might save her life, but I doubted it. Thinking of Miranda and Golden, I wished I could say goodbye to them. I wanted to apologise to my tall friend for what my sister had done to the only woman he had ever loved. Cursing myself for initially rejecting Miranda and wasting valuable time, I wished I had acted earlier before finally acknowledging what we felt for each other. Looking across the room, Tasha smiled at me, and I went to her. We held each other until sleep claimed us.

There was a noise, and I woke with a start. Tasha stood up and grabbed her bow.

"What's happening?" I asked.

"Someone is attacking McRobb's forces," Raserman said.

I ran to the wall and stood on one of the broken pillars. Looking down the hill, I could see tents burning and shadows thrusting and screaming in the flickering light. A small group of figures broke free and ran up the stairs. Tasha lifted the bow and took aim but then hesitated.

"What are you waiting for? Cut them down!" I yelled.

"They are calling in the language of my people."

I listened and caught words that were definitely dark elven and others of a tongue I didn't understand. They were yelling not to shoot and that the Snow Leopard was coming.

"It could be a trick," Raserman said.

The archer chewed his lip. Aslim held up his hand, yelling down the hill and then nodded when a voice called back.

"They are Fist," he said.

We pulled one of the pieces of the column from the doorway and four men and women dove inside the temple walls. All of them carried bows and shortswords. A thin man with a wispy beard gripped Aslim by the wrist and grinned like a wolf.

"Well met, comrade. The Snow Leopard sends his greetings."

Soon the strangers were being embraced by our group. I was caught up in the emotion and kissed a startled woman on the cheek. She smiled shyly and said something to Tasha, who laughed.

"Kyana wants to know if you greet all strangers with affection."

"Only those that save my life," I answered.

"We are not safe yet," the thin man said. "I am Rylon, leader of the Fifth Fist of the Snow Leopard. The Second and Ninth Fists attacked so we could make our way to you and riders have gone to inform the army of our situation. We were warned you might be on your way south with the Crown and it was decided to watch for your arrival."

"Who informed you we were on our way?" I asked.

"Someone named Golden, though he relayed the message through another party in Hope. You must be *Ashen*. Your father vouched for the man who sent the message, so we acted."

My friend's message had given us all a chance. I was a little surprised as Golden wasn't known for his foresight and saw the hand of Kat behind his actions.

"Your attack has given us a chance. However, the enemy will now realise we are important, and it won't take them long to work out who we are. They will attack soon," Aslim said.

Rylon and his four warriors decided to hold the southern wall while we concentrated on the northern one. Shafali and I were to provide a reserve to counter any enemy attempts to climb the walls. We rested for the rest of the night as McRobb's forces attempted to douse the fires in their camp and restore order. During this period, more soldiers joined McRobb's forces outside our position. I went to my sister and gave her some water and checked she could still feel her arms and legs.

"Your chances are still slim, brother. The Northern Crusade's army is closer than the Snow Leopard's, and ten warriors cannot hold these flimsy walls."

"We will see, Shade. At least now there is hope. The signal fire worked, and our people will send a large force to recover the Crown."

"Yes, there will be a battle, and hundreds will die for an opal and a piece of iron!"

"Don't pretend that you care. If you hadn't stolen the Crown then none of this would be happening," I said.

Her mouth snapped shut, and she strained against her bonds. I was pleased to see the knots held firm.

"Soon you will be on trial before your people, Shade, and not long after, if you're lucky, you will be shovelling manure in the prison compound."

Her eyes glittered, and she tensed, but for once, she had no answer.

The attack came soon after dawn. We watched a mixed group of men form just out of bow shot to the north and south of our position. There were hedge knights in mismatched armour, and archers and spearmen in boiled leather breastplates and chainmail shirts. I even saw two knights in full plate armour. It was the third group of soldiers that worried me; they carried ropes attached to hooks and would be coming over the wall. Most of the enemy force had shields or carried large tables in front of them to provide protection from missile weapons. They advanced slowly, and I watched as arrows fired by Raserman and Tasha slammed into the wood and occasionally into flesh. A few men crept away from the attack clutching at shafts that had pierced their legs. Then the enemy was at both doorways, and the fighting grew fierce. I couldn't see the southern opening, but I could hear the curses and clash of weapons as Rylon's command made its stand.

Aslim speared the first man who tried to force the doorway like a fish. The thrust was precise, and the soldier dropped without a sound. Then Sharhon stabbed his shortsword at the enemy, killing another warrior as he tried to swing an axe. Other men crowded into the gap, but Raserman dropped his bow and grabbed a short pike. He pierced a man carrying a shield and sword, catching him on his shoulder. The point ripped through thin leather armour and snapped the collarbone with a crack. The soldier screamed in pain and fell backward, becoming entangled with one of his comrades. Aslim's spear sped forward, striking the unbalanced man in the throat, and he fell to the steps with blood gushing from the hole in his neck.

"They are at the wall!" Shafali yelled.

One soldier was on the shoulders of another, trying to haul himself over when I shot him with my crossbow. He disappeared with a grunt, but a grappling hook smacked into the wall close by. It bit deep, and I had to drop my weapon and cut the rope with the Cold Blade. Shafali thrust at another man on the top of the brickwork, but his companion crested the wall close by and jumped to the ground. I rushed at him, but the warrior blocked my blow with a small shield. He swung at my head with a hand axe, and I was forced to sway backward. A blade thrust at Shafali, and blood spurted from a wound to her chest as more warriors clambered over the wall behind her. I caught the next blow from my opponent on the Cold Blade and lunged with the dagger in my other hand around his shield and into his ear. He screamed and fell back, clutching at the shallow wound. Another man appeared in front of me but his mouth opened and he groaned before he could raise his sword. Shafali grinned as she pulled the blade from his back. Two more warriors dropped to the ground behind her. She was slow to turn. Blood soaked the front of her shirt, and I guessed her stitches had burst. A war axe caught her between the shoulder blades, and she fell heavily.

Before the man could deliver a second blow, I thrust with the Cold Blade into his exposed armpit. His companion hit me in the side with his shield, but I rolled with the blow and came up near one of the pillars Raserman stood on. The archer turned, distracted by the movement, and then grunted. He slipped from the wall next to me with an arrow in his eye. The warrior with the shield jumped Raserman's corpse and slashed at my head with a scimitar. I caught the blow on my Cold Blade and sent a pulse of freezing energy down the steel and into his hand. The man screamed and dropped the weapon, throwing back his head in pain. I stabbed hard into his neck, and blood exploded from an artery onto my chest and face.

The wall was clear, but battles were raging at both the southern and northern doorways. I checked Shafali, but the curly-haired woman was dead. Biting back tears, I ran to the fighting. Tasha circled with her bow just behind the entrance, and in front of her Sharhon and Aslim fought.

The leader of the Fist had abandoned his spear, which was trapped in the corpse of an enemy soldier, and now used a shortsword. I reached the melee just as the two knights pushed the stones and broken column from their path, creating enough room for one of them to step into the gap. The knight stabbed with the pointed end of a halberd and caught Sharhon on the arm. The bone broke, but the big warrior sprang forward and wrapped his good arm around the knight, throwing him backward. There was a clang as the armoured man hit the ground, and spears thrust into Sharhon as he tried to roll clear. He screamed until a mace came down on his head. A man in leather tried to force his way inside, but Tasha shot him with an arrow and Aslim slashed at his face. The wounded soldier disappeared to be replaced by the other knight. This man used a small shield to ward off Aslim's thrust and then he stepped toward the leader of the Fist. The knight smashed a short-handled war hammer into his shoulder. Aslim reeled backward and fell heavily. I jumped forward and took a blow to the side of my head and chest from the armoured man's shield. Dropping to my knees, I heard Tasha yell. She swung her bow at the knight, smashing it in half and sending him back a pace. He lifted his hammer and growled while Tasha struggled to draw her shortsword. From the ground, I touched his steel shell and pushed all the power of the Cold Blade I could gather out of my weapon. The knight screamed as frost spread over him, crackling as it moved across the surface of his armour. He tried to pull the helmet from his head, but the cold spread to his lungs, and he stumbled for the stairs, knocking his men aside as he did.

With their leaders down the enemy fell back, but if they changed their mind, we had very little to stop them with. Aslim was unconscious, and I was stunned. My head spun, and small lights flashed before my eyes. Only Tasha stood, and her bow was now in splinters. I could still hear fierce fighting at the southern door and the sound of battle outside. Then Shade stepped from behind a pillar with my crossbow in one hand and a small knife in the other.

Tasha dived in front of me, and I heard the thud as the powerful bolt punched into her. She grunted and landed in my arms.

Tasha wheezed in pain as I eased her to the ground.

Still dizzy from the shield blow, I was vaguely aware of blood pouring from my nose. Shade picked up the knight's war hammer. "You should have searched me. Maybe Tearwyn was useful after all. I'm sorry brother, but you have become exceedingly annoying."

She lifted her arm and raised the hammer, and all I could do was watch. Then there was a crack, and her eyes rolled back in her head, and she slumped to the ground. Aslim stood behind her holding the end of a broken spear shaft. One of his arms hung at an angle by his side, and his face was covered in blood, but his eyes were bright.

He smiled at me and dropped the lump of wood before pointing through the doorway.

"The Snow Leopard has arrived," he said.

I made sure Tasha was comfortable before pushing aside the bodies in the doorway. Blood and corpses lay clustered around the opening to the temple with rivers of red liquid running down the steps. In the fields surrounding us, a small battle raged. Dark elves on ponies rode back and forth using horse bows to shoot down unprotected soldiers, and more heavily armoured riders duelled with hedge knights. Men screamed, and commanders bellowed orders trying to get their infantry to form a shield wall, but the horse archers rode behind the spearmen and showered them with arrows. A group of riders split from the main action and spurred their mounts up the steps toward us. On the other side of the temple, the sound of fighting died down.

A rider stopped on the landing before the doorway and grinned at me. "Well met, brother. It has been some time since I've had to pull your fat from the fire."

Anywin's steel breastplate was splashed with blood, but his teeth flashed.

"Never have I been gladder to see you, but the greeting will have to wait. We have wounded, and many brave members of the Fist have died."

"Do you have the Crown?"

That was the real reason the Snow Leopard had sent a thousand men galloping north – not to rescue our little band, but for a piece of metal and a large opal. Maybe Shade's previous observation was correct. Were all these deaths worth it?

"We do, and we have its thief."

"Shade is here?"

"Yes, she will have a sore head when she wakes up but otherwise is unharmed."

"I will order my warriors to collect the wounded. The dead we will wrap and take with us so they can be properly honoured. Are you injured, brother?"

I glanced at my blood-spattered body. "No, most of this is someone else's."

Only Kyana and Rylon had survived the battle at the southern doorway. I watched as Raserman, Sharhon, Shafali, and the bodies from the other Fist were wrapped in leather sheets and carried from the temple. Tears ran down my face as they tied the ropes around the material that held the curly-haired woman.

"Don't cry for her, Ashen," Tasha said.

Two dark elves held Tasha upright as another examined the bolt in her shoulder.

"She would be proud of the manner of her passing and will be reborn amongst the stars. We will see her again, but not while we walk the earth."

I wiped away the tears and smiled. The field surgeon lay Tasha down, and I held her hand. Another warrior gave her some leather to bite on while a device that looked like a mix between two spoons and a large set of tweezers slid into the tear in her shoulder. She groaned and squeezed my hand while the two cups on the end of the device slipped around the barbed point of the shaft and slowly eased it from her shoulder. The surgeon then started stitching.

"She will ride with me," I said.

One of the dark elves looked at me. "Are you sure you are up to it,

Sir? No offence, but you look as though you're ready to fall over yourself."

"I'll manage," I said.

Helping Tasha up onto the back of my pony, I slowly eased myself up behind her while another dark elf held us steady. I decided to keep the sturdy animal and take it back to Hope with me. The dark elf cavalry broke the engagement just as a line of spearmen from the army of the Northern Crusade appeared on a nearby ridgeline. A group of horse archers broke off to harass the new arrivals while the rest of our group trotted south. We heard later that the knights scattered the mounted bowmen after we had disappeared, but most of them escaped and re-joined the Snow Leopard's army later that evening.

21

THE TRIAL

My father wrapped me in a bear hug that threatened further injury to my battered and bruised body. *Anywin* stood at the entrance to the tent, smiling, and my mother cried with joy.

"It is good to see you alive, *Ashen.* When I received the news Golden sent, I dared to hope, but to see you here before me lifts my old heart," father said.

"He has restored our honour. The Snow Leopard has ordered that *Ashen* meet him tomorrow after he has rested," my brother said.

"It is a great day for family and clan, but it is even better for me as a father. My oldest son is back, where he belongs."

I wasn't sure about that but didn't want to spoil my father's mood.

"The Fist that accompanied me deserves most of the credit," I said.

"And yet their commander said you are one of the bravest dark elves he has met," Anywin said.

I blinked a few times, stunned that Aslim had complimented me. The leader of the Fist wasn't known for making positive comments about anyone.

"Where is Shade?" I asked.

There was silence, and my father stared at the carpet beneath his feet. My question reminded the family exactly who had precipitated our fall from grace in the first place.

"She is in chains sitting in a prison wagon. Nobody is to talk with her before the trial," my mother said.

Her eyes became large, and her lip quivered as she spoke about her daughter.

"I will speak for her when she comes before the elders," I said.

"She is not going before the Elders," Father said. "The Snow Leopard is going to pass judgment."

That didn't sound promising. My sister was going before the individual whom she had stolen from. I wasn't sure how I felt about that. It meant her chances of not being thrown from the Black Cliff had just diminished markedly. Perhaps she deserved death, as her actions had led to the wounding or death of some of my dearest friends. She hadn't actually killed anyone herself, but her behaviour had caused many casualties. She was still my sister, and even though she had been prepared to open my skull with a war hammer, I still didn't want her to die.

"I will plead her case before the Snow Leopard, and hopefully he will be merciful," I said.

"That is only proper," my father said.

I found Tasha and Aslim in a large tent surrounded by other wounded soldiers. The slim woman lay on her stomach with a large poultice sitting on her wound. Aslim sat up with his arm in a sling.

"You have both looked better," I said.

"I always thought you would prefer me in this position," Tasha said.

I laughed, and even Aslim chuckled.

"I spoke to the surgeon, and it seems you will both live, though they are sending you back to the mountains for rest and further treatment," I said.

"That is what they think," Aslim said. "I will be staying here with the army until I'm fit to fight again."

"My partner is here, so I won't be leaving either."

I must have reacted because Tasha giggled.

"You knew I was with someone, and now I'm back he has visited me, and I'll be spending some time with him very soon."

Aslim laughed. "You missed your chance, Ash."

Glancing out of the corner of my eye at the big man I realised I had never seen him smile before, let alone laugh. His face changed completely when he did.

"Then that is a regret I'll take with me to the grave," I said.

The Snow Leopard sat on a normal chair draped in the skin of the cat he was named after. Next to him, a banner carved from redwood in the image of the Great Eagle stood planted in the earth. He was average height for a dark elf, and his nose was larger than usual for our kind, but it was his eyes that captured me. They were almost black and seemed to burrow into those he spoke to. His armour and weapons were standard for someone who fought mounted, though his sword was one of the legendary Black Blades that absorbed magic. His hair was hidden beneath the crown that so many had died to retrieve. Only three others were in the large striped tent with us. A dark elf magician stood in the shadows, and a tall warrior holding a Silver Spear stood next to him. Lounging on a couch near the wall was an Original Man. He had grey hair and was wrapped in different animal pelts. His only weapon was a Blackwood Bow.

I bowed from the waist and then met the eyes of the individual who had united our people. He stared back, his mouth a thin line.

"You were cast out because you disobeyed orders?" he asked.

"Yes, Leader," I answered.

"Yet you took the blame for the error of another."

Only Tasha could have told him that. I suppose it was bound to come out eventually that Zenta had taken the command into the Demon Caves.

"Yes."

"Honourable, but foolish," he said.

"I wouldn't see her name dishonoured, Leader."

"Yet you would bring that disgrace upon yourself." He took off the Crown and placed it on a table next to him. I noted his white hair was cut short like mine.

"And you don't have to use titles here. It is only needed when I'm in public. You have lived among the humans of Hope and have knowledge of their politics."

"I have some contact with the noble families."

"Will they go to war with us?" he asked.

I thought for a moment. "That remains on a knife's edge. A few families want Hope to stay apart from the war, but other powerful groups agitate for conflict. I believe at present, the greatest probability is Hope will not join the war."

"I don't want to fight Hope, or Deeport, for that matter. I suppose if your adopted city joins the fight, then the larger northern city will assist them."

"The two cities have close ties," I said.

"And Riverside has already sent men and volunteers to this Northern Crusade."

I knew little of the affairs of the large inland city so didn't comment.

"What can I do to assist those families that wish to keep Hope out of the war?" the Snow Leopard asked.

I thought. It was obvious he couldn't do anything explicit or the Snowfelds and Lord Alder would be discredited for allying themselves with another race, but there was another way.

"Pay a criminal organisation to spread lies and rumours about those houses that support conflict. I have recently spoken to someone who provided me with information of illegal operations that have been undertaken by some of the most important families in Hope. When I pass this along to the proper authority, these households will be too busy defending their honour to worry about supporting the Southern Dukes."

The Snow Leopard nodded. "It sounds like a plan. What do you all think?" He turned and gestured to his companions in the room.

The old man on the couch spoke first. "I like it. We undermine our enemies with little cost."

"I think the man who stands before us is a valuable asset," the magician said.

"Indeed, and a fine warrior from what I have heard," the soldier with the Silver Spear said.

"His father will be glad to have him fighting at his side, leading the pikes of his clan into battle," the Snow Leopard said.

I didn't want to join the army and march against the Southern Dukes. I wanted to crawl onto a feather mattress with Miranda.

"Am I free?" I asked.

"All dark elves are free," the Snow Leopard said, "But we are at war."

"You are at war. I haven't lived with my people for over ten years."

"The reason for your exile was false. You are one of us again," the Snow Leopard said.

I didn't want to argue with the leader of the dark elf nation, nor did I want to disappoint my family, especially Father, and decided to let the matter rest, for now.

"Your sister, however, is a thief and a traitor," the Snow Leopard said.

"Shade is unwell," I said.

"What do you mean? The reports that have reached my ears haven't mentioned any illness."

"She has a compulsion to steal that she can't control. It has been with her since childhood."

The Snow Leopard stroked his chin and studied the rug in front of him. I thought the interview was about to conclude when his eyes fastened on me.

"What do you want, *Ashen*? You have done me and your family a great service, and it would be remiss of me to not to reward you if I can."

"I want justice, where my sister is concerned, and my freedom to make whatever choice I decide."

"Justice? I will consult and decide what is fair where Shade is concerned. This condition of the mind is new to me. As for your future, you are now one of us and will fight with your clan until the Northern Crusader Army is destroyed. I will need your council on its leadership and structure. You will also receive a reward of three gold bars."

That amount of precious metal would set me up for life, but not being permitted to return to Hope rocked me. Destroying McRobb's army would be no easy task for the Snow Leopard now nearly every hedge knight in the north, and a few from across the sea had flocked to his banner. My brother told me the peasants who fought with the Crusade were drilling with long spears and fought in the same manner as our pike blocks. McRobb's army didn't fight alone either. The surviving knights who served the Southern Dukes also rode with the Crusade. The ragtag force that had left the north in the middle of winter was now a formidable army.

I gave two of the gold bars to father, and his eyes lit up when I dropped them at his feet. My mother clapped her hands and spun in a small circle, and *Anywin* whistled loudly.

"This will allow us to reequip the front row of the pikes with breastplates and to pay off our debts," father said.

"With some to spare," my brother said.

"We will be able to buy large breeding males for the highland cattle herds," mother added.

I smiled and then yawned. "Could we spend some of it on a family feast? I haven't had a decent meal since deep winter."

"We will have oxen and deer. I will organise it at once," Father said.

For the rest of the day I slept, and though dim dreams of battle and blood caused me to stir, I was so tired that whenever I woke, I only remained conscious for a few heartbeats.

Shade stood with her hands chained behind her back, and her feet manacled together. She had been washed and fed, but nobody spoke to her.

"I have examined all of the facts presented by your family and from those members of the Sunspear Clan who have decided to cooperate. There is no doubt you are a thief," the Snow Leopard said.

Shade shuffled from side to side. She never lifted her eyes, and her muscles were tense.

"You have a condition that leads you to steal, and that fact was used to manipulate you into taking the Crown of Kings. You haven't killed any members of my army and technically you did not take the artefact from the King of your people as I have yet to take the throne."

I breathed out a small sigh; maybe Shade would live yet.

"However, the death of Fist member Vental can be directly attributed to your actions before the Dwarven Bridge. In your escape attempt, he was wounded by a man you had manipulated and died trying to slow the enemy you had alerted. You also wounded Fist member Tasha, though she is well on the way to recovering. It is my judgement. You are a danger to your people, and your recovery is unlikely. To protect others from harm and punish you for the death of Fist member Vental and the attack on Fist member Tasha, I sentence you to the Final Step."

I heard my mother gasp as Shade fell to her knees. My sister was to be thrown from the Black Cliff.

"Please, I never meant for any of it to happen. I didn't want anyone to die, and I won't do it again," Shade wailed.

"Yet death took one of my soldiers because of you, and you tried to kill others. It is not safe to let you walk the earth. Take her away," the Snow Leopard said.

My father's face was empty. *Anywin* and his wife comforted mother. Shade turned briefly, and her tear-filled eyes met mine.

"Save me, *Ashen!*" she yelled before being pulled from the tent by two guards.

"Not this time, sister," I whispered to myself.

My younger brother offered to represent the family at the execution, but I decided I would go. The past season I had chased Shade across the frozen north before dragging her south to face her crimes, so I thought it only right to see the journey through to the end. The small convoy that accompanied the prison wagon only took ten days to reach the cliffs, which dropped from the peaks surrounding the northern side of the high plateau. I sent a pigeon to Lord Alder asking him to inform Miranda that it would be some time before I could return to Hope, but I would be coming back. I didn't know if she would wait for me, but I believed there was a chance we would be together if the war didn't drag on for too long.

The wind whipped at my sister's hair as she stood on the Preparation Stone. The white stone was rough except for the two depressions where prisoners had to place their bare feet. My sister's black skin seemed to reflect the bright sunlight as the cloak was pulled from her shoulders. She wore a green dress, and her white hair was tied in a bun on the top of her head.

"Sabella always liked it like this," she said to me.

I stood with the sun on my back absorbing its late afternoon warmth. When its rays no longer touched the rock Shade stood on, it would be time. A row of stones near the cliff's edge would soon cover it in shadow.

"Did you love her?" I asked.

"No, but she was one of my favourites. She was tough and looked after me."

"Did you ever love anyone?"

Shade gave me a sad smile. "I always loved you. It's just that I didn't know how to show it."

"You were going to kill me," I said gently.

"I was angry with you and desperate to escape, but none of that matters anymore."

I felt my eyes fill with tears and wanted to hold her, but it was forbidden to touch a prisoner once they were on the stone.

"I think I will close my eyes on the way down. I always wanted to fly, to feel the wind rushing through my hair. At least the weather is good. It would have been annoying if it was raining."

I thought she would be able to step from the jutting rock which stuck out from the cliff face, but in the end, her courage failed her as it had most of her life. She cried and tried to run, but the guards caught her by the arms and carried her to the edge. They swung her like a bag of wheat before hurling her from the cliff. Maybe she did close her eyes and imagine she was flying because Shade didn't scream. I took a number of slow breaths, then I barley heard her hit the ground. Some of the guards stared at her body, lying amongst the jagged rocks two hundred paces below, but I didn't join them. I wanted to remember Shade as she said those final words to me. Her body would lie where it had landed until mountain jackals and vultures picked it clean. Those that were executed were never placed amongst the bones of our ancestors and their spirits wandered in torment unless a god forgave their sins. I hoped one of them would show pity to my sister and accept her soul into their keeping.

When I arrived back at father's tent many days later, we talked briefly before he took me to my company.

"The Snow Leopard has ordered we break camp. The army marches tomorrow," father said.

I scanned the two hundred eager faces in front of me and wondered how many of them would be alive when the seasons turned. In the distance, there was smoke behind the hills. Battle was coming, and I would be in the front ranks facing the soldiers of the Northern Crusade.

ABOUT THE AUTHOR

Kim Kerr is an emerging author of sci-fi travel guides. This is Kim's third book.

www.ingramcontent.com/pod-product-compliance
Lightning Source LLC
Chambersburg PA
CBHW061954170626
46813CB00006B/2643

9781928094678